Widely admired as the godfather of the British noir novel, **Derek Raymond** was born Robin Cook in 1931. The son of a textile magnate, he dropped out of Eton aged sixteen and spent much of his early career among criminals. *How the Dead Live* is the third in the Factory series, following *He Died with His Eyes Open* and *The Devil's Home on Leave*, also published by Serpent's Tail. His early novels, *The Crust on Its Uppers*, *A State of Denmark* and *Nightmare in the Street* are also published by Serpents Tail. His literary memoir *The Hidden Files* appeared in 1992. He died in London in 1994.

Praise for Derek Raymond

'One of the few novelists to bring the style of American noir genre to the London streets, Raymond was a unique stylist and a great influence on a later generation of crime writers' *Publishing News*

'A pioneer of British noir...No one has come near to matching his style or overwhelming sense of sadness...Raymond's world is uniformly sinister, his language strangely mannered. He does not strive for accuracy, but achieves an emotional truth all his own' Marcel Berlins, *The Times*

'A unique crime writer whose fictional world was brutal, realistic and harrowing in the extreme' Maxim Jakubowski, *Guardian*

'Cook's prose can make amazing stylistic leaps without once losing its balance...He anticipates James Ellroy and David Peace, among others, in this terrifying determination to disclose the skull beneath the skin...a supreme example of how nasty Britain actually is' *Time Out*

He Died with His Eyes Open

'A crackerjack of a crime novel, unafraid to face the reality of man's and woman's evil' *Evening Standard*

'A gripping study in obsession and absolute, awful evil' *Sunday Times*

A State of Denmark
'Raymond's novel is rooted firmly in the dystopian vision of Orwell and Huxley, sharing their air of horrifying hopelessness' *Sunday Times*

'*A State of Denmark* is carried out with surgical precision... a fascinating and important novel by one of our best writers in or outside of any genre' *Time Out*

'Alternative science fiction on the scale of Orwell's *1984* or Zamyatin's *We*' *Q*

The Crust on Its Uppers
'Few novels chronicle so lovingly the life and mores of 1960s London...Britain's class system was changing. Cook, the old Etonian, takes us to card-grafters in Peckham and rent collectors along the Balls Pond Road; to greasy Gloucester Road caffs and jellied-eel stalls in Whitechapel...Confession is a fashionable literary genre these days. But this younger breed of confessors, well, you can tell they are fibbing sometimes, can't you? Not so Cook; *The Crust on Its Uppers* is the kosher article by a man who was on the down-escalator all his life' *Sunday Times*

'Raymond's autobiographical account of the dodgy transactions between high-class wide boys and low-class villains. You won't read a better novel about '60s London' *i-D*

'Tremendous black comedy of Chelsea gangland' *The Face*

'Peopled by a fast-talking shower of queens, spades, morries, slags, shysters, grifters, and grafters of every description, it is one of the great London novels' *New Statesman*

How the Dead Live

DEREK RAYMOND

Introduction by
WILL SELF

First published in the UK in 1986 by
The Alison Press/Martin Secker & Warburg Limited, London

First published in this edition in 2007 by Serpent's Tail.
an imprint of Profile Books Ltd
3A Exmouth House
Pine Street
Exmouth Market
London EC1R 0JH
www.serpentstail.com

ISBN 978 1 85242 798 6

Typeset by FiSH Books, Enfield, Middx

Printed in the UK by Bookmarque, Croydon, CR0 4TD

10 9 8 7 6 5 4 3 2

To Jean-Paul Kauffmann
Christopher Moorsom

Shall life renew these bodies? Of a truth
All death will he annul, all tears assuage?
... Mine ancient scars shall not be glorified,
Nor my titanic tears, the seas, be dried.

Lt Wilfred Owen, the *Sambre*, Nov 10th, 1918

Introduction
by Will Self

'Bad writers,' Auden remarked, 'borrow. Good ones steal.' I like to think I'm a good enough writer to thieve – and do so blatantly. I ripped off Robin Cook's (aka Derek Raymond) title *How the Dead Live* quite shamelessly, and gave it to one of my own novels. He was dead, so he couldn't do anything about it. Some Raymond acolyte thought this was *a bit much* and wrote me an irate letter. Big deal. Besides, I don't think Cook would've given a toss – he was enough of a Wildean to know flattery when it was staring him in the face.

In truth, I never read Cook's *How the Dead Live* until it came time to write this introduction to it – that's how any literary blagger justifies a bit of work: he doesn't empathise with his victim – he goes in with the sawn-off pen cocked. True, I'd dabbled in a couple of his other Factory novels, the legendarily emetic *I Was Dora Suarez* and *He Died with His Eyes Open*, but it wasn't until preparing to write this piece that I gave Cook's work any serious consideration.

Some say that the so-called 'Godfather of English noir fiction' is quite distinct from his American progenitors; that whereas the books of Hammett, Chandler, MacDonald et al are characterised by lonely heroes who are committed to righting the perceived injustices of society, Cook took the detective procedural far further – down the road to full blown existentialist horror.

The nameless protagonist of the Factory novels has no truck with what he perceives as the seedy moral equivocations of the duly constituted authorities; his is a quest for perfect moments of human connection. If this means that he's condemned to a lurid shadow dance, battling with the shades of good and evil, then so be it. His is a disillusionment of not only tragic – but epic – proportions. In other words: he's exactly the same as any other middle-aged male cynic, stamping his foot because the world's gone sour on him, yet unwilling to imagine what his own mouth tastes like.

So, I say Cook was remarkably faithful to the hardboiled genre. If anything *How the Dead Live* is more Chandleresque than Chandler, right down to the incongruous quotations from Shakespeare, Spenser and Mrs Gaskell (!), and an allusion to Socrates that has to be oddly obscured in order to make it plausible mental content for a sergeant in the Met.

Then there's the lexicon of Cockney geezer slang, terms recondite even when Cook was writing in the mid-1980s. With his darlings, loves, shtucks, bunny rabbits, artists, berks and wooden-tops, Cook hearkens back to an earlier era, when 'the code' prevailed, and there was a difference between good, honest, working crims, and dirty little toe rags, an aristocracy – believe it or not – of crime, the upper reaches of which his solitary jaundiced hero feels a certain affinity with.

And then there are the lacunae with which these books proceed: the frontal lobe discombobulating occasioned by intoxication. For Hammett it was usually opiates – for Chandler, liquor. Cook's characters swim in the stuff. In *How the Dead Live* the drinking begins at 9.30 or 10.00 in the morning and pours on unabated. There's also coke, smack and dope, but you can sample this boozy stream as if it were a contaminated river running through the text: Kronenburg, vodka martinis and plenty of Bells (or ring-a-ding as our man jocularly refers to it), sherry, more whisky. When the bent copper is cornered he tries to buy his way out of it with a single malt, when the villain's catamite comes out shooting his hand is unsteadied by a tumbler of whisky. When the tragic Dr Mardy's guerrilla surgery fails, his patient is numbed by morphine 'on a whisky base'.

This view from the bar of the French House in Soho is

compounded by Cook's strangely foreshortened perception of England (or 'Britain' as he quaintly refers to it). Absent in the 1960s and 1970s, Cook's Britain is all façade and hinterland with no mid-ground: he simply isn't aware of the social context within which things happen: there are 'blacks' and 'Africans' serving in junk food places and pubs. In the shires, bumptious pseudo-squires drive five-door Mercedes, yet the saloon bar is still full of men with military titles, who bang on about evacuating from Dunkirk under fire, while in the public bar, a Falstaffian chorus of drinkers guys the town's bigwig. This is an un-time, where everything seems anachronistic – whether it's a computer, an electricity strike – or festering stately pile.

The action of *How the Dead Live* proceeds through the agency of snarling verbal jousts between the Nameless One and various hated fellow cops, debased stooges, disgusting crims and vilely ugly, whoreish women, alternating with oddly impassioned soliloquies. The only characters he has any sympathy for are his wronged sister, a ten-year-old girl beggar, a suicidal junkie he had an affair with – and, of course, the murderer. His wife went mad, his father and mother became ossified by disease, his straight-copper mates have all been savagely maimed in the line of duty.

Put like this *How the Dead Live* sounds like a ridiculous gallimaufry – and it would be, were it not for two factors: Cook could write beautifully, when he had cause to; and, more importantly, what he is writing about in this novel are nothing less than the most important subjects any writer can deal with: morality and death.

Like Chandler, Cook's very weaknesses as a writer are also his strengths – the tipsy sentimentality, the jaded eye, the poetic riff – these, when yoked to an imagination that insists on the most visceral stripping of skin from skull, produce prose of exquisite intensity.

Even Cook's weird historical perspective – sheered off like the bonnet of a bubble car – comes into its own in this novel: *How the Dead Live*, first published in 1986, teeters on a chronological cliff:

its principal characters are all irretrievably maimed by the experience of the war, and the wholesale death they witnessed. The shades of these dead haunt them, and percolate into the scuzzy atmosphere. It is this profound and now vanished era, when the dead lived among the living of grubby old England, that is Cook's true subject – the seeming police procedural is just that – and he deals with it masterfully.

As the insane Dr Mardy draws us into his mouldering fantasy and his mildewed madness, we experience a true horripilation, a rising of the hackles that indicates we are in the presence of the human mind pushed beyond the brink. Cook makes us see, that while we may cavort in the sunny uplands of life, the shades are always among us, flitting back and forth, seemingly without purpose, and yet slowly, insidiously, relentlessly, herding us towards the grave.

1

'The most extraordinary feature that psychopaths present,' the Home Office lecturer was saying, 'is the painstaking effort they make to copy normal people.' He looked happily at us. 'They make a close study of us – you realize that.'

We shuffled our feet.

'Yet the patient is unremittingly aware of his emptiness, and sees existence as an emptiness around him. He takes a scientific view of infinity. He continues to do so until he cracks; there's no slack in insanity at all. This enables us to define the patient's state. He insists on an explanation for living, and kills because he can't find one.' Absently he picked up his glass of water, gazed into it, and took a sip.

'The rest of us ride the wave of life as a swimmer does, but the psychopath can't do that. He's obliged to think everything out first, because he can't feel. He understands, from his close intellectual study of others, that he ought to be able to feel, but he doesn't know what feeling or emotion means. He can't *feel* feeling, he can only think, and this makes him clumsy compared to the general tide of life – to think you are swimming is not the same as to do it.

'He is usually highly intelligent in a formal sense and because of his emotional inferiority is violently competitive.'

Nobody in the room said anything and the lecturer pleaded: 'I'm trying to condense five to seven years' study and experience into an hour and a half. Do ask questions.' When there were no questions he said: 'The psychopath cannot afford to accept defeat; his superiority, expressed in the number of deaths he has caused, is his one defence against the void inside, and therefore outside himself. The competitive effort that the sick individual makes is his sickness. Simultaneously, though, it's a despairing cry to be rescued from it. Therefore a killer will knife or save, protect or murder, apparently on a whim – but of course there is no such thing as a whim for anyone in his condition, only a trigger. Without being metaphysical – not the fashion in this country – he kills in the role of god or devil, driven by impulses that he can neither understand nor control. That is why his judgments are far more easily and swiftly arrived at than ours; the emotion must come out somewhere, explode sometime, usually in a fugue. The results are spectacular.'

A detective-sergeant behind me muttered to his neighbour: 'Yes, and I wonder when the old geezer last found himself alone with one.'

I turned round and looked at the rows of sullen faces pointed upwards at the lecturer's dais.

'An absurd condition,' said the lecturer, 'can only yield absurd results. Let's consider the Nilsen case. He boasts of having murdered fifteen young men, cutting them up, forcing pieces of them down the lavatory in his flat, or else burning and burying them in the waste ground behind the building. He's not concerned at having been caught. On the contrary, in his mind it was necessary for him to be caught and tried, so that he could explain to the nation from the dock how clever he had been. There was also the hunting instinct, because he had had sex with them all first. But then love means death to the psychopath. A whimsical touch, he had access to these penniless young men looking for work through his job with the DHSS. Recently, in jail, he was set upon and systematically beaten up by his fellow prisoners – but his nagging complaint to the authorities was not that he had had his face cut open, but that blood had got over his jeans that he had just washed and dried in time to go in punctually to tea.

'I'm afraid that even those of us who have never committed murder are nevertheless guilty of it because we enjoy death at second hand, just as we enjoy watching a thriller on television.

After all, what's the use of a newspaper to the general public if there's not a single good murder in it? Of course,' said the lecturer, 'it must never happen to any of us.'

I knew what he meant all right. He was a pompous bore who couldn't hold a gun straight or run up a flight of stairs with an armed lunatic waiting for him at the top, but he had done some thinking.

'Or take Paolacci,' said the lecturer. 'A serious man, Fred always was serious, sharp to work at Ford's; he's now developed religious ideas and sits in his cell reading the Bible all day. Only a mediocre intelligence for a psychopath, though; I know, I've examined him. A good-looking man, he couldn't abandon women because they fancied him. Nor could he stand the sight of them – he's a homosexual. But he didn't see how he could tell his workmates that; like all psychopaths, the greatest terror he could imagine was ridicule. This condition led to three female deaths, his wife, his mistress and his daughter aged ten; he ripped them up and ejaculated in their entrails, a psychotic gesture of despair which he was unable to explain then or since.'

I sat up when Paolacci was mentioned, because it was I who had made the arrest. He had told me, after his confession, that he was much more frightened of what his mates would think than he was of killing.

Lord Longford was having a patient and unctuous time with Fred, and might get him paroled some day so that he could start up all over again.

Who has the least humour or common sense, a killer or a prison visitor? It's such a close race that I've never been able to decide on the loser.

'The psychopath,' said the lecturer, 'is someone who has been murdered in his feeling, or still-born, only he's not died. That's why his major problem is continuing to live. He is on a precipice, and determined that everyone should join him there so that the entire human race can fall with him. He has no sense of home, no sense of love. With the psychopath the death of the other affords him the same satisfaction that our possession of a living person would do.'

I remembered my own murdering wife.

'Murder gives the patient both relief and satisfaction; he avoids both shame and guilt through his conviction that he is either God or Satan; killing is his own upside-down version of being in love. His hatred, where love should be, also accounts for his contempt; the patient cannot understand, cannot conceive, why people should be sad about the dead. He takes it as a weakness to be incapable of taking human life; his own tendency is to boast, even moralize over his victims, and why not? since the difference between good and evil is invisible to him.'

The forty-odd detectives that were his audience looked at each other and one of them said: 'I'd make it fucking plain to the cunt over at the Factory.'

The lecturer coughed over the interruption and told us what we all knew the hard way: 'You can tell these people's illness, even when they're not on trigger—'

('It's not an illness,' said the same detective half aloud, 'these people are straight maniacs even if they're sober; the treatment for any kind of nut is a boot to crack it with, it's him or you.')

'Kindly don't anticipate me,' said the lecturer. 'When he is not on trigger, as I was saying, his condition becomes apparent through little manias which normal people find irritating in the extreme – for instance, his neatness and precision in banal matters. The way he arranges his pyjamas under his pillow. The sexual act to be performed just so. A glass to be washed twice at the sink, never once. The painstaking cleaning of a knife, the washing of under-wear in a classically obsessive manner, silence in the presence of others and apartness, or else pedantic speeches that have no bearing on other conversation.' He stopped. 'Now this is the moment to put questions,' he said, 'do please ask some.' Again no one did, and it was plain to me that the lecturer couldn't understand why. Yet the answer was simple. We were all brooding on our own experience in this domain; we had plenty of it.

'Very well,' said the lecturer, gazing at us through his bifocals, 'we've already seen on film earlier in this course how inadvisable it is to disturb the patient in his manic routines; this provokes stupefying outbursts which can be alarming even to the physician in charge.'

Never mind the victim, I thought.

'Yet leave the psychopath to run his own course,' said the lecturer, 'and he can be most difficult to spot.'

I felt like saying that if he were easier to spot there would be less need either for us or for his lecture, but I managed to restrain myself. All the same I reflected on what I and everyone else in this lecture hall had undergone. ('Now it's all right, son, just put the knife down now, that's right, give it to me, that's it, take it easy, yes, it's all right, you've topped her and I know you're sorry, are you ready with that straitjacket, George? That's it, just come on downstairs, why don't you take my arm, we're here to help you' – knowing that if for no reason it went the other way...)

The lecturer echoed my thinking: 'The psychopath generally kills anyone who has seen him as he is.'

'We'd almost do better not to spot him then, wouldn't we?' I said. 'Then we'd all live to draw our pensions.' I was fed up with him.

'I beg your pardon,' said the lecturer. 'I'm afraid I don't get the reference.'

'You wouldn't,' muttered the detective who had spoken before. I had placed him now; he worked in Camberwell, his name was Stevenson.

'I'll put it plainer,' I said. 'All you do is diagnose these people. We have to go in and nick them.'

'I wonder if I could take your name?' said the lecturer.

'Certainly,' I said, 'if you feel you could replace me. And you'd feel the nip in your wages even if you could, which I doubt.'

He gave me a grey look, the colour of the sea when the sun leaves it. 'You're a most insolent man,' he said.

'I'm not insolent,' I said, 'and I've got scrap-metal in me. Just cut the guff and try to be realistic.'

The lecturer was a visiting professor in psychiatry and about my own age. He dealt in his specialized way with every top security prison and hospital in the country. I couldn't stand the patronizing bastard, and I knew I wasn't the only one in the room. He constantly gave evidence at murder trials as to the prisoner's state but, unlike me, never seemed to find anything wrong with the system nor bother about the victim, only the killer. He had been called into more courtrooms than he could probably count, and it brought him a good income; evil apparently didn't mark him at all. These lectures, of which this one was mercifully the last, was the anticlimax of a refresher course occasionally ordained by the Home Office for long-service detectives of whom I, as a sergeant at A14, was far and away the most junior in rank – in fact, I couldn't think why I had ever been included in it.

The lecturer was scooping up his notes. 'Those of you,' he proclaimed modestly without looking anywhere near me or Stevenson, 'who want to know more on this subject can do no better than read my paper which appeared last August as a thickish volume, entitled *Psychopaths and the World They Live In*.'

'What about the world we live in?' said Stevenson.

The lecturer immediately glanced at his gold watch and said: 'I'm afraid I've got a lunch.'

'I reckon he's afraid of no such thing,' I said, and we all went downstairs after him out into the street and had the pleasure of watching him being whirled away in a Mercedes whose chauffeur looked as if he had been hanging about for a long time.

2

I had to have lunch too, so I went to the Clipper pub in Little Titchfield Street where I knew a few people, mostly waiters, cab- and lorry-drivers; there I was free to sit daydreaming like any man, eating my banger, scooping up my peas with a knife and drinking beer.

Only my daydreams weren't pleasant. I wasn't thinking of a naked woman with a big bum and no brains; nor of winning the pools or getting tickets for Saturday's match. I was back at my Earlsfield flat the night before last, watching television. On it I had watched the funeral of a fellow officer; he had been killed in the dark and in the back. He hadn't been putting wheel-clamps on anyone, but had been called out to help other officers save a life in a drunken shooting matter in a flat. He had cornered this artist, but then the triggers had been pulled and it had gone the other way for Ken.

And so I bad-dreamed while I ate; he had joined the others. I'd already seen enough of them – Macintosh, Foden, Frank Ballard paralysed; now this boy Ken Hales was dead.

The funeral was stiff with uniforms and held in the church of the Essex village, Sudbury not far, where Hales had grown up. What made the experience all the stranger for me was that I recognized so many of the faces in the congregation from times long before I ever joined Unexplained Deaths. My word, some of them looked grand now – there were chief inspectors, super-intendents, even a commander among those who bore the coffin, and most of them were my junior in age. In the church everyone was motionless throughout the service, his cap on the pew in front of him while the priest intoned, Forasmuch as it hath pleased Almighty God of his great mercy to take unto himself the soul of

7

our dear brother Kenneth here departed, and later, when they were round the raw clods of earth at the graveside: Earth to earth...ashes...dust; in sure and certain hope of the resurrection...Christ...who shall change our vile body unto his glorious body, according to his mighty working.

But I could only remember the dead man as a promising three-quarter in police rugby matches – big, strong, young, a man you never would have thought could go down, a fair man too, a good detective and no brute. An item on the news – a risky career wound up, a widow in black with three kids huddled round her white-faced.

I've known hard villains all right – a tiny handful of them are fun to be with, adventurers more; I don't mean the morons, cowards and assassins. I remember one of them saying to me a week before he was shot down in Whitechapel while he was out on bail: I don't see it matters a fuck whether you live thirty years or seventy, I've pulled a million's worth of strokes and spent the lot on myself, women and clubs, and I regret nothing, darling. I said you know there are people after you, and he said yes and I know who they are too, and I don't give a monkey's. I'll be thirty-six tomorrow, so why don't we split a bottle? Two, I said, and ride hard, keep riding, the way you thieve you take real risks and you're no killer, nor are you a grass.

And that's one reason I've never got far in the police – I admire one or two of the folk I'm paid to catch.

Christ, I remember the day I got out of buttons. It was June and fine weather and I walked up Sloane Avenue to Chelsea nick, where I'd just been posted to the CID. I believed I was in love, too, with my beautiful great-chested Edie, and all the birds sang double for me in the London trees that day. I dashed up the pavement wondering how soon I was going to be promoted sergeant, and wanting to know where all the villains were; the folly of youth. I hummed and sang and did a hundred silent calculations on my pay for Edie and me; my prick tingled with desire to make a child with her, and I would have gone mad, or laughed at anyone who had told me that Edie would murder our daughter.

But no one told me.

When I got back to my room at the Factory, Room 205, the phone was ringing. I picked it up and the voice said: 'What are you on right now, Sergeant?'

'I've just come off this Home Office course.'

'That's it, so you have,' said the voice. 'Did you learn anything?'

'Nothing I didn't know already.'

'You are a very cheeky man, Sergeant,' said the voice, 'and so you thought you knew it all, better than the lecturer himself, did you?'

'That's it,' I said. 'I wouldn't be alive still if I didn't know a good deal better than him.' I added: 'Have you been following police funerals at all lately? Ken Hales, for instance?'

'Yes,' said the voice, 'I was there.' There was a pause, which seemed to last a long time but couldn't have, during which I stared at the sickly green walls of my office, the plastic tulips in a corner. It was February. It had been snowing up to two days ago and the heating, which was always either flat-out or not on, was right off. I watched the north-east wind fling the snow at the roofs opposite; the dirty flakes whipped off the slates with each gust and whirled greyly down into the street; blew into hurrying people's faces.

'There's work for you,' said the voice. 'This one should fall straight into your lap. Anyway, it's going to have to, I've no one else to put on it.'

Straight into my lap – I had never known them fall any other way. 'What is it?' I said. 'Villains?'

'I don't know,' said the voice. 'But it isn't London, you're going to take a trip to Wiltshire.'

'What sort of a death is it?'

'We don't know that it is a death yet.'

'Look,' I said, 'A14 is—'

'A14 is what I decide it is,' said the voice. 'It's to do with a man called Mardy: his wife's disappeared.'

'What have the local police done?'

'Trailed their arse, a case of duck's disease.'

'That's very unusual,' I said. 'Who reported that she'd disappeared? The husband, of course?'

'No,' said the voice, 'it wasn't reported by anyone. That's what's unusual. Finally, local gossip reported it to the Chief Constable.' The voice added restlessly: 'I don't know the details, that's what you're going to find out about – we've been asked to lend a hand. First it went over to Serious Crimes, but Chief Inspector Bowman reckoned that as it wasn't a reported death it was nothing to do with him. Anyway, he's got his hands full with this millionaire's son who was found burned to death last Sunday night on Clapham Common, you've no doubt heard about it.'

Well of course I had.

'All right,' said the voice, 'get over to Serious Crimes, check with Chief Inspector Bowman, he'll give you the details.' It added: 'By the way, I do wish you and Bowman would try harder to get on together; I've had the backlash of the most frightful row you both had the other day.'

I said: 'I know the one.'

'It just won't do,' said the voice, 'it apparently nearly developed into a pitched battle out in the street.'

'People exaggerate,' I said, 'it wasn't as bad as that, but I agree – we don't see things the same way, he really hasn't the brains for the work, just the ambition.' I added: 'And I seem to worry him.'

'Unexplained Deaths and Serious Crimes are bound to have to work closely together,' said the voice irritably. 'And Bowman's your superior officer by a long way; you've got to get on.'

I said: 'I wonder if you could if you were in my place.'

'That's a ridiculous remark,' said the voice.

'I know it is,' I said, 'but it shouldn't be.'

'You could go further up the ladder yourself if you wanted to, but you will keep refusing promotion.'

'If I accepted it,' I said, 'that wouldn't solve anything, the problem in the service would still exist. Rivalry, jealousy, the struggle for recognition – the police is the same as any other organization in this country – but I'm only interested in bodies. By the way,' I added, 'it's obvious who was responsible for the burned-out millionaire offspring – Bowman's beating up every one in sight, but that'll get him nowhere. I was talking to a grass the other night in the Quaker's Head who told me that this boy's tart, a little tits and bum job, you know, page three in the Sunday press and a face like a bank statement, did you know she's got form for torture and that sonny's father likes being dragged around the floor by his cock? I'll bet you didn't, and I'll bet you none of you know how this grass found out about it. He was employed as a croupier in private baccarat games in the West End when he opened the wrong door one night in a Berkeley Square house and—'

'It isn't your case, Sergeant.'

'No, all right,' I said, 'we'll just let Chief Inspector Bowman take a long, slow lob at it and where does that get us?'

'It gets you down to Wiltshire,' said the voice, 'and that's all you need bother about. Go over and see Mr Bowman straight away, he's waiting for you at the Yard, and watch your manners, will you, for Christ's sake?'

'I'll watch my manners fine,' I said, and we rang off.

(I dream for a moment in Room 205, thinking of my uncle's letter that I have which he wrote before going off to die in '44, 'what a world, old boy, what a world'. He wrote it to my father and then he was gone – but not forgotten, anyway not by me. He foundered with the rest of the fresh blood on a brown mountainside, yet still in my breathless sleep I feel that I knew him, though I never knew him, but through his letters which he sent back from the front that I have I am still connected to him, ascending somehow to him.

My work tells me that our history is over, we are all over. I know that in my work I am supposed to represent a future, but I find that impossible when I look back at the past. At Earlsfield I watch young people at weekends dancing down the street towards Acacia Road in jeans and sneakers; they run, smile and kiss, holding hands tightly and run off laughing while I turn back into the flat to hide in the darkness of my work and thought.

The other day, having been on an inquiry till three, I got up, unable to sleep, at twenty to five in the morning and went to the bathroom; in its wrinkled mirror I saw an anxious, unshaven man. Even naked, without my worn, boring clothes, I was still a low-ranking detective, nothing at all to write home about. Yet what did the dead look like at the front? Any different?

I understand that we all were, and are, part of a most ancient history; it is only meaningless to us because we are nothing but some of the threads. This frail, threadbare picture is all that's left of us now; its strength was proud but badly led and went down – the most fertile field of all was the worst tilled.

On my days off I lie on my bed with grief for my lover and study my four small walls littered by my oversharp eye, in the paint, plaster and masonry, with the faces of my ancestors. I see the monotony of blood and nightmares and listen to the rain pattering grimly along the gutter.

Our church, my parents' burial place, is for sale and shored up with baulks of timber, and on my visits I sense the dead waiting in the tall brambles behind the graves. Later I dream of them: they point greyly at me in the pitiless rain, begging me to act for them. Since I cannot they turn hopelessly away again into the hedge, shrunken inside rotten army waterproofs.

And how will we describe our own loss and pain to others, once we have passed to join a dead father by a dead fire in the darkness of a country that has gone?)

I walked out on to my balcony at Earlsfield that was too small to sit out on and pretended it was summer again; although it was only February, I believed I felt my blood ringing in a spring mist with the sun just behind, and that I was listening to the song of a bird, young, and testing its brittle wings.

Then a truck moaned its way up the arterial road in second gear, covering the trees, everything in front of me, with diesel fumes.

I suddenly felt cold and went back indoors.

When I was small we were a united family, my mother and father, my elder sister Julie and I. We used to go out in the car on Sundays to Richmond Park, but then soon our people started to wear out, fall ill and die. My father had served in the second war and never really got over what he had seen in the Engineers; he started to get ill and die. My father liked to do everything himself, drive the car; when he got so bad that he couldn't, nor split the kindling any more, my mother turned to us in despair and said I can't drive or split wood, these are men's jobs. Yet she was sick herself and died before he did. They sat opposite each other in the sitting-room, upright, each watching the other get worse and die; or he would gaze for hours, silently, at his favourite picture, the good reproduction of a country cottage with a rose-garden which he had hung above the fire. Then Julie and I saw our mother go, after years of watching my father sit and die.

As for Julie and me, I held her tight, comforting her as she wept into a cheese plant at their home after that last row she had with her husband Harry, the get-rich-quick lad in the sports-gear game.

I love my sister Julie, I used always to look forward to going down on my free days to the villa they had outside Oxford, and it was fine for a long time until one night I saw the look on her face and I said dear, you're sick with worry, what is it, there's like a frost on your face. Oh, she said to me, I must speak to someone – I'm sickened, yes, sickened by Harry now, he has a go at all the girls and he's behind on the mortgage and he doesn't care about me and the child any more; he spends his time at the clubs. Don't worry about it, I said, that's the kind of thing that happens sometimes in any marriage. Oh no, she said, this is different. He hit me the other night for the first time in his life, and I'm really worried.

It was dreadful to see my sister so upset, we had always got on so tight and well, she was like my other self, we agreed so well, my only family, with her big arms and bustling skirt and cheerful face (hello, love, there you are at last, nice to see you, have a cup of tea, I'm making one, how are the criminals then?), and to see her now, pale and flat, pale as a candle flame in daytime. Gone her burly warmth that had been a haven, gone her sending Harry and me off to the Maid's Head (Mind you're not back late, you two, the shepherd's pie'll spoil, you know, it'll be on the table at three). All that was left of that generous affection was her worry for her child and her spontaneous tears in my arms. And yet again, as with my own wife and daughter, I was at first so blind that I could not see that between Julie and Harry many little tragedies were constructing the great tragedy that wipes out all the pleasures of our memory – a joke, a kiss, a hard night out with friends, the sensation of loved bare flesh, music hummed in the dark, kicking a stone by lamplight down a road, all small things that make existence both exciting and possible.

The day she rang me and said help me, Harry's in jail, I'm alone with the child, I went down to their flat at Oxford to find she had got worse alone, sitting rocking in a chair in her tweed overcoat with the baby on her knees with a blanket round it – the kettle and the pots she had taken pride in burned out and black and Julie herself much too small and neat now as the dead look.

I see no justice in it pissing down on the innocent under any circumstances, but it's much worse when it's your own blood, and I went in with their key I had and softly took the child from her and lit the fire and put the puzzled baby in the warmth, then took Julie by the wrists, pulling her up to take her by the waist as if we were lovers and said to her it's all right, dear, it'll be all right, as long as there's the two of us still you'll never go down, I'll make sure. I said to her, even if you weren't my sister, don't you remember what you did for me when Dahlia died and how if you, and a couple of friends at work, hadn't picked me up when you did I believe I'd have shot myself, don't you remember, Julie dear? And now it's my turn to play.

But she only smiled and said she was afraid that people get ill and die and I said no, but she said, remember Father, and I said, as if I could forget, and she said think of it, dear, a draper who defused mines. He was a part of old Britain, I said, and we can be proud of him, Julie, and she said, I know we can, and I said yes, because I can think of nothing more terrifying than unscrewing the cap off one of those, but Father did it. She drew herself up then and began to look like her old self again and I said listen, I've got money in the bank. You keep it there, she said, and I said no, don't be a fool, Julie, it's for you and the child, I'm a man on my own, I don't need it, take everything you want. No, it wouldn't be right, she said, and I said listen, I'm your brother, aren't I, whereupon she gave me such a beautiful look that I felt stung to the heart and she said do you remember how we used to play together on Sundays out at Richmond Park, and I said, of course I do. So then she looked at me very earnestly and said, dear, remember those times.

It was difficult, but I got her to take five hundred pounds at last to tide her over and she said, well, it'll be for the child, but I said, for God's sake, Julie, you're all I've got, you're my sister, and she said, veiling her eyes the way some women do, I want to repay it, would you like it if I came over to Earlsfield with the child and made house for you?

But I said no, Harry'll only draw three and do eighteen months, if that, the jails are crammed. You'll stick with him, won't you, and she said, yes, Harry's a fool sometimes but I love him, besides, there's the child to think of and I said, that's it, we're none of us perfect. After the case, when he'd only drawn eighteen months, she said, I know it's thanks to you that he's drawn so little and I said, I know the arresting officer and did a deal with him on another case. I don't think he'll do it again, he's not really dishonest, he just got desperate, out of his depth and she said, I may have been to blame too, I made him overspend – but if you knew the neighbours on this estate, how they talk. Let them talk, I said, and get a sore throat from it. When he was arrested, she said, the day they came and took him away, when I was alone in the house afterwards, for a time I wanted to kill the child and die. You'd never do that, I said. You let me know if you get depressed; you just draw on me like I drew on you and Harry when Edie and Dahlia happened. Oh I'm all right now, she said, I've got over it, but it was the shock at the time, and the shame. Would you go and see Harry? Yes of course, I said, if he'd like it. Oh he would, she said. He told me when I went to see him the other day. I know he wants to thank you; he'll send you a visiting order. She paused and said, you know what would be nice? When Harry's back, perhaps we could go over to Richmond Park one day, the three of us and the child, like we used to. We could take a picnic, it would be good for us. Yes, I said, good idea, we'll do it one day.

One day, Julie.

3

I am at Earlsfield. I go out on to my balcony overlooking Acacia Circus, its concrete pavement spattered with pigeon-shit, and watch the city stirring to the north – millions of people stirring and shifting in the anxiety of their half sleep.

This shocking loneliness! Some nights here, when I can't face going to bed, I ask the dead to sit up with me and know that they do come and listen; the air in the sitting-room is thick with them. They sit down, get up and move around just as the living do, while I try to understand the great experience they have been through. I put questions about existence to them and frankly ask them for help. I ask after my grandmother who, her brain not working properly any more at eighty-six, died in the snow one January day on the steps of a house we had long ago sold; also my cousin, an intelligent woman who died of cancer and said to me as she lay dying in hospital: 'If I just knew what it was for.'

Finally I go to bed and sometimes see my father in my dreams, rowing alone, far out from the seashore on dark water with his demob hat, which he kept as a war souvenir, cocked on the side of his head. I want to go to him but can't reach him. His boat's leaking, it's full of water, it's a nightmare; his head bobs obstinately against the twilit sky; he rows slowly away from me and sinks.

Long before I met my wife Edie I fell in love with a remarkable woman. Her father was British, her mother Arab; she filled me with a terrible excitement. We look so definite in this moment, don't we, she said to me once after we had made love and were standing hand in hand at her window. We gazed at the plane trees bowing and rushing together in the spring wind far down in the garden and she said, you'll remember this, won't you? I knew I would never forget it and I said, I'm just completely in love with you and she answered, but I'll cheat you, you know. What, I said, with another man? No, she said, giving me a strange look, there are other ways. Do you want to cheat me? I said. If so, I'd better know. It's just that there are other seducers than men, she said. I didn't know what she meant at the time.

She was writing a book (what else can you do in West Hampstead?) and was a philosophy student at University College. Her tongue was sharp, she hated errors and weak thinking; indeed, it was she who taught me to think ('you know how to, but you don't realize it yet'). My madness keeps me from going mad, she said, just after she had started to hit the cocaine (but I wasn't living with her, and was too young then to know what she meant). She was left-wing and crossed picket and police lines with a flask of whisky in her pocket; she never had any fear of people at all. I don't know how you can do it, I said, you've got more guts than I have, and she replied, it's simply trust in people and in oneself.

I never forgot that.

We broke up, but there were times when she would sit for days and nights on end in some street where she thought I might pass, graceful and dark, smoking cigarette after cigarette ('trying to get *off* it, you know').

But I had joined the police and had met Edie.

One night when she was sitting like that on a street bench the law of course came up to her and said, waiting for someone, are we? and she nodded and said calmly, of course. My lover.

She had great class. I tell you class is everything, even as you fall: your name is graven as you fall.

'My role as a writer,' she said, 'is to survive and record.' (But her work was in ruins, her book abandoned.) She was on heroin by then ('it's nothing, darling, just a kick').

On kicks get ill, on kicks get worse and die. Going up to London on the train from Maidstone where I was working when I heard she was dying, much too late to intervene, I felt her leave between my fingers at Malling, fly out into the dark air of late afternoon at Sydenham and breathe her last at Penge, marble white. At Victoria I got to a telephone and her mother explained about the overdose, the dirty needle – how she had spoken clearly of me once before coma and death. I walked up into Green Park. It was spring that terrible night and the trees in the park, buds scarcely formed, tumbled madly against each other in the wind, and there we were again by the window, her hand surging expressly into mine.

My granny used to say there was hope in any garden; but I found none in Green Park.

When I was a boy I once went down to a farm in Kent with my father and we watched three men kill a sheep with its head at the top of a flight of steps. It wouldn't stay still to die even with its feet tied together, so the owner smacked it across the face to keep it quiet – he was a big man with red hair on his chest. Then he sharpened his knife and put it straight in the animal's throat. How it bled down those steps! The farmer's wife washed the blood away with buckets of water. Afterwards, while the men were butchering it, I looked up and watched a cloud of rain coming towards us across the flat fields; it was March. Then, when the work was finished, after my father had paid for the sheep and we had put the meat in our car, we all went into the kitchen. The men talked about money and rationing (which was why we had bought the sheep), the importance of hanging a carcass properly and the best way to tan a fleece. One of the men was an army deserter from Liverpool; his name was Kevin. He had split the carcass down the spine with an axe and after he had drunk his beer carried the liver down for us on a piece of old sheet, but he kept the head for himself.

'We'll have the chops with potatoes and mint sauce,' said my father when we got home, then started talking to my mother about a dream he had had about an air raid in '43, when he was with the bomb disposal squad. He said: 'We only got thirty dead out of the building, but there were many more in there than that. The trouble was, there was a leaking gas main in the basement that we couldn't seal off.' He dreamed about that building till the end of his life: 'Of course there were children in there; we never got to them.'

Life is made of slowly composed horrors.

'Your father shouldn't worry about it so,' my mother said to us. 'It's all over now; he's distracting himself for no reason.'

But as I know for myself, some things are never over. Later I tried to get my father to talk about it, but he wouldn't; he only talked about it in his sleep and I remember Julie saying to me while she was looking after him just before he died: 'He's having those nightmares of his again.'

'About that building?'

'Yes, he was screaming about the children.'

'That's the dreadful thing about dreams, isn't it, Julie?' I said. 'It's always now.'

I try to sleep but can't, and lie awake in the dark, listening to the rumble of traffic. Just once my father said to me: 'We could hear them dying, coughing and choking somewhere under that mass of bricks. The stink of gas—'

People are horrified by death all right, but most of them don't understand it at all, including the banal element – the practised fingers of a police surgeon opening a dead eye by a road, then turning to us to say: 'She's gone, leave a constable with her, the rest of us can go and have a drink while we wait for the ambulance – that pub over there.'

Where sheep may safely graze.

4

'Hello, Charlie,' I said to Bowman when I got into his office, 'did you want to see me then?'

'Don't fucking start,' he said: 'I was just beginning to forget about you, and less of the Charlie.'

'Look, forget that business the other day,' I said, 'it's over and done with now and after all no one got hurt.'

'No, but it was close. That time it was fucking close.'

'And it will be again I daresay,' I said, 'but right now, let's get down to it.'

'There's this man called Mardy down in the West Country whose wife's gone missing.'

'Missing how long?'

'Six months' worth.'

'Yes, that's a long time,' I said. 'Missing Persons turn anything up?'

'Not a light.'

'Local law taking an interest?' I said. 'Is it efficient, does it care?'

'I don't fucking know,' said Bowman. 'The place is out in the sticks somewhere. They tried to hand it over to us but there was no body and I decided we didn't want it so I bowled it back upstairs – I've got enough on right now with this incinerated little bastard on Clapham Common, it's all on page one, you mightn't have noticed. Local law out in the middle of nothing flat – how should I know how they carry on down there?'

'All right, all right,' I said, 'don't give your garters a heart attack, where was she last seen, when and who by?'

He sighed, got a file out of a drawer and slapped it down on the desk top. He flipped the file open. 'Name Marianne Mardy,' he said. 'Last seen August 1984 at her home.'

'Seen by whom? Any names?'

'No names. The request for our help came direct from the Chief Constable.'

'But this is a carve-up,' I said, 'it's totally irregular.'

'It seems the countryside's like that in places,' said Bowman. 'I wouldn't know, I've never been hardly, except to Brighton.'

'All right,' I said, 'there's no need to go potty about our open spaces. And this woman's home, what's home like?'

'Christ,' Bowman shouted, 'I don't fucking know. You'll have to ask them down there about that. Go and find out – my life, that's what you draw your bleeding wages for. I imagine it's some old barracks where they grind out electric light by hand. I was born in Hackney, how should I bloody know?'

'Mind your ulcer,' I said. 'Who reported her missing anyway? The husband?'

'No, that's the point,' he said. 'I tell you she was reported missing directly to the Chief Constable, not the local police, the local police knew about it but did nothing.'

'Doesn't seem much point their having any local law down there at all,' I said. 'Amazing.'

'I know you're easily amazed,' said Bowman. 'I'm just telling you what we've got.'

'OK,' I said, 'and did the local people finally get pushed into moving on it?'

'Yes,' said Bowman, 'it says here they finally went up in January, here it is, the fifteenth, 1985.'

'And did they find anything? Do anything?'

'Well of course they fucking didn't!' Bowman yelled. 'Otherwise no one would have needed to send for you, would they, you stupid man?'

'You radiate police charm, Charlie,' I said. 'You're what tourists adore about Britain's wonderful coppers. Pull your skirts down a bit, though; your knobbly knees are showing.'

'I might be going to report this conversation, Sergeant.'

'Don't be silly,' I said, 'you never do.'

He said with calm ferocity: 'I'm going to try to keep my temper with you, it's an order from your Deputy Commander.'

'I know,' I said, 'I've had it as well. I don't know how we're going to manage it quite but let's have a good try, dear, shall we, and see if we can make the marriage work. Meantime, let's stick to this file. This local trainband, did they get a warrant out to search the Mardy place?'

'Seems not. And don't ask me why not!' he shouted. 'I'm not the officer on this case, I'm just handing it over to you.'

'OK,' I said, 'but you can read, can't you, and you've got the file right side up on your side of the desk.'

'All right,' he grumbled, bending over it, 'all the police down there have sent back is a load of official waffle ending up with no grounds for suspicion.'

'Sounds funny them saying that,' I said, 'when here's this woman been missing six months – everyone from the Chief Constable downwards seems agreed on that bit.'

'Look,' said Bowman nastily, 'I'm tired of this conversation. Why don't you forget about your fucking great brain and get your feet into your high-heeled boots? Get down there – do it now.' He threw the file across at me and said: 'Catch it, it's all yours.'

It seemed as reasonable an order as you could ever get from him so I stood up and he said: 'Check with an Inspector Kedward when you arrive and mind your bloody manners.'

I said nothing but picked up the file and went down into the freezing street. I boarded a bus going up to the West End; I didn't feel like going back to Earlsfield. I would buy a razor and a packet of blades at this country place. At Oxford Circus I let myself be jostled by office-leavers making in a flood for the underground in the teeth of a murderous east wind, having watched them sunk in their newspaper or paperback, frozen, exhausted in the world that meant the end of their day. I dropped off the bus in a traffic jam at a fast food; it was called the Lazy Jay. I went in and ordered a hamburger without the roll and plenty of sauce; a black girl served me.

'How you like it cooked, man?'

'Now if you like,' I said, 'I'm in a hurry.'

I paid, and a bit poorer, walked north from Oxford Street to a pub with drunks and cab-drivers sitting at raw plastic tables off Cleveland Street; it was called the Yorkshire Grey. Big black women with net bags filled with spices and ladies' fingers complained or laughed fatly in a man's ears – skinny white women examined the bar for likely punters and, finding none, settled for what wandered in and out of the gents'. I ordered a pint of lager and sat drinking it slowly. The trick about being invisible in a place like that is to be half well-known and never to look at anyone – then they never trouble to look at you, taking you for a drunk, a has-been, no matter what, or newly fired and on the dole, starting on the skids etcetera. I sat in my corner and lit a horrible cigarette called a Westminster, hoping that perhaps the straw taste would really help me stop smoking this time. It didn't; I smoked it right to the end. I tried my pint again, lit a second Westminster, and opened the file Bowman had thrown me. It was a thin file. It was a funny business; it seemed to me there had been no proper procedure in it at the local end. I didn't understand so far why the police down there couldn't or hadn't tackled it, nor where their Chief Constable came into it – all on his own to us, independently, as it seemed to me, of his own officers. It was all the more curious because no one had been reported dead, just missing – and then not by the person you would have thought most interested, i.e. the husband.

Page one of the file had the name on it – William Mardy. Profession: general practitioner. However, there was a note against this – struck off, see file that refers.

Then there was his address, Thornhill Court, Thornhill, Wilts.

Sickening errors, democratically arrived at of course, lay either side of the road as I drove west out of London. Blocks of semi-abandoned streets made dead ends of effort where people who had tried to start something – anything – had been crushed by the dull, triumphant logic of the state. I crossed the demarcation lines of two ethnic groups at Swallowtail Lane; the Regal cinema loomed up in my lights, its façade blackened by fire. I passed a series of streets that stood for political convictions. No one crossed them on foot now at night; yet they were streets that we had easily patrolled, one, two of us, as young coppers on the beat in the old days. But now there was no asserting yourself here as police unless there were fifty of you. The blindness to understanding was equally lit by the few lights that swayed in the icy darkness, and by the rows of windows, some half lit, in small streets that now no longer led anywhere but to danger. The windows all had the same mail-order leer that made a flat, to its family, whatever its colour, seem falsely safe, and each was whitened by the eyeball of a Japanese lampshade. Now, on the main road, a first-floor sash yawned, broken, open and unlit next to a traffic light that was at red. I stopped, waiting for this light to change, watching the rain sweep off the eaves in the north wind thick as a widow's tears; an Indian woman hurried down a sidestreet with a coat over her head against recognition and the rain. A block further on lay a heap of smashed cars frosted over on a stretch of waste ground; next to them, black with grime, its forecourt wet with dirty snow, stood a shut-down petrol station.

In further sad, narrow streets, beyond my car lights, half hidden by groups of old bangers with their front wheels up on the pavement, lay ruined three-storey houses that the council neither had the money to restore, nor corruption interest in pulling down. These were all dark – the power, the water cut off in them, life itself cut off there at this wrong end of winter. Yet life still did cling on in them, I knew. Uncivilized, mad life; these rank buildings that had housed self-respecting families once were now occupied by squatters of any kind – the desperate last fugitives of a beaten, abandoned army, their dignity, rights and occupations gone (or never known), their hope gone, tomorrow gone. I passed Arcade Street where there had been a machine-gun attack a fortnight ago on the wrong house (they were terrorists who had wanted the house next door) – wife and nine-month-old child killed as they watched TV in the sitting-room, terrific. But the homeless, made invisible in their misery by the frozen night, were folk that in my work I knew much too well; the ruins of their youth framed their shrieks. They screamed and robbed each other for any money or drug that would release them from their rags and bed of cement, sang, droned and wandered through these lost parts of the city for as long as hell lasted for them, and the embarrassed or absent eyes of passers-by seemed to me far worse than any well-bred laughter or liberal music heard from the snow and rain behind elegant ground-floor blinds.

What maddened me sometimes with my work at A14 was that I could not get any justice for these people until they were dead. These university drop-outs, these mad barefoot beauties that had been turned away from home, who staggered down the streets with plastic bags filled with old newspapers against the cold – wrongo's, druggo's, folk of every age, colour and past, they all had that despair in common that made them gabble out their raging dreams in any shelter they could find. They screamed at each other in Battersea, moaned over their empty cider bottles in Vauxhall, not having the loot for a night in Rowton House, their faces the colour of rotten-stucco under the glare of the white lights at Waterloo Bridge and wreathed in the diesel fumes of the forty-ton fruit trucks that pounded up from Kent to Nine Elms all night long. In the day you could see them, white, faded and stained after such nights in winter; I saw them at the morning round-up at the Factory, waiting in various moods to be taken for sentencing at Great Marlborough Street – the thin, crazy faces, strange noses, eyes, hands rendered noble by madness and hunger, the rusty punctures in their arms, their whiplash tongues and then, later, the flat, sullen grief of their meaningless statements to the magistrate. And still the politicians blag serenely on, as though poverty, since they have no policy for it, didn't exist.

Yet no murder is worse to find than a body dead of cold against a door.

5

It was a long time since I had been in any villages or small towns; London hasn't spared its own. Not that it made any difference. Where I drove into Thornhill it looked just like London. There were the same council estates, sprayed-on graffiti, closed-down factories and padlocked gates; there was also the same collection of boasting Rastas and white youths with Mohican trims leaning against dark walls, furtively drawing on anything that could be smoked behind a cupped hand. The pubs had emptied, their contents draining noisily away towards the Quikchik at the corner; I might as well have been in Tooting, except that there wasn't the city beyond and all round me that I was used to, only the empty country. I continued to drive down what was left of a seventeenth-century main street, and noticed many charming old seventeenth-century phenomena occurring around me. Five whites were chasing an Asian under the amused gaze of a pub sign called the Jolly Sailor, and a group of Angels whipped past me on seven-fifties, each with a dotty little bat in pink jeans up behind him – yes, it was almost like home.

I got to two hotels, Quayntewayes and the Saxon Arms, both built of brand-new brick, whatever the gold Elizabethan lettering said over their front doors; each stared their brightly lit windows into the other's plate-glass eyes from across the street. Fat men in their fifties, dressed as farmers only without a speck of mud on them, backed carefully out of five-door Mercedes estate cars. They wore tweed hats, pheasant feathers in the bands and all – Christ, I thought, it'll be gaiters, a pair of Holland and Holland guns and shooting-sticks next. I heard them all roaring with laughter and they looked well pissed. I slowed and watched them elbowing their way through folk on the pavement. They're the kind of people I love to watch through narrowed eyes – no class, too much money and too much noise. Red as beef in the face, they're not very nice beyond their own kind – I remember the gusto with which some of us had cleaned up the secret wargames that some very similar folk had been playing some years back. They slapped a man who was quietly vomiting against a lamp-post on the back, then staggered into the bright interior of the Saxon Arms, though it was after time down here – not that it was anything to do with me.

Next I came to a poor old church that I was sorry for, though I'm not religious. A notice said that it was seven hundred years old, but it was arc-lit at the taxpayer's expense to show where council trendies had fiddled about with it. There was also a board at the lych-gate – gold lettering on a black ground announcing many a long sermon to be preached by a Reverend Eustace Disney-Smith. I built up a glimpse of this person, minor public school and jangling some change in his blue shorts as he pounded up the field on thick but futile legs, blowing a very thin whistle in the mist, ignored by the players and righteously refusing a second shandy in the bar after the match: holy to a fault, yet mingling blamelessly with the boys.

Further on still stood a recycled cinema with space games on machines that paid out and bingo at street level, called the Lucky Jack Club. But I reckoned that the more spacious part of the building didn't bother with the unemployed and the OAPs but concentrated on punters who wanted to play blackjack, stud poker, throw dice – win, lose, but grab a bird. I knew this from long experience by the two heavies I spotted leaning on the fake marble entrance, their fists in the pockets of their tight trousers, scanning faces.

Yes, well, it was what passed for rural Britain now, once you had staggered off your RestRoads bus, whacked your way round some stately homes against the wishes of your ageing heart ('you'd have done better not to go, George, you ought to have stayed at home and watched the film on BBC2, I told you you'd be worn out if we did this'), gone round a final castle that let the rain in that was starting and anyway loathed the sight of you ('No one to cross the white ropes into the Family's area, please') and had a look at the desperately fit tigers in the park. I finally got to the police station; it was brand-new. There was also a brand-new squad car, a three and a half Rover, outside to go with it, and two scarcely used young coppers in cheese-cutters sitting up front. We all looked at each other expressionlessly as I drove by. Through the main doors I spotted a young black complaining with his arms at the desk sergeant. It was just like Poland Street; the black might as well have been skanking to his own ghetto-blaster for all the notice anyone took of him. I looked for a place to park but it was solid, so I made a U-turn on to the yellow line in front of the station, braking bonnet to bonnet with the squad car; then I swiched off and got out. The moment I did so, the copper in the passenger's seat of the squad car got out also, pausing to settle his chessboard hat in a slow and regulation way.

'Evening, sonny,' he said with a grin, 'you ever heard of the highway code?'

'Yes,' I said, 'and I could beat you on it, darling; I've been driving since before you were in nappies.'

The grin died. 'Trying to be funny, are we?'

'Yes,' I said, 'but your act isn't working, and mine doesn't have to try very hard to beat it.'

That got us straight to a silence. Into it I said: 'There's one thing about me, son. I react very badly to being called sonny – I really, really hate it, see?'

His mate, the driver, had also got out of the motor and was wandering over, pulling the armchair creases out of his tunic.

My bloke said: 'Look, can't you see you're parked on a yellow line?'

'I can,' I said, 'I'm by no means colour-blind, and where were you parked?'

'Ours is a police vehicle,' he said, 'and besides, we're in it.'

'No you're not,' I said, 'you're both outside it talking to me, so you're both committing an offence and could be reported.'

The first copper said: 'So you're telling us the law, are you? Is that it?'

'It's not difficult at all,' I said, 'if you happen to know it.'

'I see,' said the first copper. It was obvious that he didn't quite. With his mate he exchanged one of those careful looks from under his cap that you see them do on television when the producer hasn't got it quite right – he was young, and needed much more practice with a look like that. Finally he said: 'I'm going back to the car, you just stay right where you are with this officer, get it?'

'You're the great big policeman,' I said, 'and yes, I've got it.'

'Don't follow me up with any more jokes just now,' said the first copper, 'not if you want to keep your guts in where they belong.'

I said to the second copper, the driver: 'This officer has just threatened me, will you take official note of it?'

The driver said: 'I think I'd let it go if I were you.'

'If I were you,' I said, 'I probably would, only I'm not.'

'You really are looking for trouble,' said the driver, 'aren't you?'

'Yes, and I've found a lot of it too,' I said, 'more than you ever have in your short lives.'

'I don't doubt you have,' said the driver, in a voice as grey as rain.

'What you ought to be doing,' I said, 'both of you, is hop into that tax-paid motor of yours that you can't take your bird for a ride in and get into the fight I just saw three streets back on the right, five whites running for an Asian to beat him up. It looks dodgy but at least you'd be doing some good. Here, you're doing no good at all. Here, you're just wasting public time, dear.'

'I don't like the dear,' the driver said. He bunched his fists. 'Not at all.'

'It'll teach you not to call people sonny,' I said. 'Are you going to have a go?'

'It's really dark here,' said the driver, 'and there's no one watching that I can see.'

'And they call you a police officer,' I said. 'Well, that's the gullible public for you.'

I could have let them off the hook long ago if I'd wanted to; but in my shabby clothes, with my tired-looking car, I wanted them to take me for just anybody, to see how far they would go.

'Just one little smack,' said the driver, 'might teach you manners.'

'Do it if you must,' I said, 'but I should think very hard first. I could have a weak heart or a strong right – whichever it was, you'd be looking for a job.'

It was near, but in the end he flexed his arms, sighed and looked away; just then his mate came back with a drink-and-drive kit. 'Let's do a little breathing, son,' he said. 'Breathing out. I think we've been drinking a bit, haven't we? I think we've had a few, yes.'

'That's it,' said the driver. 'Very slow. Nice and hard.'

'I don't object to the test,' I said. 'The only thing is, let me just examine that kit before I blow into it.'

'Why?' said the driver.

'Because I know some coppers where I come from,' I said, 'they keep a special one in the car for folk they don't like, and that's a hat that might fit me, isn't it?'

'And where are you from?' said the second copper.

'From where you two berks would get red ears fast,' I said.

'Oh, London, is it?' They both smiled. 'How very nice to meet a Londoner on our little country patch, though they say our great capital's not the city it once was – must be on account of the people that live there.'

'In this little shithole,' I said, 'they can say what they like about London.'

'He's cheeky, this one, isn't he?' the driver enquired upwards of the scudding sky. 'Very cheeky, yes.'

'It's a habit we all have to try and master,' I said.

'I might just have to shut your yap for you after all,' said the driver.

'I'm busy,' I said. I was examining their kit. It looked all right, spanking new to me, though they had taken a long time getting it out of their car and I hadn't seen it come out of its box. Anyway, I didn't care much – there was no chance of my being over the top with a fast-food inside me and only one pint of beer, and that hours before. When I had finished they took it away and conferred by their headlights. Then the driver came back to me and said: 'It's just as we thought, you're right over the top, yes.' And his mate added: 'Oh yes, yes. Way over.'

'I didn't expect anything else,' I said, 'not parked next to you two, but can I just look at that gear I blew into?'

'No you may not,' they said together, 'as this is now, or could be, evidence in a matter that may lead to your prosecution on a charge of being drunk in charge of a motor vehicle.' The driver added: 'So now let's all go inside, shall we?'

'It certainly does look inviting,' I said, 'yet another police station.'

'Oh so you know about them, do you?' said the driver. 'I thought you might have.'

'You could say that,' I said. 'Yes, you definitely could.'

'That's it, he's got form,' said the other copper, 'you can almost get to smell it, can't you? I'll bet you it's a yard long; we've got a right runner here, Ben.'

We went through the doors and crossed to the desk sergeant, a hatless middle-aged man with a rash in his hair. 'Well?' he said, 'what's this, then?'

'Drink and drive,' said the copper called Ben, 'way over the top, bang to rights.'

'How I do love a country Londoner,' I said. '*Bang to rights!*' I mimicked. '1950s slang, I lap it up.'

'And cheeky with it,' said the same copper, reddening. The desk sergeant looked up at me and said: 'You'd better realize, laddie, you're doing yourself no good with that kind of talk.'

'What you'd better realize,' I said in a leaden voice, 'is that I've got an actual name, and I strongly recommend you to use it. It's neither sonny, laddie, darling nor dear, what do you take me for? A sheepdog starring in an old B-movie?'

'All right, all right,' said the sergeant warily. He pulled his pad of charge sheets towards him. 'Since it seems you've got a name let's have it, if you're sober enough to give it.'

So I gave it to him.

'Address?'

I told him Earlsfield.

'Place of work?'

'Poland Street.'

'Poland Street?' he said, creasing his eyes up. 'What number in Poland Street?'

I told him the number.

'That somehow rings a bell,' he said.

'It ought to.'

'Oh well, never mind,' he said. He yawned. 'Any profession?'

'You bet,' I said. I dropped my warrant card on his desk. 'You can see what profession.'

An extremely long silence followed. To end it I said to the sergeant: 'Your apprentices here have really got their goolies tangled up in the high wire this time, eh, Sarge?'

'Why the fuck didn't you tell us?' yelled the driver.

'Because I'm in the business of extracting information,' I said, 'not volunteering it.'

'Let's all keep calm, shall we?' said the desk sergeant.

'You can screw the calm,' I said. 'I may well bring a charge against these officers, in that they knowingly made and preferred against me and conspired to make a false drink-and-drive charge against me.' I said to them: 'Now bring me that kit I blew into, and double.'

'You've got to realize,' said the desk sergeant, 'these are my men.'

'I realize that all right,' I said, 'and I don't give a fuck about it, so you'd better put your weight behind me, otherwise it'll be your head on a plate too, and new jobs aren't so easy for old men to find in these hard times.'

'All right,' said the desk sergeant. 'Get it, the pair of you, and snap it up.'

They trooped out and were gone for a while. When they did come back the one called Ben said: 'Sorry, Sarge, but I'm afraid it got trodden on on the way in.'

'Well that's that then, isn't it?' I said. 'I like it better than an outright confession.'

The desk sergeant said: 'What are you going to do about it?'

'Nothing,' I said. 'But you take bloody good care that none of you ever do a thing like that again. Now get both these artists out of here, there must be something for them to do other than warming their arses on a yellow line.'

'OK,' said the sergeant, 'there's the report of a fight come in over at 10, Wakefield Road, so get out there the two of you and create some peace, now move.'

At the door the driver turned to me and said: 'You're a right bastard, you are.'

'I prefer me to you,' I said.

'Christ, you must be fun to work with, that must be really amusing.'

'It wouldn't be if anyone did, sonny,' I said, 'however nobody does, and looking you two over I like it better that way. Now do what your boss tells you, jump on your bike, remember you're a public servant the same as everyone else in here and don't take the piss, otherwise it'll be your head next, now get out of here.'

When they had gone the desk sergeant said: 'All right, now what are you down in Thornhill for?'

'Isn't it obvious?' I said. 'What do you think?'

'The Mardy business?'

'Well of course it's the Mardy business,' I said. 'A few syrup of figs have started to get on back to front over this. What I want to do right away is see Inspector Kedward.'

'Well you can't,' said the desk sergeant, 'he isn't here.'

'Why not?' I said. 'Is it his night off or somethmg?'

'I'm spelling him.'

'Get him on the phone, can't you?'

'I've instructions not to, unless it's really urgent.'

I said: 'Listen. You can take it from me that if overworked detectives from A14 get sent down from the smoke to a little rat-trap like this, it's for something the brass thinks is urgent.'

'Inspector Kedward didn't consider the Mardys urgent.'

'I know,' I said, 'but your Chief Constable does, and that's all that need concern muddleheads like you and me.'

'Why don't you get on to him then?'

'Don't be stupid,' I said, 'and don't take the piss. Now get your inspector on the phone.'

'I wouldn't know where to reach him, not at this time of night.'

'You mean he hasn't got a home to go to?'

When the sergeant gazed down at his desk without speaking I said: 'What you mean is, at this time of night he's seldom there. OK then, is he married?'

'Of course.'

I didn't myself see why of course but I said: 'All right, well then get Mrs Kedward on the line for me then, else leave a message, or do I have to do it myself?'

'Doesn't matter which of us does it,' he said, 'you won't reach her, she won't be at home either.'

'Hardly seems much point in having a detective-inspector here at all quite frankly,' I said, 'does there, if he's never on the job.'

'He's here in the daytime.'

'Yes but the trouble is,' I said, 'that a good many things that should interest detective-inspectors happen at night.' I planted my elbows on the desk and put my nose up close to his. I said: 'Now listen, are you telling me the truth, or are you covering up for your inspector?'

'I tell you I'm standing in for him,' he said neutrally. 'Nobody said you was coming, otherwise doubtless he'd have waited here to see you.'

'Nobody said I was coming,' I said, 'because I didn't say so myself, I like it better that way. I find detective work depends on being sudden at times and that's me, do you see? Sudden.'

'Very impressive,' he said. 'I'm flabbergasted by it.'

'I don't think you quite understand,' I said. 'I'll put it this way. The more you don't tell me right answers to what I want to know, the more I start to suspect – and as another police officer I'd better remind you straight off, you be careful you don't pot the wrong colour on this one, darling. Because if you do you could lose the whole of this frame fast and find yourself out on your ear with a pension worth five times fuck all. Now your best course is to start telling me what I want to know immediately, otherwise I'll dig it up by myself in which case God help you, are you reading me? It's London that wants the answer to this Mrs Mardy business fast, and I mean very fast. I've got a firework up my arsehole from my folk, and that means I'm going to have to put one up yours, it's called self-help, all right?'

When he didn't answer me at all but looked stubbornly down at his blotter I said: 'You really are giving me a dreadful pain, you are. I haven't a hundred years to deal with this but about two days, three at the most. I've got a stack of work on back where I come from, I've no time for your sweet old country ways. You're either straight or you're bent, copper – I'll give you the benefit of the doubt for the time being and assume you're straight. In that case, if you won't talk about Kedward leave him to me; tell me about the Mardys instead.'

He stared at me for a long time and said in the end: 'My name's Turner.' He opened a drawer in the desk and got out a flask of Bell's. 'By the neck,' he said, 'I've no glasses. Does that suit you, Mr fucking London man?'

'It'll do,' I said. I picked up the bottle and took a good drink out of it.

He did the same and said: 'We might finish this bottle, if you're in the mood.'

'Watch your inspector doesn't catch you at it,' I said as he drank, 'you on duty and everything.'

'There's no fear of that.' We were getting on better now.

'I'm in the mood to finish your scotch,' I said, 'but you tell me about these Mardys.'

'I'm Mr Kedward's man, don't threaten me.'

'I'm not in the threatening business,' I said, 'I'm in the inquiry business.' I added: 'You don't like detectives, do you?'

'No,' he said, 'frankly, they stink.'

'I'm sorry to hear you say it.'

'I've seen worse than you,' said Turner, 'but to me a proper police officer goes in uniform, he's not afraid to be seen in it. I don't like it when they go skulking around in shabby clothes like you.'

'No more than I like it when I see you sitting around here not clearing up the business of a woman disappeared from right under you,' I said.

He had a drink; it took him some time. Then he said: 'Old family here, the Mardys.'

'How old?'

'They came over here with Charles II in sixteen sixty and been here ever since.'

'What's the house like?'

'Burned down and rebuilt in 1860. It's a ruin now, though, and that's putting it mildly.'

'Have they got money?'

'I don't know,' he said, 'but I wouldn't think so. Anyway, not now.'

'All right,' I said, 'so now what about Mrs Mardy?'

'We never called her that in Thornhill,' he said. 'We used to call her madam because she was French; it was the nearest we could get to the French, which of course we can't pronounce at Thornhill. It was to her face we called her madam, but among ourselves we always called her by her name, Marianne. She was beautiful, but what was more, she had a wonderful singing voice and gave concerts in the house; Dr Mardy used to accompany her on the violin. Anyone from the town was welcome, and afterwards there would be wine and sandwiches in the hall under the organ; the girls would come in and help her with the sandwiches, and some of the men would bring a bottle. It started small as things do, but in the end people would come a long way to hear and watch them. They were great evenings as long as it didn't rain in. People you never might have thought would be interested used to come – people from as far off as Birmingham and Oxford, London even. Then, after she had finished singing, she would come down with the doctor off their makeshift stage, the doctor with his violin in his hand and an arm round her waist and she joking and laughing with everyone, sometimes trying out a new song in a corner with someone while we ate and drank. Oh yes, they were wonderful evenings, they were, wonderful – people got together and talked, quite like old times, much better than watching the match on the telly. I tell you, we're no great lovers of the French here, but she really won us over with the songs of her own land and ours, and I tell you that hall was packed, packed it was. People wanted to give money sometimes but she would never accept it; she said, give it to something important, like the cancer fund. Yes, yes, with her character she wiped out all prejudice, she was so kind and natural. You know if I shut my eyes I can hear her singing now and see the doctor behind her, his face bent over his bow as they changed key. They did love each other. Some people only came to jeer at them but you can be sure they never stayed long, because Marianne and the doctor had gained our deep respect here at Thornhill.

'When I think back towards the last concerts they gave you could see right across society in that hall; the whole of our people was somehow there, all joined in their music. You take me for a sentimental idiot, but it was beautiful; I love good music, true music. Sometimes, carried away herself by what she was singing, she would reach out to us all with her arms, smiling radiantly, and then at the end wave as though she were saying goodbye, saying remember me.

'No, I never missed a single one of her concerts, and I can think of dozens like me.'

'What do you think's happened to her now?'

He didn't reply at once, but took another drink and then said:

'I think she's most probably resting with the doctor up at the house; she hasn't been well for a long while.'

'How long?'

'I'd say a good year.'

'You believe she'll come back?'

'Come back?' he said. 'Marianne? Of course she'll come back.'

'There are people that doubt it.'

'I can't help that,' he said obstinately. 'If anything had happened to her we would have known.'

'I wish life were that simple,' I said. 'I've been in my disgusting game for years. It hardly ever smells of lilac and I can tell you, it doesn't this time. This Mrs Mardy's not been seen for six months, six months, and people are worried for her, don't you see? Worried enough to have me come down.'

'She's got the doctor to look after her. He's her husband. He loves her.'

'Six months' disappearance can mean eternity.'

'No, no,' said Turner, 'I tell you, she's just resting up at the house.'

I said: 'It's late, but I think I'll just get in touch with the Chief Constable.'

'You can't,' said Turner, 'he's in hospital, he's had a stroke.'

'You're seriously undermanned around here,' I said.

6

I was booked into Quayntewayes and lay down on the bed in Room 21. After a while I put out the light and stared at the uncurtained windows; presently I began to smell dead flowers. There was a bad photograph of Marianne Mardy in the file I had and in the darkness of my head I reviewed it, going over her laughing features one by one and adding to them everything I had just learned about her. It wasn't easy for me to fix her face in my mind because in the photograph the face was blurred; the camera had moved. However, I could see that although she was not beautiful as the cinema thinks of beauty, there was a tenderness in her eyes which was its own beauty. She was in a garden, dressed in old clothes, a skirt and jumper, and running her hand through her hair; she was looking as if towards someone out of shot – her husband, surely. It wasn't the first time I had smelled dead flowers – they were always the same flowers, chrysanthemums, and every time I smelled them it meant that somebody was dead.

I fell for a time into a mood, not sleep, until I found that I was murmuring words so old that I couldn't think for a time where I had heard them, but in the end recalled them as Spenser's, verses of his that I had learned at school:

> 'She fell away in her first age's spring,
> While yet her leaf was green, and fresh her rind,
> And while her branch fair blossoms forth did bring
> She fell away against all course of kind;
> For age to die is right, but youth is wrong;
> She fell away like fruit blown down with wind.'

I felt myself in that hotel room, prosaic as it was, racked by sorrow, and in the half-dark was aware of arms opening spontaneously to me. I remembered those words of hers that Turner had cited: *I am Marianne, remember me*. Spenser continued:

> 'Yet fell she not as one enforced to die,
> Nor died with dread and grudging discontent,
> But as one toiled with travel down doth lie;
> So lay she down as if to sleep she went,
> And closed her eyes with careless quietness.'

I had a dream sometime in the night. My mad wife Edie and I were walking through the outskirts of a foreign city, going away from it. There was an atmosphere of terror and sadness everywhere, also an ominous silence broken only by the sound of shuffling feet. We walked into a corner grocer's shop to buy food. The big woman who served us said: 'This used to be the administrative part of the city,' and added: 'I'm shutting up shop after you. Everyone's leaving, those that haven't already left.' When I asked her why, she laughed and answered 'Murder,' and turned off into a corner. I packed what we had bought into a bag we had with us and then we walked back out on to the boulevard we had been following before. People, thousands of them, were hurrying down it, all going in the same direction as ourselves. I wanted to try to reason out why we were doing the same, but couldn't seem able to. At fifty-yard intervals bodies were lying against the walls. A man in a business suit had collapsed under a sack of cabbages; further on an old man in rags sprawled on a toppled heap of garbage cans; he was dying. A monk in a brown habit stood beside him, holding a syringe; near them stood a shabby woman in her forties, wringing her hands as the crowd went past her, repeating the same unintelligible phrase over and over. No one took any notice of her; they hurried on, heads bent, walking swiftly away from the city centre. Neither Edie nor I spoke to each other – face shut inwards, lips pursed, she moved so fast that I had trouble keeping up with her. We just had Edie's handbag and a case each.

I knew we were going on a very long journey that we would never repeat and that like the others we would fall when we could no longer go on. I didn't know where we had come from, or why, or where we were going.

I must have picked Edie up from the asylum at Banstead, for when I looked closely at her I saw there was something very wrong with her clothes. She had stout black shoes on and a rubber bib showed under her coat.

7

I drove over to the police station at seven in the morning and walked into the reception area; there was a different sergeant on the desk. I asked where Kedward's office was and he told me, adding: 'He's expecting you.'

I went in and said to the inspector: 'I'll identify myself.'

'Don't bother,' he said sourly, 'I've had a phone call over you.'

'You know what it's about then.'

'The Mardy business – Christ, what the hell does London have to worry about that for?'

'You don't find it unusual, Mrs Mardy having gone missing for six months?'

'They're just a couple of middle-aged eccentrics.'

'I see – not worth troubling about then.'

He said: 'Watch your tone.' He looked dull, was about ten years older than me, and had a thin face. His wrinkled suit looked wiser than its owner; the material was a light, bitter shade of grey, and it seemed to know what it had coming to it – early retirement from Thornhill, end of line. He said: 'Have you been up to see Mardy yet?'

'No,' I said. 'I want the background down in the town first, I only got here last night.'

'Background?' he sneered. 'Some of you junior officers want to get your bloody skates on.'

'Mind out when I do,' I said, 'I go far and fast.'

He laughed: 'Convince me.'

'I will,' I said. I could tell Kedward and I were never going to get on. 'Meantime I'd like to hear anything you can tell me about the Mardys.'

'Before we go into that,' he said, 'I'm told you had a run-in with

43

two of my men last night, a squad car crew.'

'PCs 281 and 183,' I said, 'that's right. But it was all amicably fixed.'

'They breathalysed you, did they not?'

How I detest people who say things like did they not. I said: 'Yes. It was negative. Some of these youngsters are over-keen.'

'You used strong language to them.'

'I use it all the time,' I said.

'Don't try it with me,' said Kedward, 'I'm not going to have you London people treating us like yobbos; get that straight, Sergeant.'

He was another rank addict. I said: 'Well, the best thing you can do then is ring my Deputy Commander and tell him that, why not do it now? The answer might really surprise you.'

He flushed; his hand did not reach for the phone.

'All right,' I said. 'Now let's cut out the crap and get back to the question. Are you asking me to believe that you delayed investigating Mrs Mardy's disappearance until last month, January, that makes five months since she was last seen, because you thought she was a middle-aged eccentric? Now come on, it's incredible.'

'We'd no grounds for suspicion,' said Kedward. 'That was my decision and I put it in my report.'

'I've got your report and I've read it,' I said, 'and a skimpy little document it is too; it's a skirt that wouldn't cover a gnat's thighs. Now try harder.'

'Look,' said Kedward, 'everyone in Thornhill knew she was sick last year.'

'What do you mean by sick?'

'Appeared in town less and less often.'

'Did you see her when she did come in?'

'Sometimes.'

'Make an effort with this, will you?' I said. 'I keep asking you.'

'Well, she just looked sick.'

'How sick?' I said. 'Come on, you're a detective, you've got eyes in your head, haven't you? White, you mean? Thin and drawn?'

'Didn't speak much latterly,' he muttered, 'or else just in a whisper. Always wore a veil in the end round the lower part of her face. But you hardly saw her.'

'Not exactly the person she'd once been then, was she?'

'How did you know what she had been like?' he said, sitting up.

'Never you mind,' I said. 'What we're talking about right now is that a local woman who used to be pretty, happy, vivacious, first starts to wither away behind a veil and then totally disappears. And you don't find that reasonable grounds for suspecting anything?'

'I told you it was well known she was ill!'

'Was she going for treatment? What was she ill with?'

'How should I know?' Kedward shouted. 'Her husband's a doctor, isn't he?'

'Oh he is, is he?' I said. 'Do you know when he last practised?'

'No, why should I?'

'You really freak me,' I said, 'you're meant to monitor this patch.'

'That doesn't mean sticking my nose into other folks' business.'

'It's what the public pays your wages for,' I said, 'I'm always being told it. All right, let's get on to something else. What sort of a man is this Mardy?'

'Now you're down here,' he said, 'you can be the judge of that.'

'I will be. Now, did you eventually go up Thornhill Court?'

'I did.'

'And when was that?'

'You must have read my report. It was January 15th. Last month.'

'And yet it seems Mrs Mardy had been missing since August last year.'

'Thornhill Court isn't the sort of house anybody just goes into.'

I was getting weary of this. I said: 'Why isn't it?'

'It's not a bloody council estate.'

'Bollocks,' I said. 'You call yourself a copper. Council estate, high rise, country house, the law can go anywhere it likes any time it likes, as you know full well.'

'The Mardy family's been here in Thornhill for three centuries.'

I said: 'I don't care if they moved in with Julius Caesar.'

'You work in town too much, but you're ninety miles from London here.'

'People don't seem to change, though.'

He shouted: 'Will you mind your manners with me, you cheeky bastard!'

'I'm not into minding manners,' I said, 'but solving cases. I tell you I'm here to find out what's happened to Mrs Mardy, how when where and why, and I'm going to, with your help or without it. Now then – you never got a warrant out to search the Mardy house. Why not? Why didn't you?'

'I don't have to explain that to you.'

I said: 'I think you'd better, and I'm asking you that question again.'

'Because I had no grounds for suspicion, I keep telling you!' He added: 'All right, we both know it came from the Chief Constable for me to go up there.'

'And didn't it take some pushing for you to do it,' I said, 'what you should have done anyway months before. What was the reason you gave Mardy for your visit when you finally did get up there?'

'That I was acting on information received.'

'But what information?' I shouted. 'Whose information? Why isn't any of this information to be found in this pathetic report of yours I've got here?'

'That's just it,' said Kedward, 'in my view none of it was information, just gossip.'

'Well, with a local woman having disappeared for six months like that,' I said, 'yes, I'll bet there was plenty of it. Now, did you go up to the house alone?'

'Certainly not. I went up with Sergeant Turner.'

'All right. And did you turn the house over?'

'We did not.'

'Why not?'

'Because I formed the opinion after talking to Dr Mardy that there was no necessity for it.'

'And what was that opinion based on? The fact that his wife was nowhere to be found? Or did you find her? Did she appear? If she did, what the hell am I doing here?'

'No, she did not appear.'

'And what was Mardy's explanation for that? Or didn't you ask him for one?'

'He told us that his wife was absent for a time, that her health was not all it might be, and that she'd gone abroad on a long visit, back to her home in France.'

'And you were quite satisfied with that.'

'Why shouldn't I have been?'

'I don't know yet. Was your sergeant satisfied with it?'

'I don't ask my sergeants for their opinions.'

'What a pity,' I said. 'You know, Inspector, as one detective to another, I'm frankly wondering if you've ever tackled such a thing as crime in your life before. Or are you wilier than you make out?' I added. 'Are you concealing anything from me, Inspector?'

He had taken a beating from me; his gaze slid across the room. 'No.'

'Because if you are,' I said, 'I very strongly advise you not to do so.'

'Sergeants don't give advice to detective-inspectors,' he said. 'They take it as a rule, if they know what's good for them.'

'I've never known what was good for me,' I said. 'That's why I'm in my mid-forties and still a sergeant. But don't be an idiot, I'm working for the Yard on this one. I'm not local law.' I didn't believe what I was going to say next but I said it just the same: 'Of course, I've no grounds yet for supposing that you are holding anything back, but what I'm confronted with so far is your investigation into this business, which is so fucking inept that it doesn't even deserve the name. I can't believe that you're as stupid as you would like to make me think you are – I think you could have done much, much better than this if you'd wanted to, and of course it's natural for me to want to know why you didn't want to.' I pointed my finger at his nose. 'And if it turns out at the end of this case that you were withholding information from me all along, and if I have to find out what that information was all by myself, then you are going to find yourself in very, very serious trouble, do you understand?'

He snapped: 'I'm not withholding anything from you.'

'Well, I've given you your chance.'

'Yes, thank you so very much,' he said poisonously, 'I am grateful.'

I let that slip on by. 'There's something else I want to know,' I said.

He looked at his watch. 'I haven't much time,' he said, 'I've got an appointment.'

I said: 'It'll have to wait,' and he looked at me in a silence that I enjoyed. 'What I want is some background information on Dr Mardy – does he have any staff up at his house?'

'Not any more.'

'What staff did he have?'

'A part-time jobbing gardener called Dick Sanders, local boy.'

'Were the dates of his employment there relevant to the period we're discussing?'

'I suppose so.'

'Well? Yes or no? Come on – I can quickly check it.'

'Yes.'

I made a note of the name. 'And by the way,' I said, 'the day you and Sergeant Turner went up to the house, did you ask Dr Mardy why his wife had been seen around Thornhill with a veil round her face?'

'No, I didn't.'

'Why didn't you?'

'Because I didn't think the way Mrs Mardy dressed was any of my affair. I knew she was ill and I didn't want to press or upset Dr Mardy.'

'You may have been dead wrong not to press him,' I said. 'Another thing – weren't you at any time ever intrigued by Mrs Mardy's illness? Her face?'

'I don't probe into other people's misfortunes.'

'Then you're in the wrong job,' I said. 'Now, what about this veil she wore?'

'Well, what about it?'

'Oh for God's sake,' I said, 'I want to know more about the veil. Was it a thick veil? Could you see her face behind it?'

'It covered her face below the nose, and you couldn't see through it, no.'

'And none of that interested you at all.'

'No.'

'You knew her quite well?'

'Reasonably well.'

'But you never asked her what was the matter with her.'

'No. I tell you I never—'

'In fact,' I said, 'you didn't do anything. Not even before she disappeared.'

'I prefer to wait for people to come to me.'

'How very cooperative of you,' I said. 'Did you go to any of her concerts?'

'How do you know she gave any?' he said quickly.

'Oh,' I said, 'her fame spread, you know. Now then, going back to this illness, this trouble with her face—'

'I've told you all I know. All right, she was ill. Unfortunately, there's nothing unusual about illness.'

'That depends,' I said. 'Some people in this town appear not to have agreed with you about her illness. They seem to have thought it was very unusual.'

'Just town gossip in my view.'

'Your view's the kind that needs strong glasses,' I said, 'and the Chief Constable evidently thought the same. Now, is there anything else you'd like to tell me about the Mardys before I find out on my own?'

He looked stiffly away at the wall and said: 'There's nothing more to tell.'

I said: 'You must be the most uncooperative officer I've ever had to deal with.'

'Deal with it on your own, then!' he snarled. He banged his fist on the table. 'I've been overridden. It's your case now, so why don't you just get up there and dig up what you want to know?'

'Let's hope no digging will be necessary,' I said, 'as much for your sake as anyone else's.'

'You can work on your bloody own!'

'I'm going to,' I said. 'I'm used to working on my own – in fact, I like it that way. I'll put it all together, you'll see.' I stood up. 'And thank you for all your help.'

'The reason you've not had much help from me,' he said, 'is that I don't like you.'

'Most people don't,' I said, 'but I don't think that's the reason at all.' I turned at the door and said: 'I believe that this woman is dead and, if it turns out that she is, your pension will add up to a bag of rotten nuts and it could go bluer than that. No, don't get up, Inspector.'

He hadn't, and didn't. He didn't say or do anything. He didn't look at me even.

I went to my car, which was on the yellow line where I had parked it the night before. The squad car, with the same two specialists in it, was also parked there.

I waved to them cheerily; but they didn't wave back.

8

I got back to the hotel and rang the voice.

'I want a bank account checked.'

'Whose bank account?'

'Inspector Kedward's.'

'Oh Christ,' groaned the voice, 'don't tell me you've got up his nose already.'

'I'll get further up than his nose,' I said, 'I'll get up into his brains and make them yelp.'

'Why didn't you get on with him?'

'We got on like newly-weds,' I said, 'I don't think.'

'Ended in early divorce, did it?' said the voice. 'I might have known. What have you made of it so far? Have you seen this man Mardy yet?'

'Look, I only got down here last night,' I said. 'No, I haven't seen Mardy yet. There's no rush over Mardy for an hour or two; he isn't going to run away. No, I tell you, I've been busy with Kedward; I find him very interesting.'

'What does interesting mean?'

'You know what it means,' I said, 'it means bent. I want his bank statements checked out right over the last twelve months.'

'You really are a dreadful man,' said the voice, 'cheeky and self-opinionated. I send you down to look into the business of a missing woman – no, you pin this inspector to a card instead.'

'It's a pity you weren't with me when I saw him just now.'

'What would that have told me?'

'I keep telling you,' I said patiently, 'it would have told you that he was bent. Bent, crooked, not straight, as bent as an old banger's front bumper.'

'He's the law in that town. What's he got to hide?'

'I don't know, but I'll find out.' I sighed audibly into the phone. 'Now can I have his bank statements checked, please?'

'Wait a minute,' said the voice uneasily, 'you just look out what you're doing, Sergeant. You're not noted for tact.'

'There's no point being tactful with villains,' I said. I described the interview I had had with Kedward and in the end even the voice saw what I was driving at. 'He's a nice loose thread to tug on to start with,' I said, 'so I'm going to give him a good hard tug.'

'You mind what you're doing,' said the voice even more nervously. 'You tug a corrupt police officer out of all this – well, you know what the press are like.'

'You handle all that side of it,' I said.

'Indeed I will, Sergeant.'

'All the same,' I said, 'whichever way you look at it, if he's in there he's in there, being corrupt.'

'I'll agree about this much,' said the voice, 'I find Kedward's attitude to this Mrs Mardy incomprehensible. Why, when I was on the CID myself—'

'Oh, not incomprehensible,' I said. 'There's a perfectly good reason for it; Kedward's no fool. It's just a question of finding out what reason, and you can be sure money comes into it somewhere.' I repeated: 'So can I please have his bank statements checked? I'm not being tactless – he'll never know his account's been checked.'

'I'm thinking about it,' said the voice, 'don't ride me. Listen, did you accuse him of anything to his face?'

'I'm not in a position to yet,' I said, 'but I asked him if he was hiding or withholding information from me about the Mardys, yes, because I had the feeling, as strongly as possible, that he was.'

'Oh God, why is it,' said the voice, 'that every case you handle, something frightful blows up in it virtually straight away?'

'Because there's something frightful in every case, sir.'

'Just calling me sir isn't going to make me any better tempered,' said the voice, 'though I'll make a note of it – the last time was Christmas Eve, and I got the impression that you'd had a few that day.'

'Kedward's bank statements,' I said. 'I want to go up and see Mardy now.'

'All right,' said the voice, 'yes.'

'You'll get the results down here to me as soon as you can? By courier?'

'Yes. You're not to get in touch with his bank directly, do you understand?'

'It's all right,' I said, 'photocopies are all I need.'

'Tell me,' said the voice, 'I know it's early days, but what's your instinct about this Mardy woman? What do you think may have happened to her?'

I said: 'I feel there's every possibility that she's dead.'

'Well,' said the voice, 'that's what we're here for. All right, keep at it. You're cheeky, I had a half-hour hate from Chief Inspector Bowman about you this morning, but you're an energetic officer and you've got brains, I'll say that for you.' He rang off on me, muttering: 'A corrupt police inspector he digs up – oh God, who ordered any of that?'

9

With the map I had I traced my way through the lanes north of Thornhill. I made mistakes, first driving up rutted tracks into a blank, frostbitten field, then turning off wrong at an unmarked crossroads. It had got completely dark with sleet, then icy rain, turning to hail, battering the high ground.

But at last I was speeding past an old brick wall with most of the coping gone and reached two stone pillars that supported half-open gates. I got out with the torch that I kept in the car. There was a mailbox screwed into the wall by the gates that read Thornhill Court, so I opened the gates, got back in the car and drove up five hundred yards of mud.

The house didn't look beautiful in the headlights even while I was far from it; when I got up close it was hideous, sombre and huge. Fallen masonry, a lot of it, sprawled across the left-hand edge of the drive's circle under the façade. I got out of the car; not one window was lit. All round me wild trees prayed soaking in the rain, their bare arms nagging the sky. I walked past a rusty Ford van with a flat front tyre and looked up at the five storeys, streaming with wet, that stooped over me. Then I noticed that one of the plate-glass front doors was swinging ajar in the gale, so I went up the porch steps and stood on the threshold. I shone my torch round the hall beyond; it was vast, unlit and empty. Rain spilled on to me from the balcony overhead.

I called out sharply: 'Mardy? Dr William Mardy?'

There was no answer. I went in and stood in the hall. Facing me was an organ, its loft very high from the floor; the windows I picked out were stained glass, black now against the blackness outside. Far down from me was a marble fireplace, its breast rising to lose itself in false beams high above from which rain pattered down everywhere, dripping at logical intervals on a table built to seat twelve.

I called out again: 'William Mardy? Are you there?'

Nothing.

Now that I was in out of the wind my hearing adjusted itself to the house. At first I thought the place was silent except for the droning of the gale, but presently I became certain that this was not so. A long way off, it sounded as if it might be high above me upstairs, I was sure I heard the murmur of voices, muffled, as though coming from behind closed doors. The voices sounded like those of a man and a woman, alternately strident and persuasive on both sides, though there was no making out any words.

What could be easier than to stand in a pub with a few drinks inside you and tell everyone that you've got solid nerves? All I know is that when I saw a feeble light wavering down the staircase from the gallery that ran away above each side of the organ, I was glad I had the open door behind me, the torch and the car. However, I stood quite still and turned the torch off. There was no sound of any voices now. The light came slowly nearer down the stairs, appearing and disappearing at the bends. I thought of Hamlet – *I'll cross it though it blast me.* The light shivered, throwing patches along the sick walls; then it descended the last stairs and came over to where I stood. Above the lamp was the face of an elderly man.

I said: 'Are you Dr Mardy?'

'Yes. Who are you?'

'I'm a police officer.'

'You surely don't want to talk to me,' he said. 'You should go and see Inspector Kedward down in the town. He knows all about my affairs.'

'No, it's you I want to talk to.'

'I don't generally talk to anyone very much.'

'This is going to be different,' I said. 'You and I are going to have a long talk.'

He sighed. By his dim light I watched him shuffle towards a corner. I heard his hand feeling along the wall; a switch clicked and a light sprang on. I looked at Dr Mardy. He was a hollowed-out shadow of a man in his sixties, as white as if his face had been dusted with chalk; his eyes were black and intense. He was dressed in an anorak, slippers and shapeless corduroys and had a dirty yellow scarf round his neck. He put his gas-lamp down on a table and turned it out; then he faced me. 'What is it?' he said in a dead tone. 'Why can't you leave me be? Are you a local man?'

'No. From London.'

'From the Yard?'

'Yes, I'm working from A14, with Serious Crimes.' I showed him my warrant card.

'What is A14?'

'Unexplained Deaths,' I said. 'I'm here to inquire about your wife.'

'About Marianne,' he said. 'Yes, I see.'

'Perhaps we could go somewhere and sit down,' I said. 'This'll take a minute.'

'Everything's very primitive here, I'm afraid,' he said. 'I seldom receive people now.'

'Why is that? You used to, you and your wife.'

'My wife isn't here.'

'All right,' I said, 'we'll go into that presently.'

'We could go into my study,' he said, 'it's warm and hardly leaks at all – it's my base here now.' He relit his lamp, picked it up and said: 'This way.' He turned out the light in the hall and I followed him upstairs, We passed through suite after suite of rooms; they were all ruined. In some, books, reviews and medical magazines stood in piles up to the ceiling. In others the ceilings themselves had been shored up with beams. In one, a mountain of sodden books had collapsed.

When we had gone a reasonable way I asked: 'How many rooms have you got here?'

'Eighty.'

Everywhere plaster littered the floor; the house stank of wet. Curtain rails, the curtains themselves, lay where they had fallen.

Furniture leaned against beds steaming with damp; mould, green and black, had spread across the walls.

'Be careful of this piece of floor here, there's some dry rot.'

'Since when was the place in this state?'

'I never noticed,' he said, 'I suppose that it slowly declined. My wife and I each had our own work. We were never ones for detail, and there would have been the cost.'

Had, I thought. We were never ones for. There would have been the. 'You're not a rich man,' I said to him, 'why do you live here?'

'Where else would I live?' he answered, confused.

Rain, which I could see pelting through a glassless window, had now set in for the night. It tapped monotonously on floors, on tables and broken chairs as we passed – a gilt clock without its dome and smothered in verdigris stood with its hands forever at twenty to ten on a dripping mantelpiece. Pictures, eighteenth-century prints and maps, askew on the walls, some lying on the floor in their own glass, gazed at us in the light of Mardy's gas-lamp – light that also glanced across a tallboy with jammed and swollen drawers, on a stricken chandelier with half its lustres missing. It danced over a music-room with a concert grand in it; moss choked the blocked teeth of the keyboard. It slid over partitas spread wetly on a stand, on a drenched metronome with its pendulum rusted out to the left, and the water streaming down the walls glittered in it.

'Why don't you get the roof done at least?' I said.

He stopped to look at me. 'Don't you realize?' he said, shaking his head. 'There's an acre of it; life's hard and I'm sixty-three.' A gust of wind swept past us, slamming a door. Mardy's eyes fixed me from his disordered, unshaven face. I studied the hairs that curled out of his ears and nose – the mouth that slipped down one side of his face in an expression that was not a smile.

We walked on.

'Don't you feel lonely here?' I said.

'No. I'm never lonely.'

Finally we were confronted by a door which he opened. 'Here

we are,' he said. 'I'll go first and put the light on, then you'll be able to get on with your questions.'

'There's plenty of time,' I said. The light came on. The room was warm after the damp we had walked through, and I smelt cooking. The smell was stale, the bad cooking of old people.

'Sit down,' he said, pointing to an old armchair.

I did so and said: 'Where we've been through, was there any wiring in those rooms?'

'There was,' he said, 'but it's rotten so I don't use it. It's old and the wet gets through into it if you don't look out.'

'The wiring looks new in here, though,' I said.

'Yes, I've had some of it redone. This is my study in here though it's half a kitchen now.'

Bookshelves covered two of the walls, a cooker stood against another next to a sink, and there were saucepans on a draining-board. It was a low room compared to those we had come through, and vaulted.

'This is the old part of the house,' Mardy said.

In a corner was a partner's desk covered with papers. I just wandered over and had a look at what lay there. There were a lot of bank statements in Mardy's name with the name of his bank on them. None of the statements looked very promising. There was other correspondence too, but I didn't bother with any of that.

He took off his anorak. 'You're starting your questions?' He looked thinner than ever in his cheap shirt – his ears, the too large ears of an old man, showing through his grey, uncombed hair.

'Tell me,' I said, 'do you ever hear people's voices in this house? I'd been told you lived alone, yet I thought I heard voices when I arrived.'

'The only voices I hear are past voices,' he said, 'that begins happening to you when you get older.'

'So you've no one living in? No staff?'

'No, I've no staff at all.'

'But you did have a gardener for a while called Richard Sanders.'

'He's gone now.'

'Why?'

'I wasn't happy with his work.'

'No more to it than that?'

'No. I weed round the house myself now.'

I was sure he was lying; his answers were pat and too short. I said: 'Until your wife returns?'

'Yes.'

'So in the meantime you live alone here in eighty rooms.'

'As you see.'

I said: 'Have you any idea where your wife is at this moment?'

'All I know is that she's gone on a long journey.'

'Do you know where? Come on, she must have told you something.'

'She's not been well; she's gone until she gets better.'

'But how long was she going for, and where to?'

'I don't know how long for, but I think she's probably gone to France since she was French, though she didn't say. She was ill, and tired of our existence here at Thornhill for a while.'

'But you only think she's in France, is that it?'

'That's all I can tell you, yes. She was a mysterious woman.'

'Even so,' I said, 'you must have had some news of her, her whereabouts, since she left. No? Nothing at all? That's what I find mysterious. Aren't you worried about her? Don't you miss her?'

'Miss her?' he said. He choked right to his lips, a most sinister sound. 'Excuse me.'

I said: 'What family has she got in France that could be contacted for news of her?'

'She had a brother but we haven't written for years, I couldn't tell you.'

'So all you know is that you believe she's in France somewhere, but you don't know where, and you haven't had as much as a postcard from her. That is what you're saying, isn't it?'

Tears came into his eyes. I said: 'Look, I'm only trying to get at the facts. That's my work; that's why I've been sent down here, people are worried about your wife.'

'She's resting,' he said. 'She just got tired in the race.'

'I'd like to hear more about her illness,' I said. 'What exactly was the matter with her?'

'A general malaise.'

I don't know why, but instinctively I didn't believe a word of it. 'Did she go for treatment of any kind? A local doctor here? Or to London?'

'No, she said she'd rather go home to France for a long rest,' he said, 'and visit a doctor there. To France.'

I try to act out of disinterest, which nearly always clashes with my superiors' ideas of what my work should be; but I can always tell when something's hiding from the light.

'Why did she wear a thick veil round the lower part of her face?' I said. 'What was she concealing, do you know?'

'She had begun to hide from the world.'

'Why?'

'I don't know.'

'She was your wife, and you don't know? Did she take the veil away in front of you?'

'Never.'

'You realize I can't be satisfied with answers like that.'

'They're the only ones I can give you.'

'Why?' I said. 'Because they're true, or just convenient?'

He said nothing, just looked away. I could have threatened him, but I was no Bowman – I wasn't in the business of smashing down the resistance of an old man at the end of his tether, for I knew I was in the presence of a profound sorrow. So I stood up and said to him: 'I've got other inquiries to make,' since I was sure I could get at the answers I wanted by applying different methods to other people – I didn't want to drive anybody mad. I only said: 'I'll have to come back again I'm afraid in the next day or two, you can be sure I'll know a great deal more by then.'

'There's nothing to know,' he said. 'My wife's just ill and abroad in her home country – if only you could all just leave me alone.'

'I'm afraid that's not possible now I've come down,' I said. 'I've no choice – I either have to get to the bottom of something or else put in a report that'll wipe it off the books.' This reminded me of his bank statements I had just seen on his desk. I said: 'You've got money worries, haven't you?'

'Hasn't everybody?'

'Who is it?' I said. 'The bank?'

'Yes.'

'And what else?'

'Tradesmen.'

'What sort of tradesmen?' I said. 'Who are they? What are their names?'

'No one I could pick out.'

I said: 'Look, Dr Mardy, I can see you're in some trouble you're not telling me about.'

'I'm not, I'm not.'

I said: 'Be honest with me, because then I think I could help you.'

'Isn't that what the police always say?'

'Some of them mean it,' I said, 'but if you won't help me, I can't help you, and I have a feeling I want to.'

'I'm in trouble I can't really explain,' he said, 'yes, I admit that.'

'You mean you can't explain it because you don't know what the trouble is?'

'Oh no, I know what it is all right,' he said bitterly.

'But you won't tell me about it.'

'I can't. I'm literally not able to tell you.'

I said: 'Come on, Dr Mardy, it can't be that desperate.'

He said: 'It is.'

'I'll find it out, you know,' I said. 'Not just from you, from all sorts of people here. I think there may be a villain or two about.'

He was quiet for a while, then he said: 'What will Inspector Kedward have to do with your inquiry?'

I said curiously: 'Why do you ask?'

He only shrugged, but the shrug was perhaps the most important answer he could have given me. Not for the first time, I was impressed by the association of words. No sooner did I mention the word villain, than up he came with the name Kedward. I picked up my torch.

'Tomorrow, then?' he said. 'At about this time? I've no telephone, I'm afraid, but the front door will be open.'

'That'll be all right,' I said, 'I'll have found out plenty by this time tomorrow.'

He relit his lamp and led me back through the rotten house and down to the entrance. 'Goodnight,' he said.

'Goodnight.'

I went back to the hotel and spent the rest of the night thinking.

10

I came down the Quayntewayes staircase next morning at ten to ten. The steps had a way of making their concrete known to your feet under the cut-price carpet, and the reception hall, as it was named in green electric lights, had that enticing British habit of reminding you that you were on the away ground here.

An old blonde whose head looked as if it had been left behind in a train and whose bra was too big for her breasts sat behind the switchboard. She wore a ring with a big enough stone in it to deter a sex maniac, but had a nose like a peashooter that would have put him off anyway.

'What was you wanting?'

'Breakfast.'

'Too late!' she crooned triumphantly. 'Kitchen shuts sharp at half eight, nothing till lunchtime now. Here,' she said, pointing at a notice behind her with a finger that looked as if it had been borrowed from an archery course, 'can't you read?'

'I'm good at it,' I said, 'and I could show you some card tricks too if I had as much time on my hands as you have, but I haven't. Do you know a man called Dick Sanders?'

'What do you want to know for?'

'I don't know,' I said. 'I might want to tell him he's won the pools; on the other hand I might want to tell him he'd been done for shagging sheep. What bloody business is it of yours?'

'I don't like your manners,' she said, turning a dull orange colour.

'Then you can think yourself lucky you don't have to live with them,' I said, 'and not getting any breakfast makes my temper worse. Now do you know him or not?'

She said: 'If you aren't careful I'll call the management and have you thrown out – you're insulting, you are.'

I showed her my warrant card and said: 'It'd take a little more than you, dear, to get a police officer thrown out of anywhere, so just answer the question, it's quickly done, you either know the man or you don't.'

Her whole manner turned coy. It's always the same with people like that – they either spit at you or else go over on their back. 'Of course I didn't realize you were a police officer,' she said, looking thoughtfully at me and nibbling a nail that curved sharply inward to get at the finger it grew on. She considered, lips spread across indifferent teeth. 'I know him by sight,' she said finally, 'most people in Thornhill do.' She shuddered delicately; it made her look like something being carried by a paraplegic waiter. 'The Sanders are all just slag.'

'I don't care about that. Do you know where he lives?'

'Somewhere out by Lakes Mill, who cares?'

'I do for one,' I said. 'They on the phone?'

'How do I know?' she said. She nearly sniggered, then thought better of it. 'I'm not in the habit of ringing people like the Sanders, my husband wouldn't like it. He's very strong, my husband is, and works for Cashabout, the security firm.'

'I don't care about your husband or where he works,' I said. 'Give me the local directory.' I drifted through the S's. The Sanders were listed OK, so I dialled them.

'My husband, he works right through the night sometimes,' said the receptionist.

I got the ringing tone and said to her: 'Be quiet, will you?' The phone answered the other end and a woman's voice screamed down it: 'Well?'

'Dick Sanders there?'

'No, he's not in!'

'He lives with you, doesn't he? You're his mother?'

'Yes I am, no I'm not, yes he lives here, no he doesn't, who the hell are you?'

'I'm his uncle Bill, tell him.'

'My Dick's not got no uncle Bill.' Then she got it and screamed backwards from the phone: 'My life, it's only the old bill on the fucking phone.'

I said: 'I'll be round to see him today, this afternoon most like, make sure he's in, ma.'

'More of you interfering bastards!' .

I rang off. I made a note of the Sanders address. The receptionist said: 'You like quick results, you do, don't you?'

'They're the best kind,' I said. 'Do you know a house called Thornhill Court?'

'Who doesn't?'

'Did the Mardys come into this hotel?'

'Sometimes.'

'Did you see Mrs Mardy about with a scarf or veil round her face?'

Her own face went deaf and blind. 'No.'

'All right,' I said, 'I see there's no point my pressing it. You just take my messages for me, all right?'

'This isn't the Policeman's Arms.'

'Just do as I say,' I said, 'and you'll spare yourself a big pain in the fundament.' I walked out of the hotel and into the morning. The weather was sharp and overcast with ice in the gutters. I walked up what was left of the old high street past the arch of the coaching-inn, now a boutique on one side and a fast food on the other – now, I guessed, the only carriages to be seen there were on veteran car club day, the only horses when young bank managers came down holding their children's bridle on a Saturday morning. But why be bitter about progress? I walked past cottages converted into offices, with soft-looking men and breastless little brides hard at it on their IBMs behind bow windows. I looked at the business signs – Walter Baddeley, Estate Agents, HM Inspector of Taxes, a Listening Bank, W. Baddeley & Sons, Funeral Directors, until I got to the Jolly Sailor. His picture looked just as bucolic and amused as it had done last night while it swung benevolently over the five whites chasing the Asian, except that by morning light his smile and chubby cheeks looked improbable and hung-over. I went through into the public bar; the place was empty except for an African who was sweeping up.

'Good morning,' I said.

He let that drift.

'Place is open, is it?'

'Look, man, you're in it, ain't you?'

'I mean open for a drink.'

'Don't know about that, I'll have to see.'

'That's not difficult,' I said, 'try turning round, the clock's right behind you.'

'So am I,' said a rich voice, 'and I'm the governor here.'

But he said the word governor as though he bad beeen at some pains to learn it.

'Fine,' I said. 'Well, are we fit for a drink then?'

'You're starting early.'

'That's got nothing to do with it,' I said. 'What I'm asking you is, are you serving? It's gone half past ten.'

He looked at me carefully to see if I was sober; I looked at him carefully to see if he was a villain. He wasn't. He was one of those people who try to turn a pub into a Battle of Britain officers' mess, though far too young ever to have known one. I could practically hear him running my accent through his mind; with my grammar school background I don't suppose I scored high.

'Yes, very well,' he said at last, 'what'll it be then?'

'I'll have a pint of Kronenbourg.'

'You ought to try some of our real ale.'

'I prefer the Kronenbourg,' I said, 'we're used to each other.'

The governor pulled the pint and said: 'Busy day ahead of you?'

'Very,' I said. 'I won't outstay my welcome.'

'Commercial, are you?'

'Not quite,' I said. 'More of a surveyor really.'

'Sounds interesting,' he said, struggling not to yawn, 'that'll be one pound twelve.'

'Tell me,' I said, giving him the money, 'do you own this place or are you just the tenant?'

'I'm the tenant,' he said, 'not just the tenant.' He gave me my change and looked my tired clothes up and down. 'And tell me something,' he added. 'Do you go round like this every day, asking people you don't know personal questions?'

'Yes,' I said. 'It's all part of being a surveyor.'

'I thought they worked with theodolites. Is it about the new road at Hope Street corner?'

'No it isn't,' I said, 'and some surveyors just use notebooks. I'm one of them.'

'Well, to put this bluntly,' he said, 'I'm accustomed to receiving gentlemen in this bar, everyone else goes next door. And the mark of a gentleman is that he doesn't stick his nose in where he isn't known.'

'You're full of mad dreams,' I said, 'but cherish them if you like. Speaking for myself, I'm certainly no gentleman, but I ask a great many questions and what's more, I usually get answers to them.'

'You'll find I'm the exception,' he said in his public school tone, turning red.

'I won't, you know,' I said. I identified myself. 'I'm a police officer; can't you spot them yet?'

He pulled out a handkerchief and made a moist noise into it. A fragile old man with a stick, pork-pie hat and suede shoes slipped past us saying: 'Good morning, Captain Goodinge, a rather dreary day again.' He sat down at a cane table under a repro sporting print, dropped his stick on the floor together with an empty shopping bag and said to the African: 'My usual, please.'

'What's that, man?'

'You know perfectly well, Selim,' said the governor. 'The colonel's is a double vodka, dry martini, two drops of angostura and plenty of ice.' He turned to me and said: 'Of course I'd no idea you were from the police.'

'I try to foster that idea,' I said. I added: 'Surveyor. I tried to mark your card. Quaint, that, I thought – but you didn't catch on. I don't think you've been in this business long. What are you? Trainee manager?'

He turned red and said yes.

'Always get on good terms with the law if you keep a pub,' I said. 'That's iron rule number one.'

'You're not local,' he said.

'Nor are you.'

'You're down from London, then?'

'That's right,' I said. 'I've come down over the Mardys, it's to do with his wife's disappearance.' I made no attempt to keep my voice down and the governor, the old man in the corner, the African, the whole pub were all suddenly very still. I said to Goodinge: 'Did you know Mrs Mardy personally at all?'

'I wouldn't say that,' he said quickly. 'The wife and I used to go up to their concerts at the house, of course. Weird place, but you had a lovely evening.'

'Many people in Thornhill went up for the concerts to listen to Madam Mardy sing,' said the old man. He spoke slowly, and his face above the regimental tie and the expensive tweed jacket had the purplish look of a cardiac case. 'You'd leave feeling full of song, and different somehow.'

I said to the governor: 'Have any of your regulars seen her around since last August? You yourself, or your wife? You, Colonel?'

They said no.

'And how was she, how did she strike you both the last time you did see her?'

'That was back in last June for me,' said the governor, 'and she looked dreadful, terribly ill. She'd whisper past you in the street with that veil round her face, and her hand to the veil, face turned away from you to the wall by the pavement side, and she'd got so thin ...oh, good morning, Major,' he added to a grey, straight-haired man who strode through with a grey flannel dog on a chain. 'The usual? Straight away.' Filling the major's order at the optic he said with his back to me: 'Yes, Madam Mardy was a remarkable woman all right.'

'Was,' I said. 'Everyone keeps saying was.'

'What else can you say of her when she's been gone six months like that?' said the governor. He set the major's drink on a tray and picked it up. 'Nobody's saying we weren't all worried, mind.'

'Well,' I said, 'my people are worried too and so here I am come down to worry about the worry.'

The governor went into the other bar with the major's drink and the old man said: 'Will you get far, do you think?'

'Yes,' I said, 'I'll go the distance, but only slowly on my own – useful help, like information, will speed everything up.'

'Yes, but you know how things are,' said the governor, returning, 'it's not for us to pry into the affairs of other people.'

'It's the old story of the road accident,' I said. 'Everyone drives on saying it's none of our business, while the victim dies in the hedge.'

'Don't talk like that, Sergeant,' said the old man sharply. 'Even if we hadn't liked the Mardys as much as we do we'd still have reacted.'

'The people who should have reacted,' I said, 'were the local police. Has either of you any idea why they didn't?'

'Ah well, I—' said the governor, and stopped.

'You, Colonel?'

'Where there's no proof,' said the old man, 'I'd rather say nothing.'

'That's all right,' I said. 'Now you say that people in Thornhill generally liked the Mardys. When you say the Mardys, does that include Dr Mardy?'

'Well of course,' said the colonel, 'poor William Mardy.'

'Why poor?'

'There's a man who'll come in presently could explain that to you if he wanted,' said the colonel, and the governor said: 'Now easy, sir,' but the colonel said: 'We are talking to a police officer; it is our duty to give him all the help we can; he is here to investigate this matter.'

'Perhaps you would point this individual out,' I said, and the colonel said yes, I will. He added: 'William Mardy is a very troubled man,' and I replied: 'I know, I've met him.'

'Time ran on,' said the old man, 'and the local police did nothing, so that in the end a group of us signed a petition and I—'

'Colonel Newington got up the petition,' said the governor, 'and went to see the Chief Constable with it.'

'Ah,' I said, 'I wondered who had.'

'The colonel used to be a magistrate until he retired.'

The old man ordered us a round. There were just the three of us in the little bar; it was early yet. A fire of beech logs spat sharply in the grate and a flight of crows wheeled in the grey sky outside, making for the naked fields. The old man downed his drink and crooked his finger for Goodinge to bring another.

'It's a question of seeing men die,' he said presently, 'and of feeling responsible; it's also a matter of running the same risk, otherwise you can't know what the danger means, and that's how I felt over Marianne, watching her fade and the rest of us powerless to intervene.'

I understood all right.

He said: 'I was on Dunkirk beaches in June 1940 with the Royal Artillery, 31st Light AA Battery. We were trying to hold off the Luftwaffe; we were some of the last to get away. The French did well,' he muttered into his glass, 'very well. We all did well but we were defeated, what else can you say? I was just a lieutenant then, but most of the senior officers were dead, and when at last we got orders to abandon our guns it was up to people like me to make sure that everyone got properly organized on the beach. I'd had no experience of combat anything like that before, so I remember thinking the whole time that I had to look as if I knew what I was doing, which mostly consisted of standing upright among the bullets, keeping calm and arranging the queues that were waiting to wade out to sea where the boats were. What a bloody nightmare. I wanted to dig down into the sand the whole time, but was even more afraid of being thought a coward, of being court-martialled and unable to face my family if I ever got home.' He had turned grey, and wasn't really talking to us at all. 'A great many dead,' he whispered, 'a terrible lot, French and ours. But there was no panic hardly, no mutiny – I shall never know why not. Everyone behaved so well; they should all have been decorated, every man of them. Those bloody fighters shot them wholesale in the sea; I remember part of the water turning pink by the shore. Then I had the language problem too – try evacuating men under fire in schoolboy French. Orderly retreat, orderly retreat kept coming through from Gort at GHQ. They didn't know what they were asking for, and the staff-work had become appalling under the pressure, a shambles. At the very end I was hit in the right foot and had to sit down. There was another man beside me; he'd been shot in the leg. We managed to get to the shelter of a dune and lay back to rest for a time in deep sand. I tried to dress his wound, but he was losing blood at a dreadful rate. I kept telling him he would be all right, and in the end he rested his head on my lap for a time. I put my hands and cap over his face to protect him against the sun, then there was a great explosion and his chest was gone, there were only his head and legs left. I was red all over from him and my own boot was full of blood. I don't remember after that, but it seems they came for me and took his head out of my hands and got me to the boats on a man's back who told me later on that I was reciting the Nunc Dimittis. Of course I didn't remember that either.'

'Don't take on, Colonel,' said Goodinge, 'it's forty-five years ago now, all that.'

'Not to me,' he said. 'It's as if it were yesterday to me and I should add that I was terribly in love at that time. Her name was Claire, lovely Claire from High Court. She was the only girl I ever knew who could jump the great fence at Toll Shaws; she did it on Thistle, her father's big roan, gay as a spark, looking back at me with a grin while the other men fidgeted on their hacks, biting their nails – they had told her not to be so silly as to try it. That same night at the hunt ball at Castle Carey we danced together all night, on fire with love for each other, with eyes for no one, till dawn came up to greet us with breakfast and more champagne. There were candles everywhere and much punch and music; she was an image like a dream, her long skirts collected behind her in a bustle, a pink top, an onyx against her breast on a silver chain. Blonde, she was, and straight as a little stick: it was in thirty-eight.'

'Another drink, Colonel?' Goodinge said.

'Yes,' said the colonel, holding out his glass, 'and for the sergeant here, thank you, Goodinge.'

'And tell me,' I said, 'did you marry Claire? Claire from High Court?'

'No,' he said steadily. 'I didn't.' He lit a cigarette in the flame that Goodinge held for him. 'She was killed, machine-gunned by a fighter in Plymouth in August 1940, on the steps of the hospital where she was working as a nurse.'

'And did you never marry?'

'No,' he said. 'Some of us can only love once.' He looked at his cigarette for a minute and said: 'Have you ever been shot at?'

'Yes,' I said, 'and hit too. In the arm, bloody painful. I took a knife too, once.'

'Have you ever been married?'

'Yes,' I said, 'but I'd rather not talk about it. What I'd rather talk about is a young man I want to interview called Dick Sanders.'

Goodinge murmured to me: 'Go easy. The old gentleman will have had a few before he came in, a skinful; he often drinks all night.'

'That's a lie, Goodinge,' said the old man in his even voice. 'I'm not as deaf as you think I am. The fact is that I drink all night and all day. I drink to the eyes of a malt so clear that I'll leave her a widow; but she'll remarry, I've no doubt.' He added: 'Yes, I employed Dick Sanders, but not for long.'

'Why was that?'

The colonel made a savage gesture at the table in front of him and his glass fell on the floor. 'Because he was a spy and a thief. In the end I put a twenty-pound note where I knew he'd go looking for it, then watched and caught him with his hand in the drawer and the money in it.'

'And what did you do about it?'

'I had a glass of whisky in my hand and I threw it in his face, and that was the end of that.'

'And did he go to the Mardys after that?'

'Immediately after. I told William not to employ him, but he did so just the same.'

'That was last year?'

'January last year.'

'Can you tell me any more?'

'I could tell you lots of things,' said the colonel. 'I could tell you about treachery; I could tell you about people who come in here every day that stain the dead, of words that give a mouth the expression of dishonour as it speaks them, of eyes sly as money over the lip of a pint, the pupils almond as a cat's, you'll find them.'

A man in a black suit went by into the other bar and Newington pointed at him and said: 'Him! Look at him!'

'That's Baddeley, the estate agent,' Goodinge muttered to me, 'one of the main people in Thornhill, there's a rumour he's going to run for mayor.'

'Nothing known?'

'What?' he said.

'Never mind,' I said, 'it's a police phrase.'

'Let the colonel off,' Goodinge whispered, 'he's had enough. I'll ring for his taxi.'

The colonel said blindly to the wall: 'Let me alone, Goodinge, it isn't lunchtime yet.' He said to Goodinge: 'Be a good fellow and take me to the loo.' Goodinge came round the bar, the colonel took his arm and they went off together.

I watched them go; but now suddenly a new voice whispered into my ear: 'It's very sad about the colonel; he's not what he was, of course, old age.'

'What used he to be?' I said.

'A war hero,' he said gravely. 'Thornhill is proud of its Colonel Newingtons.'

He had his hand on my shoulder, something I hated; I disengaged myself and turned to look at him. It was the man in the black suit that I had seen just now going into the other bar, where he could listen to us. Meanwhile time had run on and the big bar had filled up with the roar of young voices ordering beer from the staff at the other counter that had come on, asking for darts and cards – suddenly the pub was full up. I looked at this man. He was in his fifties, mostly bones inside his black suit, and gave off an odour, if you were as close up to him as I was, of a long-closed keyboard opened suddenly in an empty house. Now he smiled at me with a set of expensive false teeth, but above those his eyes didn't smile at all; they were slaty and still, like hundreds of eyes I've seen in villains' pubs in London.

He looked as if he had had all the practice on earth backing out of five-door Mercedes estate cars.

'What's done in youth,' he was saying to me, feeling for my elbow, 'can never be undone in age – that's what my old grandparents always used to tell me, you know.'

'Well, if your grandparents ever really did say that,' I said, 'I can only tell you that they copied it from Mrs Gaskell.'

'Eh?' he said, dumbfounded, and it was perfectly obvious to me that he had never heard of Mrs Gaskell, but had unconsciously drained the allusion off as an appropriate undertaker's platitude in the presence of a bereaved family, from the recent TV adaptation of *The Old Nurse's Story* – his grandparents be damned. He had a fruit juice on the bar beside him, and took a sip of it. The white fingers, the colourless but cracked nails held the glass delicately and also jealously away from me and he beamed on me as one does on an evident inferior. He took another sip, and his stomach growled in him somewhere far down: 'I should like it if you would join me in a half of bitter.'

'No,' I said. 'I never drink halves. Or bitter.'

'Something stronger, perhaps?'

'Nothing at all.'

'I hear you're a police officer.'

'That's correct.'

'Might I ask what you're doing down here in Thornhill?'

'I'm doing what I always do,' I said, 'minding the public's business.'

A titter went up from the big public bar whose counter I could see opposite us; people were leaning across. 'What's your name anyway?' I said to him.

'I'm Baddeley, Walter Baddeley,' he said. 'Estate agent.'

The titter became a gust of laughter. A young man from by the dart-board shouted: 'He's Baddeley, Walter Baddeley, an agent of this town! He owns it, he loans it, he's known for miles around!'

'Nice to have an audience,' I said.

Baddeley didn't appear to think so. He stopped smiling, his hand fell away from me to his side and he said: 'Young, well young some-things, only I naturally won't say it.'

I said: 'Are you also the Baddeley whose name I noticed over the undertaker's place up the street?'

'That most certainly is me,' he said. 'Yes.'

The crowd in the other bar roared out: 'Going out to bury, makes Walter Baddeley merry! He sends in his bill, gets a clause in the will, and then he's happy, very!'

Baddeley started moving away, furious, but I caught him by the arm on an impulse and said: 'What do you know about the Mardys?'

'I'd rather not talk about them,' he said. 'It's too sad.'

'What's sad?' I said. 'Come on, you start getting familiar with police officers in a pub, you can't complain if you get asked questions – I'm here to do that.'

'They were going downhill,' said Baddeley. 'Of course, I went up occasionally for Madam Mardy's concerts.'

'Oh,' I said, 'you like music, do you?'

'All I can tell you,' he said, 'is that the Mardys were both very, very special people.'

'And of course you were upset when Mrs Mardy disappeared last August?'

'I was naturally very distressed, like everyone else here in Thornhill.'

'And what did you do about it? Did you go up to see her husband, try to console him at all?'

'We weren't close friends,' he said primly, 'I didn't feel I had the right to intrude.'

I knew instantly that he was lying. 'I find you quite interesting,' I said. 'I hear a rumour you're running for mayor, yet something bad happens to quite prominent fellow citizens of yours and you just let them drop, if I'm reading you properly. You enjoyed their hospitality and their music while it lasted, showed your face because it was the thing to do and then, when things went sour, you forgot all about them, terrific.'

'You're bending what I've said.'

'No I'm not,' I said, 'but you might be; I think you might be quite wicked.' I added: 'Just tell me something as a one-off, did you ever have any business dealings with the Mardys?'

'Why should you think I had?'

'Instinct,' I said. 'I didn't order you in this bar, but you saw Colonel Newington pointing at you just now, and my bet is that you've also heard that I'm down from London to inquire into Mrs Mardy, and now by Christ you're sticking to me suddenly like shit to a blanket, you can't keep away from me. There must be a reason for it, and of course I want to know what it is. It's just routine, Mr Baddeley; you know how we always say that.'

'I'm not obliged to answer!'

'No you aren't,' I said, 'it's merely that if something turns up later on in the course of what I'm doing here and you haven't cooperated with me, you could find yourself hanging upside-down by your balls and having to answer me under what I'll call disagreeable circumstances, so why don't you do it now?'

'I don't like your manners,' he said.

I said: 'That's why I cultivate them, they're specially for you, now answer, cough it up, it might be a gold watch and chain.'

I was enjoying myself. I can tell a villain when I see one, no matter how well he's disguised.

'I'm not answering questions of any kind in front of all these people,' he said, 'that is absolutely not on.' He was very pale, and his right hand was shaking where he had rested it on the counter. 'I cannot and will not answer questions of a private nature in a public house – any business transaction, if there were one, is complicated, and can't be answered by a straight yes or no.'

'Oh yes they can,' I said, 'and if you had any with the Mardys they're going to be.'

He said: 'I think the best thing would be if we were to discuss anything that needs to be discussed out at my house, privately.'

'I get results better the way I'm going,' I said, 'but still, very well, I'll ring you and make an appointment convenient to both of us; I'll be round.'

'All right,' he snapped. 'Meantime I'd like to point out that I simply imagined you were new to the local police and I approached you because I thought that, being a man of some standing here in Thornhill, I might be able to give you a few tips.'

A face peered round at us from the other bar and I said: 'Well, you couldn't have got it more wrong. I'm nothing to do with the local police, I'm working from the Yard.'

'All I wanted was to give you some advice, Sergeant.'

I said: 'I'm afraid in my job I don't take much of that.'

In the other bar the crowd that was listening had got going and roared out: 'He wanted to give him advice, but got his cock caught in a vice! He thought he'd found someone to fleece, then found it was just the police!'

'It's nice to be liked in your local pub, isn't it?' I said to Baddeley.

'You have got the most abominable cheek,' he said.

'I need it. Now then, do you know a man called Richard or Dick Sanders?'

'No.'

'I'm going to pretend you didn't say that,' I said. 'Take plenty of time over your answers, don't just snap them off. OK, now play that one again.'

'I know who you mean, of course.'

'Did he ever work for you?'

'Whether he did or didn't,' he said furiously, 'it's not going to be discussed in here.'

'We'll save it up for our appointment, then,' I said, 'by which time I'll doubtless have the answers anyway. Try and understand, Mr Baddeley. I work for a department called Unexplained Deaths, and I'm inquiring into Mrs Mardy's disappearance. I have to dig till I find the right place to drill into.'

'I wouldn't drill hard into me,' said Baddeley, 'whoever you are. You're just a police sergeant, and I could give you a hard time down here that you'll never forget.'

I said: 'This is more like it. Now you listen to me. After years of the work I do, I find that a terribly bald line, besides you've missed out half of it. The rest of it goes: if you don't shut your boat I shall report you to your superiors and have you busted. Well, don't bother. It's all a load of blag and I'm not in the market for it.'

'This is the first time I've ever heard of a police inquiry being carried on in a public house!' he shouted.

'You'd be surprised how many are,' I said. 'Thieves, grasses, heavy villains – I see them in pubs all the time. It's better than an office at the Factory. It's a good way of getting results fast.'

He went spare. 'Are you putting me in the same bracket as people like that?'

'I don't know yet,' I said. 'I might be.'

'You're libelling me! Slandering me!' He poked me in the shoulder.

'Don't do that,' I said.

'I've been publicly defamed! You've made me look an idiot in my own town, you'll pay for it! I shall speak to my solicitors, Messrs Carrow & Carrow—'

Many of the people who had been in the public bar were round the door of our small one now. They were loving the scene. They roared out: 'Carrow & Carrow, their credit's very narrow. They'll defend you, they will, and send you the bill, and cart you away in a barrow!'

'How many times have I told you that this has got to stop, Captain Goodinge!' Baddeley shouted to the governor above the din. 'This is an impossible situation!'

I said to Baddeley: 'Were you in the forces too? What was your rank? Everyone else in here seems to have one.'

Baddeley said loudly: 'I too was a captain!'

The crowd, intoxicated with beer and delight, began to chant: 'When I was a captain, a captain, a captain, when I was a captain, I got 'em in a fright!'

'That's another song I've told you about!' Baddeley screamed at the governor. 'Can't you do anything about this, Goodinge?'

'Well not really, Walter,' the governor said mildly. 'As far as I'm concerned it's within permitted hours, and you can't expect the lads not to talk and sing.'

'But they're insulting me!'

'Why don't you sue them?' I said.

'These ignorant people,' said Baddeley, 'they can't help it, I daresay, they're jealous because I'm going to run for mayor of Thornhill. I don't care about their vote; they're all on the dole anyway.'

'You'll make a very fine mayor,' I said, 'if I may express the opinion.'

'I have certain ideas for the town,' he replied smugly, 'yes.'

The mob in the public bar, the folk that couldn't get into ours because the doorway was full to bursting, had put in for another round, and when the beer came up they started singing again: 'We'd march for Captain Baddeley, for Baddeley, for Baddeley, he doesn't run too badly, he runs the other way!'

Then they all cheered.

'It's going to be a close contest for mayor,' I said. 'I can see that.' I had trouble making myself heard.

'All right, lads and lasses,' Goodinge shouted, 'that'll do. Little place like Thornhill,' he added to me confidentially, 'you know what a little place is like.'

I wasn't sure if I did, but I knew it was like any other place when you had to pee. I went out through some plastic panels, one marked toffs and the other toffees. I ended up by deciding I wasn't a toffee. Beyond the doors was the usual freezing draught I was used to in pubs from Stoke Newington to Battersea – also the smell of urine, disinfectant, vomit and wet concrete.

I wasn't thinking of the Mardys in the splashback, nor of Sanders, Baddeley or Kedward. I thought of Claire from High Court, straight as a little stick in thirty-eight: She led me back to my dead philosopher girl who said to me: if you're too tired for love, I've something else in a drawer to speed up our frightful experience. I was back with her in West Hampstead again, questioning her for what she knew, and I heard her all over again saying: Despair? But there's no intelligence without despair. To find yourself as a good brain in this world and then be ended in a random way, it defies all logic, it's no better than a fucked-up orgasm. Naked thinking, she said, is the last indignity – the dead breast covered by your only lover long after he has died, been run over, gone mad or gone away: in the end what we name love is nothing but a thin remembrance, a deferred loss. Great ghost, you are a broken officer, our spirit is denounced, stripped and reduced to the ranks where it can shuffle unseen; bitterness, disgust and self-interest remain. All defeat, all battlefields are the same. Even Napoleon after Jena, even Wellington after Waterloo finally learned how to weep over the waste of trust, over faith in death lying where it fell, the lazy eyes, the broken arms and the stink of last meals bursting open for the rats into fresh, uncaring air – birds, flies, sun settling expertly on ideas according to earth's primitive necessity, her sanitation and her plan. Our pub arguments were settled with a shell – our gods, our politics and beliefs picked over by lame men in tears, cracked skulls turned over, the brains gone, great pain. True, the remains were dealt with in style at a convenient date, a few children following to ask why and to learn, and some women white with grief, asking themselves why they had ever let him go.

So we spoke once as our thighs locked in the night – love's own old lost story.

11

I went back to the hotel; the woman that looked like Pinocchio had gone. Instead, a young man with flat disappointed cheeks was sitting reading a soft porn mag, his chin confused in a little beard. His narrow chest was sheltered by an army woolly, patched in places where woollies never wore out. His eyes were sharp, though, and gave me an unkind look that I think was copied from the new series that television was running on the SAS.

'What do you want?' he snapped.

'Not a bullet,' I said, 'not tonight. Just the key to Room 21.'

'Oh that's you, is it,' he said, 'the great detective, how's the case going?'

'Not the same way as you are,' I said, 'now mind your own fucking business and give me the key.'

He took on a shaken look. I said: 'Now you can make yourself useful for once. I want a direct line from my room twenty-four hours a day, and I don't want anyone listening in, OK?'

'It's not hotel policy,' he said, 'that isn't. Normally they—'

'Do yourself a favour with the law, darling,' I said, 'and change the policy, do it right away.'

'I'm not sure if I know how,' he said. All the same, he pushed a few plastic buttons on his switchboard and finally said: 'That seems to be it.' Then he opened his mag at a much folded page and murmured: 'Hey, look at these snaps, see, you can look right up her. I love it – she's a little wanker from the cradle up, she says here; it really makes my knees tremble, this little mystery does, she tells it all on page thirteen, she can't leave it alone, she tells the whole lot in here.'

'It's very sexist,' I said, 'what you're saying.'

'I know,' he said, licking his thin lips, 'and don't I just love it.'

I went up to my room, took my jacket and shoes off and called the voice. It was out; I got the deputy voice instead. I was pleased; it was easier to get on with than the real thing. All this voice wanted was good manners, so I gave it some of that for a minute or two. 'I wonder if you could give me a hand over this Thornhill business I'm on,' I said. 'I'm sorry to bother you when you were probably just going home.'

'That's quite all right, Sergeant.'

In spite of my rare effort to please, urgency got into my tone. 'I'm afraid it's a question of more banking,' I said. 'William Mardy, get the name down. I think there'll be a drain on his account. Any big transactions over twelve months back will do for the present.'

'Every withdrawal?'

'No,' I said, trying not to shout at him, 'I mean the kind of withdrawals that people normally can't afford.'

'Say so, then,' said the deputy voice, 'and wait while I get it down.' Presently he said: 'OK.'

'Now if you could just get the computer on it,' I said, battling with my temper, 'it'd be a lot of help.' I gave him the name of Mardy's bank, which I had got at the price of a few phone calls. 'I want to know who cashed any big cheques he drew over the period – where and when.'

'You want to know everything,' said the deputy voice.

'It's my silly job.'

'Things breaking where you are, Sergeant?'

'I think a heart,' I said.

I braked the car beside an elderly man who was walking his dog down a road outside Thornhill. I said: 'Could you tell me the way to the Sanders' place?'

'You want to go up there?'

'That's right,' I said. 'Are you local here?'

'I suppose so,' he said, 'I've lived here sixty-eight years.'

'That's all right, then,' I said, 'you're local.'

He scratched his head under his cap. 'What do you want to go up there for anyway?' he said. 'Are you a friend, or related? Do you know them?'

'No.'

'Are they into you?'

'No.'

'Why do you want to have anything to do with them, then?'

'Never mind that,' I said, 'just where do they live, these people, do you know?'

'Of course I know. You're on your way there now. Go on a mile and the road turns left uphill. I hope your tyres are good,' he added, 'they need to be – it's rugged, that road.'

'Old place?'

'Old? Broken down, you mean. We call it Arnold's farm. The Sanders rent it – pay the rent to Oldford's the solicitors in the town. Sometimes, that is. There's a gaggle of them up there.' He spat across his dog's back. 'Since you're not related nor a friend I'll say it – they're a load of rubbish up there.' The dog barked and wagged its tail. The old man added: 'Got a weapon with you?'

'Why? Do you think I'm going to need one?'

'Wouldn't be the first time folk did. Still, if you're anxious to be shot at you can have my ration; I had all I could stomach in the war and it earned me nothing.'

'You think I could get shot at up there?'

'Wouldn't be the first time folk had come howling down from that place with some number nine up their arse. Writ servers, mostly. Are you one of them?'

'No.'

'None of my business,' he said, 'you could be a copper for all I care. Anyway, old Ma Sanders can't show her face in Thornhill – she owes too much money, she's made too much trouble, been in too much. Most of the money she owes is for alcohol – Christ, she drinks. Her old man fucked off years ago. I don't blame him; she's handy with a shotgun when she's drunk. Or a kitchen knife.' He looked at me again. 'Another thing. If you don't mind me giving you some advice, the first thing I'd do in your place would be to turn straight round and leave anything you've got on you that's valuable somewhere safe – that load of no-hopers'll have it off you somehow or other if not, they'll find a way. And don't turn your back on your motor while you're up there – next thing you know, it'll have no engine in it, no radio and no wheels.'

'Relaxing,' I said, 'the countryside.'

'Same as the city now, nearly. You a Londoner?'

'That's right.'

'You sound like one.' He shrugged. 'Well, what's the difference now? I'm just the remains of Thornhill; the best went into the two wars and stayed there – maybe they were lucky after all, at that. I just walk the dog round, still see the fields as they were, not the semi-detacheds on them. Horse and cart, traps I see, no cars.' Rain started to drive through the hedge on a cold wind, coming down through two ragged hills the shape of half-empty breasts. The old man began coughing and turned his coat collar up. 'No weather to be staying outdoors,' he said, 'the dog and I'll be getting back into the warm.' He coughed again and spat into the hedge; it was painful to listen to him. 'German gas,' he said, 'and I'd take the bastards on again, give me a rifle. Yes, well up you go, son, and a mile on your left you'll see a track with a post marked Lakes Mill. It runs out at a farm and that's the Sanders' place. Leave me something in your will if you do get killed,' he added, 'if you've anything to leave. I'm an OAP on thirty a week, and I find things tight at eighty-eight.'

He turned back with his dog and I watched them go away, two shapes on the road in the last pallor before the night, and drove on until I found the track that ended up, as the old man had said, in a neglected farmyard. I parked with a ruined barn on my left; ahead of me was a low building not much better than a barn itself, but still a house, a patchwork of mouldered bricks and breeze-blocks. There were no farm animals about, but four big dogs, no, five, came bounding over as I got out of the car; they were of no known breed, but they were savage, surrounding me whining and snarling, showing their teeth. Now, near the barn, standing so still that I hadn't noticed him before in the gloom, I saw a young man holding a rake with his hat on the side of his head. I said to him: 'Is your name Sanders?' He didn't move and I went up to him so that I could see his face. I instantly wished I hadn't; he presented me with vanished eyes and a mouth open to show black, shattered teeth, a cheek covered with bruises. The dogs circled him contemptuously; it was me they were interested in. The boy's jeans and jacket, never made for him, were in rags, and where they weren't wet through with the rain they were rotten. His pants were soaked with his piss, and he smelled worse than a pig.

I shouted up at the house. The boy in front of me never moved but just stood with the wooden rake in his fist as if I wasn't there, gazing away from me. I shouted again, and this time a huge, dirty woman rushed out of the main door of the farmhouse. She had a moustache and stockings that only reached to her swollen knees, and the whole of her body that I could see was ingrained with dirt among the dents in her fat. The dogs ran to her, their bellies and tails flat, and she grunted at them as they came to her: 'Down, Flossie. Down, Bess. Down, Fiver,' and they turned their muzzles up at her to growl in answer. She held a spade in her hand in much the same way as the boy held the rake. I had been looking at the dogs, but when I saw the woman's hating expression as she looked at me, I didn't bother about the dogs any more, but concentrated on the spade.

'What do you fucking want?' she said. 'Get out of here.'

'I will when I've seen your son,' I said.

'Who the hell are you?' And when I showed her she screamed: 'Police? Was that you on the phone? Ah, the fucking law.'

'That's right,' I said. 'Now get those bloody dogs away and get your son Dick down here for me to talk to.'

'He isn't here!'

'Then I'll wait till he comes back,' I said, 'though for my money I shan't have to wait long because I think he's upstairs behind that window there. But whether he is or he isn't, the longer I have to wait the rougher it'll be for him.'

'What do you want to see him for?' she shouted.

'Could wind up being a judge's business.'

'You fuckers never let go,' she shouted, 'you miserable load of bastards.'

'No, that's right,' I said, 'we don't let go.'

'You're on your Jack Jones,' she said, 'and I've got four more sons hanging around this shithole besides the half-wit there.' She jerked her great chin at him.

'Thinking of setting your mob on the law, are you?' I said. 'I should think about it very hard first, if I were you – that carries five years bottom weight.'

'I know,' she said, 'but by Christ I've a mind to.'

'I know,' I said, 'you old villain.'

The woman shook with fury at me, her thick grey hair falling down her back over her army fatigue jacket.

'Well,' I said, 'there's no point in us going on like this all night, though we can if you want to. I don't care – it's the taxpayer looks after my wages. But your boy Dick's a tealeaf, I've had Records phone his form through – he's been in bother with the law since he was a muppet. A petty thief, and too stupid not to get caught.'

'All right,' she said, defeated. She turned towards the house, and the blazing eyes of the dogs beside her followed every single thing she did. 'Dick?' she shouted up at the darkened house. 'Come on down, you'll have to come!'

Nothing happened except that a tattered curtain moved at the window I had spotted on the second floor. The old woman said: 'Look, what could I offer you to go easy on him?'

'Nothing,' I said. 'It's to do with this Mardy business.'

'I knew it,' she said. 'I just knew.'

'It looks like a death to me,' I said, 'and Christ help anybody that's been in any way mixed up in it if it is.'

'You mean it can't be smoothed.'

'No,' I said, 'it's gone rotten now and too far up, otherwise I wouldn't be here.'

'You bastard,' she said. 'Time was when I could have pulled my skirt over my tits and shown you something that would have sent any cunt down the dark path.'

'Too late now,' I said, 'on either side.'

'All right,' she said, 'but Dick's trying to go straight, he's done his time.'

'He's making a strange job of going straight if I'm reading this right,' I said.

'You bastards,' she said, 'you come on so hard.'

'And the Mardys, who cared about them?'

'We've got to live how we can,' she said, 'these days there's no other way to protect your own.'

'I know,' I said, 'I'm getting on in life and I'm no bastard. But the law's what it is, now get that boy of yours down here.'

Beaten, she turned, the coils of her hair twisting down to her great arse, and called up at the house: 'Come on down, Dick, Dick, hey, you'll have to come.'

I could see how drunk she was; and still I thought, what do I truly represent? In my job I couldn't afford to think like that, which was just why I did it. And the idiot still stood motionless in the yard. I took stock and saw that this place that had begun by looking threatening and dangerous was really just what it looked, very sad, very hopeless.

At last I heard someone coming downstairs in the house, and a young man came out. He looked like any of the other youths I'd seen trailing about in Thornhill – or in the East End for that matter.

'Are you Dick Sanders?'

'Suppose I said no.'

'Let's get this right – I'm saying are you?'

'You're looking at my hair. Just because I grow it long, preacher.'

'Don't swop language with me,' I said, 'that'd be the silliest thing you ever did. It's the length of your form that interests me, not the length of your hair – I'm a police officer. Now are you Dick Sanders or not?'

'Yes all right, I am,' he said, 'and so what's it about this time?'

'You know bloody well,' I said, 'it's not about a TV set that fell off a truck – you've got to where you might be going to star in court, you're in the big time, Dick, so let's just go over it and see if you know your lines.'

He thought that lot over, and I watched him do it. 'You're going to be headlines exactly where you don't need them,' I said. 'It's down to the Mardys, you're gone, now work that out, I want to know everything, OK?'

He stroked his wiry hair, long and tied back with a ribbon, in a weary way; his face was pinched and tired, his lips like a machine that refuses a credit card.

'I'm just a gardener.'

'No, not just a gardener,' I said, 'more an odd job man, and very odd jobs. So odd that I've come all the way down here to find out more about them – now let's start.'

'You nauseate me,' he said, 'I find you nauseating.'

'The smell a corpse makes is worse than all the smell of us put together,' I said, 'and I believe that there's one around here some-where in Thornhill not far that'll make me vomit if not you. Now don't be arrogant and look at me in your funny way, it'll get you nowhere. You just tell me what you know about the Mardys during the time you worked for them and realize you're in deep trouble.'

He began to get afraid. 'I tell you I just gardened for them.'

'And that was it? Just planting and digging?'

'That's right.'

'I don't think that's right at all, my darling,' I said, 'so speak up before I tune you to the song – there was a lot more to it than just that, and I'm going to pitch your strings to the point where you'll sing me the lot, so get going.' The old woman was still standing near us, silent and weaving with drink, and I said to Dick: 'Is your mum strangling your throat? She can go or stay as long as you talk, I don't care.'

I didn't; he did though. He turned to her with eyes like a swivelling shotgun and said: 'Fuck off out of this, Mum, will you.'

She screamed at me: 'Don't you go victimizing my boy, do you hear?'

I said: 'I'll do what I have to,' and the boy said: 'Just go back indoors, Ma, didn't I say – I can manage.' I said: 'Yes, and take your dogs with you.'

'Why? They bother you?' she sneered.

'Yes,' I said, 'they stink, now get them out,' and at that she turned heavily away towards the house, trudging across the mud of the yard on swollen ankles. She said backwards to her son, the words streaming on her frozen breath: 'You mind yourself with that cunt, Dick, my son, he's a copper and he's got an evil mind,' and so she slunk off back into the house, dogs and all, and the warped door banged to after her.

'That's better,' I said to Sanders, 'much better. Better for me definitely, and maybe for you too – if you spill about the Mardys we could perhaps do a deal.'

'Money?' he said.

'Don't be stupid,' I said, 'what, you? It's your liberty I'm thinking of, you'll be lucky to keep it.'

'Still, a few quid greases the wheels.'

'You are an idiot first class, you travel free to the nuthouse,' I said. 'Didn't I just tell you? You've got a lot to learn.'

He said: 'If you've the money for it, they say you can do that in bars.'

'Not in your case,' I said. 'In your case you won't learn it in them but you'll be buried and forgotten behind them, so try and play lucky for once. Now tell me what I want to know and we'll see what we can do, all right? OK, answer these questions. What was Mrs Mardy doing during the time you worked up at their house? How did she behave? How did she look? What did she wear? Come on. Talk.'

'I can't. I didn't see. I was just there.'

'You lying bastard,' I said. 'Look, I know how thick you are, a man has to be thick with the form you've got, but you can still see the difference in the woman who employs you when she's got a veil round her face and when she hasn't, surely, can't you?'

'All right,' he said, 'all right, let up, will you?' Now he was really frightened.

'I don't see why I should,' I said. 'You didn't.'

'Yeah she wore a veil,' he said, 'but what you said just now is threatening.'

'I haven't begun,' I said. 'A worm like you, I could have a W in my jacket for you right now, so really sing, it's the disappearance of a human being we're talking about, you're getting the message at long last, so speak, speak, fuck you.'

He knew when he was beat. 'All right, well, yes,' he said, 'while I worked up there, like over a period, you know, I watched her getting weaker, kind of drained, it's dificult to know how to put it, trundling about in the garden and that, yeah, her face veiled – she'd always go into what they called the rose garden, all overgrown, no roses, no man could keep up, it was all just weeds but you could see where the flowers had been, and she'd turn her veiled head away if I was around and stretch her arms up a moment into the sunlight, it was always afternoon, and then go back into the house. As for the husband, poor old gent, he'd be fumbling somewhere behind her, bending to pick wild flowers, there were no others, and he'd have made a bouquet of them which he'd always give her on the balcony at sunset, there above the front door.'

I said: 'Had you any idea why she always covered her face?'

'No,' he said, 'nothing to do with me! No, Christ, of course I don't fucking know!'

'I hope for your own sweet sake that you're telling the truth,' I said, 'because if you're not you could find yourself being stood in a concrete corner for a very long time. Your best option now is to tell me the entire truth over what you know about the Mardys. Do it now, Dick, while you've still got a chance.'

'You mob never let up,' he said.

'No, never where there's a death,' I said. 'Use a little imagination and try to see what it means to die.'

'I'd never thought about it,' he said and I said start before it's too late, Dick.

'You folk from London are really murder,' he sobbed.

'It's the filthy business we're into,' I said, 'like it or not – so how did you get the job up at the Mardys?'

'I was recommended. All right, I'll talk – have you ever heard of a man here called Walter Baddeley?'

I said: 'Where do you fit in with him?'

'I fit in with him where everybody else in Thornhill does, nearly,' he said. 'We're all on sup. ben.'

I said: 'Was it Baddeley sent you up to work for the Mardys?'

'Yeah,' he said, nodding and bowing his thin head. 'Yeah, it was.'

'And you didn't just garden,' I said. 'You spied, listened and watched.'

'This is very tiring,' he said, 'all this is.' His face set obstinately.

'So is Canterbury,' I said, 'specially since it'll be the third time round for you in there, now choose.'

He laughed in my face. 'You think you're so bright and so tough, you think you can do anything with a warrant card. But I reckon you're just a cunt.'

My voice turned grey on him and in me and I said: 'You're a fool to take me for a cunt, you know nothing about me, what I've done, what I've been, what's happened to me. But all right, let's play cunties, now supposing I were to take this' (removing the rake from the hand of the motionless figure beside us) 'and hit you so hard with it that you had to wear a scarf round your face for the rest of your days, then what?'

'Oh come on,' he said, sniggering yet backing off, 'you'd be in dead trouble if you did that, now you would, wouldn't you? Hey, man, that's enough.'

'You're so right, it is,' I said. I was never going to hit him and didn't need to, for he broke slowly over on his knees in a corner of his own accord, sobbing, covering himself up with his hands. 'You pitiful man,' I said, 'get up, get up.'

He wouldn't, though, but screamed 'Hey! Mum!'

'She won't save you,' I said, 'come on, you little actor, what have you all been doing to Mrs Mardy? Tell me what you know – I don't need any more of your sweet old country lies.'

Now the old bat leaned out through a cracked window upstairs. 'Are you all right, my Dick?' she crooned to him, 'are you seeing to that nosy copper, my son? That's right, my dear, I heard him sobbing, you see to him, you give him a right taste of it.'

Then she saw it was all the other way round.

'You shitbag,' she shouted down, 'have you hit my boy?'

'You bet your fat tits I will if I have to,' I said.

'Fuck the Mardys!' she shouted, 'and fuck you, my Dick was just a gardener.'

'A laughing gardener,' I said, 'he giggled in the wrong place. He knows what I want to know over this business, and he knows that I know it. As for gardening, he wouldn't know one weed from another unless he could roll it up and smoke it.'

'You want him seen to, Dick?' she screamed. 'It's easy done, I'll get the banger to him now!' Her shadow staggered back out of the light. Sanders moved to get up, but I pushed him backwards. 'You're dead,' I said to him, 'but not buried yet. You do exactly as I tell you and you'll stay healthy, and not a moment longer.'

Old dreadnought was back at her window with a twelve-bore; I watched the barrels switch about in the half-dark, narrowing and shortening on us, the blue steel glinting from the bulb behind her as she tried to find the range. I took hold of Sanders and started dragging him out of the light, saying: 'She's going to fire, but let's hope she's too pissed. Let's get into that barn, now come on, sweetheart, move, I want you living so you can speak to a court.'

'All right,' he muttered, 'anything. I'm frightened of my mum when she's got a gun in her hands.'

The old fool upstairs fused the bulb in the room with a blow from her furious head and there was no more light in the yard, but I could feel the twelve-bore aiming for me and I yelled, pushing Dick behind me: 'You fire on a police officer, you old bag, and that's the rest of your life gone rotten.'

'I don't fucking care!' she shrieked, 'you can both of you go and wank yourselves!'

I got Sanders into the barn doorway and was about to back in too when the first barrel went off. I like playing snooker and it wasn't the right angle for the shot, but it was fucking near. It was full choke and took a lot of brick off the wall about five inches from my swede. The cold air filled with the smell of powder, and old straw suddenly flew about the place. When I got inside I said to Sanders: 'That was nasty. Buckshot, that was.'

She heard me and yelled down: 'Of course it's buckshot, and it's all for you, you pig.'

'You're wrecking the building, not us,' I said, 'so put that gun up and get lost, will you? You're finished here, missis, I'll see to it, now sleep on that.' I peered at Sanders; he was white-faced and weeping. I was sorry for him now. I felt that we were all of us, without exception, filled with errors and that we knew it, yet had to live through them. It would have been better to be stupid, perhaps even mad. It's the capacity of knowing that's the real agony of existence; maybe we would all of us be more honest without knowledge. Yet it was a hall of mirrors: I had a job to do, and do fast in the allotted time, and I was as disturbed over the Mardys as I could ever be. I found I had some Kleenex on me and gave them to Sanders for him to wipe his face, finding rain water in a bucket and saying, are you all right, Sanders?

He looked at me and said: 'You know Baddeley. I'll tell you about Baddeley. You know he runs Thornhill?'

'Yes.'

He sighed: 'I feel bad at what I've done.'

'What have you done?'

'It's as much what I've not done.'

'Over Mrs Mardy?'

'I wronged her.'

'Was it money?'

'Money,' he breathed, 'ah yes, money.'

'Wronged her how?'

93

'Wronged her memory, and for money. But when you haven't any money then you have no memory.'

'Look, we're alone here, Dick,' I said. 'You can say anything you like, it'll go no further than it would anyway, I swear.'

'How far is that?' he said.

'That I can't answer,' I said. 'The more I find out about the world by what I do, the more I see how much I don't know.'

'I got in the wrong hands,' he said, 'young broke people do, we're used, and then we still have to pay. We pay the Baddeleys, we pay you coppers, why don't people just finish us off, or better still not have us?'

I had no haven to offer him; in a way I was as helpless as he was. I was strictly bound by the terms of my inquiry into a disappearance, a suspected death. I had to grind on and live, even if I didn't know why. My silly idea about absolute justice, I wonder if it's not just an excuse so as to go on talking to people, continue on in the light so as not to have to die, go into the dark. How balance my interest against disinterest? But as a police officer I couldn't possibly tell Sanders, not even my lover if I had one, any of that. And yet I saw Sanders in that vague light, in that barn, both of us fresh from that drunken fire, exhausted by the shock of it, and I knew by looking at his face that he was begging me, reaching to me for the one thing that I couldn't give him – help. How alone we are! The one real risk we run is to understand our state: the rest are stupid smiling, cruel or uncaring people, all of them idiots, broken into the confused tragedy of a herd driven forward across hard country to be killed, and at a profit.

'Don't ask me if I'm all right if you can't help me,' he said. 'You'd just be taking the piss, I couldn't stand more jail.'

'I'm not,' I said. 'This has all turned out to be very serious, and I'm in as tight a corner as you are because I have to find out about Mrs Mardy's fate, and also those responsible for it. If we people didn't do it, it would really be as if folk died for nothing, might as well never have lived, and then there'd be no such thing as civilization left at all.'

'I'd never thought of it like that,' he said, very white and tired, 'never had such an idea in my life at all.'

'You're exhausted,' I said, 'you must get some proper sleep.'

'I seem to have suddenly changed,' he said, 'I can't tell how, but I can't go back up to sleep in the house now after what's passed, my mum'd kill me. Anyway I'm better now and don't feel like sleeping, I'd rather go out and wander while I think.'

I knew what he meant; I often did the same. But I said: 'It's no good, I can't let you do that just yet. Whatever my feelings are I must get an answer to this case, and you're a key to it; I'm also in a hurry because I'm being hard pushed from London.'

'I can't do a deal with the law,' he said, 'that's flat. It would get me killed.'

'You'll have to,' I said, 'you've no choice. I want to keep all this in my own hands; I don't want you passed over to other officers I know. But the problem for you is, you'll have to talk.'

'But I'm afraid.'

'I know,' I said, lighting us both a Westminster, 'but we're all afraid. Best thing I could do for you is to arrest you for your own good and put you somewhere where you'd be safe but the trouble is I've nowhere to put you; I don't like the police stations out here.'

'You know about Kedward?'

'It's what I feel about him so far. But feeling can turn out to be fact.'

Sanders said: 'Christ what a mess this is.' He put his head in his hands and groaned with despair: 'And I thought it was going to be so easy.'

'What did you think was going to be so easy?'

'Making the money.'

'Money for doing what?'

'Up at the Mardys last year.'

'What did you do up there?'

'It started with me reporting on them.'

'Reporting to who? Baddeley?'

'Yes.'

'How much did you get paid?'

'A thousand down, cash, for a gardening job – I thought, this is wicked this is, it's fantastic, Christ, a thousand quid? Of course I had to watch on them. That's how I knew madam was so sick. Sick?' He tried to vomit.

'And then what?'

'It was the electricity strike last September, and the doctor came to Baddeley for some dry ice.'

'Oh? Dry ice what for?'

'It wasn't to make ice cream,' he said bitterly. 'What do you think it was for?'

'There are very few answers to that,' I said, 'and I find all of them far out. Is she up there?'

'I don't know for sure,' he said, 'but I think so. I helped deliver this ice and I see now I was in something too deep for me. If and when it comes to court wouldn't you put a word in?'

'I might if I can get a few more words out of you,' I said, 'I don't know. Let's try this one. Was Mardy being blackmailed over this dry ice?'

'Yes. Baddeley was doing it through a firm called Wildways Estates.'

'What a pretty name,' I said, 'and how did the trick work?'

'Mardy paid the cheques to Wildways, and that was a way for Baddeley to try and kosher them – you know, lose them so they wouldn't show in his accounts.'

'Laundered cheques,' I said, 'dirty laundry, it's nothing but cheques in this bloody business. Still, it's lucky how stupid these people are just when they think they're being so clever, I'm always telling folk. All right now again – where the hell is Mrs Mardy? Do you know?'

'That I can't tell you,' he said, 'and that's straight up, but I tell you I'm sure she's up there at Thornhill Court somewhere.'

'Can't you tell me any more than that?'

'I would if I could,' he said, 'I swear it.' He swallowed and said: 'Aren't I being any use to you?'

'Some,' I said, 'not much.'

'Look, over me, be human, will you?'

'That depends,' I said, 'it's no real part of my job. My job is to help put an end to this case. It's a snake I must spike and kill.'

'Try and see it my way,' said Sanders. 'I'm twenty-seven with no future – I probably never had one, I was fucked before I got off the ground. Look at this shit-heap. We barely eat here, and the troubles we've got are enough to cut your appetite even if you had food in the fridge. Landlord's solicitors working to get us out, no money for the rent. If not it's trouble with you lot, or else it's the council and trouble with the rates, trouble and thunder everywhere. I tell you I wouldn't mind if there was a way out. But I can't see one so I thieve because I must live, I've got to find a way. There's Mum and her bottle on one hand, idiot out in the yard on the other, then there's four more like me with two of them doing bird. The sun never shone on me; I was born to be screwed.'

I knew what he meant; I knew that no matter how much music you played in the motor it could never drown out your trouble, all the trouble of your state.

'They say our family was respectable down here once,' he said. 'Farm labourers, a reputation my grandad slaved his guts out to build, but that's all finished now. I'd still just like to work, settle down and marry like normal folk do. But there's no work for a half-skilled man in Thornhill now. It's not as if we were breaking the law when you take us away; there is no law in Thornhill, only the big villains we try to copy. You people are pissing in the wind when you send us down, and it's not as though all of you were honest either. Bent or straight, it makes no difference to the hours you do, but at least you know you'll draw a month's wages. Only you try getting up at six in the morning without a penny to go plodding out in any weather on foot, hitching down this lane, hacking up that one, going to farms in the season and pulling your hair saying 'scuse me, missis, just looking for work, I'll tackle anything, and all she says is sorry, we're not hiring right now but here's fifty p. Fifty p, hardly enough to buy you half a pint to drown in. Listen, I've got a bird you know and we really get on, only her dad drives a truck for a firm down in Thornhill and they've got savings, which puts them in a different class straight away from me. Sally's dad? Christ, he and his old woman wouldn't give me the skin off their shit. What, me, with three years' bird behind me? What would they want their only girl to marry an ex-con for? So what they say is, you come round here again looking for Sally, cunt, and it's guaranteed birdshot right there where you plant it, darling, now fuck off. So all we can do is go off and be happy with a cassette-player I've got and dance to beer in hedges and screw in ditches and that's our marriage, stars crossing overhead when there are any, and they call that a summer wedding down here because summer's short. I don't know whether we're the new poor or if it was always old; the difference is that they don't recognize us any more the way they did in the old days. There's no solidarity here any more, just your own hell; yes, it's wicked, man.'

'I'll do everything I can,' I said, 'but you know I've got my own folk upstairs to think about.'

'I know that,' he said, whereupon I walked straight out of that barn door shouting up to the woman like a fool: 'You've got the other barrel, use it, now's your chance.'

Nothing happened. 'Will you be all right?' I whispered to Sanders in that freezing dark.

'I've got my brother Brad,' he said, 'down in town, he'll look after me.'

Even the idiot had gone, and the house was as lightless as we are in a state of disaster or sleep.

I said to Sanders: 'Contact me if you're in bother, but I'd better tell you that we're short-handed, there's only me.'

'Considering who you are and what you do,' he said, 'I think you're all right.'

'None of us are ever all right,' I said. 'We're all just waiting for the death express.'

12

The clerk at the hotel was absorbed in the new issue of *Dare*, but he dropped it under the desk when he saw me coming (as if I cared what he read). He didn't look pleased to see me, but some people never are.

'Any messages?'

'Yeah, there's all this lot,' he grumbled, pushing it at me. 'Hey, look, we're not an answering service here, you know.'

'Any good citizen's always anxious to help the police,' I said.

'Yeah but there's a limit to it. There's been nothing but messages, more messages and still more messages since you got here, and this is supposed to be the slack season.'

'And I'll bet it's the one you like best. And aren't you bloody lucky, because there's never any slack season for me.'

'Why can't you just do the whole lot through the police station?' he moaned.

'Because I don't want to,' I said, 'and that's all you need bother about.'

He turned his pair of hopeless eyes up at the ceiling and said, 'Is it all going to take long?'

'It'll take as long as it takes,' I said, 'and think this over – I'd go to exactly the same amount of trouble if it was you who had disappeared.'

I went upstairs, sat down on the bed, took my shoes off and looked at the top message. It was an order to ring the voice, so I rang it.

'At last,' it said. 'What the hell are you doing down there? Have you found out anything about this Mardy woman yet?'

'A good deal, yes.'

'Like what?'

'That's bad grammar, sir.'

'As long as you understand it,' said the voice, 'my grammar's good enough. Well?'

'To start with, the husband's been blackmailed over her.'

'What for? Who by?'

'I've got the name, but I need some checking done into some banking transactions.'

'Oh, not more banking.'

'Banking and vanishing are often very closely linked,' I said, 'you know that as well as I do. Anyway you can take it that it's to do with this voyage that the man says his wife went off on.'

'Will you try and be a little clearer?' said the voice. 'What sort of a voyage was it? Sea? Air? Rail? Have you tried tracing the ticket?'

'It was the kind of voyage you don't need any ticket for. Last autumn Mardy took delivery of a load of dry ice, and you know what you use that stuff for.'

'Yes, corpses,' said the voice. 'Let me think, dry ice will freeze them right down to—'

'And where do you get it from?'

'It's not easy – the morgue, I suppose.'

'Yes. Or?'

'I don't know – wait – an undertaker's, maybe.'

'Now we're getting there,' I said, 'an undertaker's. Exactly.'

'Stop flourishing your logic in my ear,' said the voice, 'will you? Anyway, this woman's dead, is that it?'

'You can be one hundred per cent sure of that,' I said. 'You don't need to freeze the living.'

'Where's the body, then? Anywhere near you?'

'I think so, yes.'

'Why do you think so?'

'Because I've got a witness – a lad who helped deliver the dry ice. He's a no-hoper in his twenties with three years' form called Dick, or Richard Sanders. He's an accessory to murder, of course, when we find the body, because even counsel with L-plates on could prove that Sanders knew what that delivery was and what it was for.'

'But why would the man want to freeze his wife?'

'That's the part I don't know yet, but I'll find out if I do it my way. Sanders also, on his own admission, says he received a thousand quid cash for his part in the job and what's more, he worked for the Mardys over the period that interests us as a gardener.'

'Sounds as if he's in trouble,' said the voice, 'people like that always are. Have you arrested him?'

'No,' I said. 'Firstly because it doesn't suit me to just yet and secondly because I've nowhere to put him.'

'What the hell are you talking about?' said the voice. 'What do you think a police station's for?'

'The first thing it's for in my view,' I said, 'is to lock Inspector Kedward up in, and that's where he'll end up by the time I've finished with him.'

'Oh Christ, is he really bent?'

'I haven't the proof yet, but I'm convinced of it. It's the only way to explain his behaviour over Mrs Mardy that I can see.'

'The whole thing's very confusing the way you're telling it,' said the voice, 'and I don't like the Kedward part of it at all.'

'It's not my fault the man's bent,' I said, 'and any case is confusing no matter who's telling the story, especially if you're in the middle of it.'

'All right,' said the voice, 'what else have you got?'

'There's this blackmail angle.'

'Any names there in the fairy tale?'

'Yes, I've got one good fairy and one very bad one, apart from Kedward and Sanders. The good one's a very interesting man called Colonel A'Court Newington; he knows a lot about the Mardys and I've a message here asking me to contact him. The naughty one's a man called Walter Baddeley and he runs a company whose finances I want checked out – Wildways Estates, with registered offices in Thornhill.'

'Tell me more about Baddeley.'

'He's a man of many activities,' I said. 'He has political ambitions, he's an estate agent, a property dealer, and guess what else he is? An undertaker. Have you put Kedward on the computer yet? Because while you're at it I want every payment made to or by Wildways Estates checked. And talking of Wildways, the computer can go through Baddeley's personal account as well.'

'You've got an obsession about banking in this case, Sergeant, it seems to me.'

'Yes, and with some reason,' I said, 'because money, murder and blackmail often jingle happily along together hand in hand; they make a sweet little nursery tune together – it's called motive. Sometimes another pretty little instrument joins in too,' I added. 'It's called greed, and I certainly think it's joined in here.'

'I just hope you're not giving the computer a lot of work for nothing.'

'It's no work for the computer,' I said irritably. 'They link it to the appropriate bank terminal and it'll whip through that lot in a few seconds. Tell them to search back to January eighty-four and then ask them to get me the photostats of any cheque made out for more than a hundred pounds – and how soon can I have it, five minutes ago could be too late.'

The voice sighed. 'I'll have it sent down by courier.'

'Good,' I said. 'Once I've found what I think I'm going to find in there I'll get along a lot faster.'

'I'll say this much for you, Sergeant, you usually do get on fast,' said the voice. 'Tell me another thing, now – what about this man Newington, where does he fit?'

'Newington's a retired colonel, served throughout World War Two in the artillery; he was at Dunkirk. He was also a magistrate and a man whose word I would accept without thinking twice, and that's something I very seldom say about anybody, you know me. He's old and very sick and lives on his own in a big house. His fiancée was killed in 1940, machine-gunned by a German fighter outside the south coast hospital where she was working as a nurse.'

'I've never heard you be so poetic over anyone before,' said the voice. 'You seem to think a lot of him.'

'I do,' I said, 'he's the kind of man I'd like to be when I'm old.'

'All right,' said the voice, 'leaving all that aside, what makes him so interesting?'

'First, because he knew the Mardys very well and liked them. Second, it was Newington who went to the Chief Constable about Mrs Mardy. It was not, I repeat not, Inspector Kedward.'

'How do you know it was Newington?'

'It's ridiculously simple,' I said. 'He told me. You've got to remember,' I added, 'how popular Mrs Mardy was in the area, particularly with her concerts. Everybody liked and respected them. But it needed a man with Colonel Newington's authority to take action when the local police did nothing about her, and he took it.'

'Quite irregular.'

'Yes, but it worked,' I said, 'because here I am.'

'Yes, all right.' The voice paused. 'You feel this case is right for A14, do you?'

'I'm afraid so,' I said. 'I believe the Mardy case is an unexplained death all right. You get a nose for—'

'Keep going,' said the voice. 'I'm not interested in your nose,' it added, and rang off.

I looked at my nose in the mirror; I wasn't interested in it either. There was a fridge bar in a corner of the room. I opened it and found a make of dark beer I didn't like but no lager. Still, there were some miniatures. I got a Bell's and added ice and water to it. I stared into the drink for a while, then rang Records and asked for Sergeant Harrison. 'Hello, Barry,' I said, 'how's things?'

'I was just going to ring you,' said Harrison. 'To start with, there's nothing at all on Marianne Mardy.'

'I'd be surprised if there had been,' I said. 'OK, then, what about him?'

'Ah, William Mardy's more interesting. Born 1921, medical student. The war interrupted that. Joined the Medical Corps at the end of thirty-nine, qualified with them. Went on active service –

North Africa, Sicily, Italy, Austria, finished at a military hospital, Potsdam, in forty-five. Practised in London till nineteen forty-seven as a GP, then started to train as a surgeon. So far, fine. But then things went wrong.'

'How?'

'He carried out an operation on a woman patient while he was still a student.'

'When was this?'

'October forty-nine.'

'What happened?'

'The patient died.'

'What was the operation?'

'An abortion. Illegal here in those days, which is why she went to Mardy. Also, they were cousins. She was a Miss Dorothy Martens; he operated on her in her flat. He performed a D & C. It didn't come off, because the girl had some sort of gynaecological abnormality – I forget the medical details. When he realized this he did rush her to hospital, but too late. She died of septicaemia.'

'Christ,' I said, 'he should have known better than to do that.'

'He doubtless did, but he equally knew he was breaking the law operating at all.'

'Why did they go to such lengths to get rid of the child?'

'In his evidence at the inquest Mardy merely stated that he carried out the operation because she begged him to. There were family reasons too – her dad was a vicar – bringing shame on her parents etcetera.'

'Any suggestion that the child might have been his?'

'Well, of course the coroner put the question to him, but he denied it. Blood samples were taken of Mardy and the foetus, but the results weren't conclusive. I don't think the coroner thought he was.'

'Did she have a reputation for jumping in and out of bed? Vicar's daughters sometimes behave like that.'

'Don't I know it,' said Harrison. 'I'm married to one, or was. But there was nothing definite.'

'Criminal proceedings?'

'Of course,' said Harrison. 'But he got off lightly – eighteen months at Ford Open. He had good counsel, and the judge remarked during his summing-up that he'd already been sufficiently punished by the death of the girl and a wrecked career.'

'Anything known of him after he got out?'

'He's never turned up here again.'

'He wasn't short of money until I think recently,' I said. 'Only child, old local family, inherited this barracks of a place down here. His wife seems to have had money too, from France.'

'Well, I hope some of this has been helpful.'

'Of course it has, Barry,' I said. 'Thanks a lot. Everything I can find out helps. Remind me to buy you a drink when I get back.'

'That's fourteen you owe me,' Harrison said. He added: 'What sort of a case is it?'

'Nasty.'

I had hardly put the phone down when it rang again. 'Reception here. There's a Colonel Newington waiting to see you in the bar.'

'Has the bar got a phone?'

'Of course it has.'

'Then put me through.' I said to the barman: 'Ask Colonel Newington to come up and see me in Room 21.'

When he arrived I said: 'I hope you didn't mind my asking you to come up, but we can be private in here. As for bars there's one in the corner here; what can I get you to drink?'

'Whisky.'

I made the drink for him and said: 'Is there something you wanted to tell me?'

'About the Mardys, yes.' He was sober but looked dreadfully grey, very frail. He said: 'I drink a lot because I'm in pain most of the time.' He finished half his whisky at a swallow, put it down and lit a cigarette. 'I'm not supposed to smoke or drink as far as the doctors are concerned.' He smiled absently. He stared up at the ceiling for a time before looking at me – when he did it was a look out of eyes the colour of gun-metal. 'Since we met in Goodinge's pub,' he said, 'I've been doing a lot of thinking.' With the edge of his thumb he pushed his cigarette from the edge of the ashtray into the middle. Without looking away from the cigarette he said softly: 'What do you think of Kedward?'

'Probably what you think,' I said, 'but I haven't enough facts to back my opinion yet.'

'Very good,' said the colonel. 'What do you know about Walter Baddeley?'

'Not as much as I shall do in a few hours' time.'

'One fact I'll bet you haven't got,' said Newington, 'is that Kedward's wife is Baddeley's sister.'

'Ah, really?' I said. 'That's golden information, that is.'

'I hate that whole pack of bastards,' he said.

'Does the name Wildways Estates mean anything to you?'

'It does.'

'Would you care to tell me exactly what it means to you?'

'It means rackets,' he said. 'There are two directors – I mean working directors – the third's just a broke peer on the letterhead. Wildways pays his bar bills. Sometimes.'

'Would you tell me who the working directors are?'

'Certainly. Walter Baddeley and Anne Kedward. But she uses her maiden name.'

'This Anne Kedward's a new piece in the game.'

'She's a bitch,' said the colonel, 'Kedward's completely under her thumb. Mind,' he added, 'it's his own fault; he's weak and greedy and just does what she tells him.'

'They don't make good police officers.'

'No,' he said, 'but you get them just the same.' He added: 'Any more whisky in that fridge of yours?' I got it for him and he remarked: 'It was difficult for me to start talking to you. I had to balance giving people away against what I thought to be right.'

'You'd already started when you contacted the Chief Constable over Mrs Mardy.'

'I didn't give Kedward away,' said Newington, 'I want you to realize that. But I decided that the inquiry into Mrs Mardy's disappearance needed, what's the word I want? A boost, and I know the Chief Constable well; we used to play billiards together, and of course I saw a good deal of him as a magistrate.' He added savagely: 'Now I wish I'd gone and seen him before; Marianne Mardy might still be alive.'

'You think she's dead?'

'I'm sure of it.'

'So am I,' I said, 'but try not to blame yourself. If you hadn't gone to the Chief Constable it would have been an age before anyone else did. Now look, would you tell me how you found out that Walter Baddeley and Anne Kedward were on the board of Wildways Estates?'

'Yes, they wrote to me with a proposition. I've got the letter.'

'The proposition was what?'

'I have no heir,' said Newington. 'You know that; I told you I wasn't married. The substance of what they wanted to know was whether I had enough capital to keep my house and two farms going and whether I was fit enough to do it and, if not, whether I would be prepared to accept a piddling annuity from Wildways on condition that my entire estate reverted to them on my death.'

'And did you reply?'

'Yes,' said the colonel, 'I told them to fuck off, though I didn't put it quite like that.'

'And was that the end of it?'

'It was as far as I was concerned,' he said, 'but one or two other cases turned out differently. Lady Eleanor Crosby of Wood Hall, for instance, had neither a husband, a penny, nor an heir. She needed to go into hospital for her chest, but wouldn't unless she could afford private treatment. She couldn't, so she accepted Wildways' annuity.'

'And?'

'And she went into a London nursing home and died there, so that now Wildways owns Wood Hall, everything in it, and the land – they got the whole lot for practically nothing. And that's not the only example.'

'It's very strange, I know,' I said, 'but legally there's nothing wrong about Wildways, as you must realize yourself. You and I find it ghoulish, but it isn't against the law.'

'I'm not saying it is,' said Newington. 'It's like any successful racket. What I'm saying is, that it is a racket. Wildways specializes in old, sick, lonely people with property to leave. He manages them, he cheats them, and as often as not he buries them too.'

'All right,' I said, 'let's go a little further now. Have you any reason to think – I'm not asking for proof – that Wildways have overstepped the line anywhere?'

'Well, they're greedy,' he said, 'very greedy.'

'Getting careless? Annuity-holders not dying off fast enough, so give them a push?'

'I don't know what's happened to Marianne Mardy,' he said, 'so I can't be positive. But I believe it's possible.'

I had a desire to tell him about the dry ice delivery, but I knew I couldn't – I wasn't far enough on yet.

'Yes, I think they've made a mistake somewhere,' I said, 'and I'm here to find it.'

'Now we've got on to the Mardys,' he said, watching the smoke of his cigarette drift up to the ceiling, 'there's something you'd better realize. She came to see me.'

'On her own? When was this?'

'This is the most difficult and painful part. Yes, I can tell you exactly. It was July 22nd last year.'

'At your house?'

'Yes, I was having a drink before going in to dinner. I detest meals,' he added inconsequentially, 'I've no appetite. Well, I was just facing up to the idea of eating when the lady who looks after me in the evenings came in to say that there was a Mrs Mardy to see me. I told Mrs Whittington to show her in at once; I was in the library.'

'And how did Mrs Mardy seem?'

'Not at all well, I'm afraid, and carelessly, poorly dressed, which was unheard of with her, though for months before I had noticed how she was letting herself go.'

'Money problems?'

He shook his head. 'Marianne would still have looked smart, no matter how badly off they were. She would have kept up appearances. No, it wasn't that.'

'Was she wearing her veil?'

'Yes, she never went anywhere without it.'

'She didn't even take it off when you and she were alone together?'

'Oh no.'

'Can you describe to me how she spoke to you? I mean, what did her voice sound like?'

'She didn't speak,' he said, 'she would only whisper. She came quite close up to me, but even so I had great difficulty in making out her words, and I'm not deaf.'

'Can you be more precise?'

'It's hard,' he said. 'The nearest I can get to it – it was an indistinct whisper.' He said, looking straight at me: 'I can't describe to you how bad it was to listen to her, remembering the other times when she used to sing and be so happy.'

'Can you tell me what she whispered to you?'

'I must,' he said, 'that's why I'm here. She asked me for help, and yet when I asked her how I could help her she began to cry and said she was beyond help.'

'And then?'

'Well,' said the colonel, 'then she clung to my sleeve for a while, and I made out that what she wanted most was just to be with someone she knew and could trust for a little while. I offered her a sherry, not knowing what else to do, but she stepped back and shook her head with a horrified look which surprised me, because she always enjoyed a dry sherry in the old days.'

'Perhaps it was because she wouldn't, or rather couldn't take off her veil to drink the sherry,' I said slowly.

'I'm afraid so,' said the colonel, 'yes.'

'I'm sorry my questions are so painful,' I said.

'It can't be helped,' he said. 'I had got myself ready for them.'

'Did you ask her why she didn't remove the veil?'

'That's where I feel so culpable,' said Newington, 'no, I didn't. I felt I couldn't. I daresay if I'd been anything but British I would have done. But I felt it would have been an intrusion.'

'All right,' I said, 'I understand.' There was a moment's silence. Then suddenly he said: 'She smelled funny.'

I said: 'I'll have to ask you this, but could you put a name to the smell?'

'I could,' he said, 'but I'd rather not. It's something I haven't smelled since the war.'

I said: 'There's no need to go any further.' I knew it was the same smell as we found when we broke a door down to find a body that had been behind it for several weeks.

'I'm glad I don't have to talk about it,' he said, 'I don't know that I could. I've hardly slept since that evening and for the first time in my life I've grown afraid of the dark.'

'And was that the last time you saw her?'

'Yes.'

'Did she say if her husband knew she'd come out to see you?'

'She said he didn't know.'

'How did she get to your house? By car?'

'No, on foot; she couldn't drive, and their place isn't far – about three quarters of a mile.'

I had a sudden image: the veil fluttering by the hedge that night, feminine steps walking quickly down the dark road, the fitful beam of a torch.

'Did you ever, at any time, ask her about Baddeley?'

'Yes, I did. I hinted at the same things that I've told you about him, but the name meant nothing to her, except that she'd met him at her concerts, of course.'

'This isn't just idle prying,' I said, 'but could you tell me whether or not the Mardys were well off?'

He closed his eyes and thought for a moment. 'Judging by the state their house is in, general opinion is that they haven't a penny – yet no one ever heard that there was a mortgage on it, which is the kind of gossip that gets around in a small town like Thornhill, and they never seemed to have any trouble meeting their bills.' He shook his head: 'It's really impossible to say.'

'Never mind,' I said, 'I've got other ways of finding out about that if I need to. One last point – do you think we could return to the Kedward angle for a minute? The question is this – Wildways is clearly making a lot of money, in which case I can't see that a detective-inspector's salary makes much difference to the Kedwards one way or the other, so why didn't Kedward just jack the police in, I wonder?'

The old man smiled. 'Now come on, Sergeant, for once I can do your job for you. Weren't we saying a minute ago that Wildways is operating, at times, anyway, on the edge of the law? Supposing they did go over it, don't you think it would be a good idea to have a tame local copper around?'

'Yes it would,' I said. 'Risky for a copper to play that game, though.'

'You could assume his wife gave him no choice,' said Newington, 'she's a first-class bitch – and now do you see why the police here dragged their feet over Marianne Mardy?'

'Yes,' I said, 'but Kedward must have realized things wouldn't stop there.'

Newington said: 'I believe that Baddeley and Anne Kedward panicked over Marianne and played their police card – Kedward was so deep into Wildways through Baddeley and his wife that he'd no option but to do what they told him.'

'I'm having all Kedward's and Baddeley's banking affairs gone into,' I said. 'I'll get the information by courier any time now.' I added: 'I wouldn't mind finding out more about Anne Kedward too, by the way.'

'That's easy,' said Newington, 'why don't you go over to the gambling club she runs? It's only a hundred yards down the street from here, and it's called the Lucky Jack.'

13

The Lucky Jack Club was part of the bingo hall I had seen when I first drove into Thornhill, the one with the heavies leaning against the wall by the doors in tight flannels and blazers. If gear like that was meant to make them look like guards officers on leave it failed to impress me. As I went up the steps they closed in on me and one said: 'Sorry, members only.'

'How much for the evening?' I said, 'just to lose a few quid?'

The big blond one gave me a blank stare all over and said: 'Too much for you, sweetheart. Nobody knows you and nobody wants to, now get lost.'

'You know, I get the feeling you might have been a copper once,' I said.

'I might have been,' he said, 'now fuck off.'

Behind him I could see a thin gent with wavy grey hair coming towards us across the foyer; he wore a weary red dinner coat with a small burn mark over the breast pocket. He weaved through the doors and said to the other two: 'What's this, then? Have we suddenly got into the business of turning punters away?'

'I don't like the look of him,' said the blond heavy.

'What do you mean?' said the manager. 'You've never seen him before.'

'I still don't like the look of him.'

'All I'm trying to do is lose some money,' I said to the manager.

'That's reasonable,' he said. 'Where are you staying?'

I told him and said: 'Will you take a credit card?'

'I will if it's good.'

'Check it.'

'We always do,' he said. 'Meantime, come in and have a drink.

Girlies and bar are down here – the serious stuff is two floors up in the lift.'

'Good idea, the drink,' I said. 'When you've checked the card out, join me in the bar and bring me a couple of grand in cash.'

'Done,' said the manager. He disappeared through a door marked Private. I let the entrance doors swing to in the heavies' faces and went through to the bar. It was small and packed with people, what they call intimate. I don't. Crimson lamps like candles fluttered hotly on the walls; frozen women sat at the tables near the back with punters chatting them up. I went up to the counter and parked on a stool. A barman came up who looked as if he had worked in a mental ward; he had the build for it. It turned out later that he had worked in one.

'What'll it be, sport?' He had trouble talking and I soon saw why; the teeth in his lower jaw had been wired up.

'Ring-a-ding,' I said. 'Two glasses.'

He produced them with the bottle and a bowl of ice. He said: 'You a London punter? You sound like you was London to me.'

I said: 'Well? What of it?'

'That'll be twenty quid.' I gave him the money. 'Which part of London you from?'

I said: 'The part with a lot of fucking hospitals in it.'

'Oh yes,' he said, 'West End.'

'It could be the very end for folk who ask too many questions,' I said.

He understood that all right and pissed off; he may have been frightened for his jaw again, which he had probably opened too often for its own good. Soon the manager joined me, gave me the credit card and the slip to sign. When I'd done that he took the card back out of my hand and compared the two signatures. 'Can't be too careful,' he said.

'No, not these days,' I said. I put the card away and said: 'So let's have the money.'

'It's waiting for you upstairs in chips.'

'Look,' I said, 'what's the rush? Can't you see I've got a bottle in front of me?'

'They'll keep it for you here.' I could see the man had me marked as a mug punter and couldn't wait to get me at it.

I said aggressively: 'I told you I wanted the money in cash here. I'm a big boy; I'll buy my own chips, so bring the notes to me here and now.'

He didn't argue. When he came back with the money I counted it; there was fifteen quid missing.

'That's for the entrance fee.'

'Nice business you've got going here,' I said enviously, 'you cop all round. The boss about?'

'Daresay she'll be in later. Why, do you know her?'

'That's it,' I said. 'Now let's see, it's Anne, wait a minute, Anne—'

'Kedward.'

'No,' I said, 'that's not it. At least it wasn't in the old days. In the old days it used to be, I've got it – Baddeley.'

'Course it is,' he said. 'I must be getting pissed.'

'You must be well pissed,' I said, 'if you don't know the names of the people you work for.' I pushed the bottle over to him. 'Have a drink. By the way, talking of names, what's yours?' I was letting my voice become slurred.

'You ask a few questions, don't you?'

'Why shouldn't I?' I said, squinting at him. 'What's strange about asking the name of a man you're having a drink with?'

'I'm Charlie,' he said. 'Charles Masters.' I doubted if that was his real name but he had to say something; he didn't want to lose me, didn't want me to reel out of the place in a drunken temper.

'Oh, yes. Charles,' I said. I stubbed my cigarette out, missing the ashtray and doing it on the bar. 'Charlie. Now that's a really nice name. You know, I work with a bloke called Charlie. Lovely man, my best mate.'

'What work do you do?'

'I'm in steel chain,' I said. I slopped out two drinks and pushed one over to him. 'All the best, Charlie, good luck, and may the best man win.'

'I must go,' he said, 'we're busy tonight.'

'I think you've got a dolly upstairs,' I leered, 'don't let me keep you. Good old Charlie.'

'Enjoy yourself,' he said coldly, 'see you later.' He left.

I finished my drink slowly. After a while a girl in red Bermuda shorts with bad legs under them and no bottom came over. 'Hello, stranger,' she said, 'I'm Honey, I look after lonely men.'

'I'm not lonely,' I said in a thick voice, 'but I've got a thing. I can't stand Bermuda shorts, particularly on a man.'

'Are you a masochist?' she shouted.

'No,' I said, 'and you're certainly not.' She stormed off and sat down sulking at the far end of the bar. I looked at the time; it was ten past one. I didn't care. I hadn't counted on getting much sleep in Thornhill.

After a while another girl came up. 'Hi there,' she smiled, as though we had been childhood sweethearts, 'I'm Gail, don't you like it in here?' Her features were good – the trouble was, they looked as if they had been set in concrete. Her nails were bitten to the quick, but at least she knew how to dress.

'I don't know till I've started to play,' I said.

'Would you like me to come and play with you?'

'It would depend what the game was.'

'Look,' she said, 'frankly, are you gay? I love doing things to gays, I'm good.'

'I'm not gay,' I said, 'but as we're getting so intimate, are you a dyke?'

'Oh, I love rude dominating men,' she said quickly, 'my first boyfriend was like you.'

I didn't want to hear about him, so I sat watching while she gave her eyelashes some exercise; she let her mouth have a go too. She could make it turn into something like a cushion; it was remarkable how she did it.

'Do that again,' I said.

'What?'

'What you did with your mouth.'

'Oh, that,' she said. 'Why, do you like it? Does it turn you on?' She did it again, only it didn't work as well as it had the first time. First Honey, now Gail – news of my credit limit must have got round.

'How expensive do you come as a cards partner?'

In spite of herself she spoiled her act; her eyes snapped alert. 'I'd take twenty per cent of your winnings, and you'd pay me the same, cash, on the amount you lost.'

'Your mind works like a chain store executive,' I said. 'Sounds cheaper if I play on my own.'

'Maybe,' she said, 'but not so much fun.'

'You'd be a distracting influence,' I said. 'Any bed in the price?'

The great red mouth cushioned regretfully. 'You know I could really really fancy you, but I've got a steady boyfriend.'

'I'll bet you have,' I said. 'I'll bet you're a pushover for layabouts on what you make – your troubles won't start till you try getting rid of him.'

'Are you trying to be insulting?'

'No,' I said, 'though it wouldn't be hard. What's more, I've got another piece of advice for you.'

'What's the advice?'

'Get lost,' I said.

She stared at me in disbelief as if I had thrown my scotch over her; then suddenly the manager was beside me again. He said to the girl: 'Fuck off, you.' He said to me: 'Having a good time?'

'Average. How do these women know my credit's good, Charlie?'

'I don't know,' he lied. 'Now wouldn't you like to go upstairs and play? There's poker, blackjack and baccarat, all three going.'

'In a minute,' I said. I patted him on the back. 'You're good, Charlie,' I said, 'generous with the credit, now why not have a drink?' I watched him watching me in the mirrors across the top of his glass, trying to gauge how drunk I was; he wanted me to go far, but not so far as to have me pass out. 'Right,' I said, hurling my drink back in one gulp, 'poker.' He nodded approvingly. I did a practised stagger away from the bar and yelled: 'Which way's the lift?'

He got in with me, pressed button two and fed me out into the gaming room. I tottered about among the punters and in the end flopped down in a chair at the poker table. 'Dealer's choice?' I said to the lipless blonde girl in charge. She nodded. 'Right,' I said, giving her a hundred pounds, 'let's have the chips for this.' There were three other punters at the table, and I sat out till the deal came round to me. 'New cards,' I said.

'OK,' said the girl. She took two new packs from under the table and slit the seals with a thumbnail like a kitchen knife that had done murder. 'House'll sit in,' she said. She shuffled the cards and cut to me. 'Five pounds in the kitty,' she intoned, 'minimum stake five pounds and multiples. Sky's the limit.' I dealt a hand of five card, nothing wild, to see what would happen. I won on a pair of tens but the betting was lethargic and I only cleared sixty pounds. The deal passed to my neighbour and I sat back, juggling with the chips in my pocket. The little bat said to me sharply: 'Are you in?'

'No,' I said.

'People could use your seat if you're not playing.'

'They can have it,' I said, and stood up. I murmured to her as I left: 'Never force a punter, it's the quickest way to lose him, you've a lot to learn yet.' She hated it.

There was someone like a court-martialled army baker standing by the door in a velour jacket waiting to deal with trouble, and I said to him: 'Is there a garden out there?'

'Most people use the toilets.'

'Just answer the question,' I said.

'Back down in the lift – they'll show you. Why?' he added spitefully, 'fancy some exercise?'

'Only the mental kind,' I said, 'nothing you could help with.' I went out into the garden. I felt sorry for it. It was lit electrically at that time of night when all life wants to sleep. I walked about in it. The trees were old – perhaps two or three centuries – and there were borders, carefully planned flowerbeds, now harbouring arc lights and electronic speakers that must have been there for a very long time, long before the Lucky Jack was built on the site of some other house. Water, lit from beneath, glittered uneasily in a stone pool. Cigarette-ends and the stub of a cheap cigar floated in its bilious greenness, and every tree, even at this time of year, had interrogators' lights pointed straight at it. Cold though it was, people whooped drunkenly behind the shrubs; a man and a woman were having a fight, hitting out toe to toe on a circular patch of grass. Omnidirectional music harangued everyone, and the trees swayed as children do in their effort to stay awake late at night – there was too much noise for any rest. I watched this corner of our tragedy pass me in the cold electric dark; I believed that for a moment, surrounded by the corruption I was trying to expose, I could see in the untruth of that garden everything that we had ever tried to defend flying away from me. A singer called out from among the blackened plants:

> 'Ev'ry night that you don't come
> I care a little less.
> Every night you cheat on me,
> Is there anything left to say?
> Living, doing –
> But ev'ry night
> My body turns to die,
> You have always been a star,
> I have always lived in storms,
> I have always been next door.'

I went back indoors, and there was the manager with me again. 'Everything OK? You going to play some more?'

'I might.'

'I'm glad,' said the manager, 'because just now Janine—'

'Who's she?'

'Our poker table manageress.'

'Oh yes.'

'She seemed to feel you weren't happy.'

'There was something troubling me, but on the whole I was happy all right, yes.'

'You should have been. Seems you picked up a few quid.' He added: 'You don't seem quite as merry as you were last time I saw you.'

'You mean drunk,' I said. 'I can drink an awful lot, Charlie; you've got to be able to if you work in steel chain like I do.'

'Is that so?' he said indifferently. He thought for a while. 'I'll tell you what, if you're feeling blue, how about a girlie? I can give you a room on the fourth floor – just point out the bird you fancy as we go by.'

'Later maybe,' I said. 'I'll play poker right now, and why don't you come and watch me?'

'Nice of you, friend, but I've a lot on.'

'You might have even more before the night's over,' I said.

He gave me a puzzled look as if he knew he'd lost me, but couldn't believe it. The look lasted the tenth of a second. 'You're not really a mug punter,' he said.

'Who said I was?'

'You came on as one.'

'You read me all wrong. I've been playing poker for years. I find excitement relaxes me.'

'You weren't drunk in the first place either.'

'No crime in being a natural actor,' I said. 'Now come on, Charlie, cheer up – I'm going to play everything I've got on Janine's table and I want you to come and watch it, you'll be really sorry if you don't, you'll be missing something.'

'I'll certainly escort you to the table and stay a minute or two,' he said. 'After all, that's part of my job, making our guests feel at ease.'

'And friendship makes work a pleasure,' I said, as we got into the lift. 'Besides, I have a feeling this won't take long.'

'I don't think it will either,' the manager said.

'That's it,' I said, 'there's no stopping me once I feel lucky.'

Nothing to speak of was happening on Janine's baize; three punters, one of them new to me, were playing a desultory game of five card for low stakes. When the girl saw me she gave me a look and said: 'Back to play?' In profile her lipless face was as sharp as a meat-cutter.

I said: 'Well, I'm not here to talk about the weather.' I counted two hundred pounds and said to her: 'Chips for that.' I said to the others: 'Do you lot want a real game or are we just going to play fairies?'

'Why not just you and I for a hand?' said the new punter.

'OK,' I said. 'My money's on the table, let's see yours.'

The girl said frigidly: 'The house will vouch for Mr Earle; he can play for what he likes.'

'Good,' I said, 'because you never know, he might need to.'

Behind me the manager made a noise.

'I'll take three ton of chips,' said Earle.

'No problem, Mr Earle,' Janine said, and pushed them over to him.

'Well, well,' I said to Earle, 'just you and me.'

'Why not?' he said.

'No reason,' I said. 'Cosy.' He had a thick mouth in a thin face; neither of them liked me. His clothes were expensive but had been on him for a while and could have gone to the cleaners.

But he had no limit with the house.

I said to the girl: 'I believe your name's Janine.'

'That's right,' she said, 'what about it?'

'Let's have fresh packs about it,' I said. 'I don't like putting new money on used cards.'

Her lips, never obvious, got lost in her distaste, but she got two sealed packs out. She was about to cut them open with that sickle-shaped thumbnail of hers only I reached over and said: 'I'll have a look at those if you don't mind.'

'What the hell do you think you're doing?' said Earle.

'You can see for yourself,' I said, 'I'm risking my money with folk I don't know, and I'm no Santa Claus.' All the time I spoke I was feeling the seals, passing the ball of my thumb and index gently over them, to see if they had been steamed off and replaced. I hadn't done a year on bent Soho gambling clubs for nothing, and in fact I was nearly certain that—

'You want to watch your manners,' Earle said.

'Don't we all?' I answered, 'only mine are like yours, the kind I can't help.'

'Try to help it,' said Earle softly.

I let that one strain its greens and said to Janine: 'House sitting in?'

'No.'

'Just you and me, then,' I said to Earle. 'Cut for deal. Aces high or low?'

'High.'

He cut a nine; I cut an ace, one feel of the pack and I knew how to. 'Wasn't that lucky you called aces high?' I said cheerfully. 'OK, then, a nice little game of seven card with a wild five.'

'We don't much go for wild cards in this club,' said Earle. 'We're country people.'

'Sorry,' I said, 'it's dealer's choice, let's see if the city can't make some sparks.' I dealt us two cards down and one up and watched Earle pick up his hidden ones. I watched how he handled them and remarked to Charlie without looking behind at him, without taking my eyes off Earle's hands: 'Do you see how Mr Earle actually feels those cards, Charlie? Look at his fingers really caressing them.'

The manager stirred. The girl's face was blank. Earle stopped his fingers on his cards.

I said to Earle: 'Do you feel them bringing you luck when you brush them with your fingers like that? Maybe your old granny was a witch.'

'Just play your hand,' he said, 'and stop the chat.' He had an eight showing; I had a seven.

'Go on, then,' I said, 'it's you to bet.'

'I'll go a score.'

I'd nothing in the hole – that didn't surprise me at all. I said: 'Your score and raise you a score.'

The manager coughed. He had no means of knowing yet that I was playing with the taxpayer's money. They none of them in that room realized that I was playing cards to prove a point that would end better than winning any hand. I dealt us another card – I knew his was a king by feeling it and sure enough, up it came on the table. By chance I dealt myself a five – not that, with what I knew about the packs, it would have mattered if I hadn't. 'Ah,' I said, smiling round the table, 'that makes it all more equal, doesn't it?' The girl gave me a look like an unripe plum. I said to Earle: 'Well, on the strength of it I'll go fifty.'

'Your fifty and raise you fifty.'

'I'll raise you fifty over that,' I said, 'a ton if you like.'

'No,' he said, 'just the half ton.'

'All right,' I said, 'I'll let you down gently till the next card if you don't stack.' His face had begun to glisten like a hundred-day egg. I dealt the next cards; his was only a two, mine another five. 'Oh, well fancy that,' I said, 'three sevens I'm showing, must be my bet.' I was enjoying myself.

'You going high?' said Earle.

'Couple of ton,' I said, 'if you like.'

'I don't like.'

'Well, I'm doing it all the same,' I said, 'I don't give a fuck about your likes and dislikes. If you choke on it, darling, I remind you you can stack.' I said to Charlie: 'You still there?'

He was there. I said: 'How much credit did you say I had? Two long ones?'

'That's right.'

'Go and get it all,' I said, 'in cash. Do it now. I'm going to play this man under the table.'

'Your signature will be enough.'

'All right,' I said, 'but I shall need to see this punter's money.'

'You'll see it,' said Earle, 'but not to go into your pocket, now deal.'

So I dealt myself a seven, which gave me four of them showing – Earle was beaten on the table. 'Make that last remark again,' I said, 'I didn't quite hear it just now.' Even if Earle had two fives in the hole, which I was sure he didn't, I could see from his face that I couldn't be beat. I said to the manager, still without taking my eyes off Earle: 'You know, I find this game dull, Charlie.'

'Dull?' he mumbled, 'what, with money like that out in front?'

I said to Earle: 'All you can do now is stack, that's the logic of the game.'

The little bat said: 'You mean to say you find this boring?'

'Yes,' I said, 'because it's bent. Blokey here has two aces in the hole.'

'How do you know?' she shouted.

'Because I dealt them to him,' I said. 'All the cards are marked from ace down to ten, pinpricks at the top left-hand corner.' I reached over and flipped Earle's hole cards up. 'There you are, see? Two aces. And the card he was about to get would have been a king, which would have given him full house aces and kings, but not enough to beat four sevens, you see them?'

I scooped up all the cards and all the money, the chips, the packs, the seals; I stowed it all away in my pockets. 'It's pitiful,' I said, 'it died out in cities years ago – did nobody ever tell you that sharp poker players often come on as drunks? And didn't you ever hear what a wild card's known as in the cardsharper's trade? It's called the mug punter's insurance policy, because no one can tell which card in the pack the punter's going to choose. But dealer's choice is dealer's choice, and Earle here, who works for you lot, never should have said he didn't like a wild card – that marked my card – my Christ, what a load of amateurs. Here, while I'm about it, let's have a look at that roulette wheel you've got over there, and I'll show you where that's bent as well, if you like. Do you want me to speak louder so that your miserable losers can hear, or would the rest of you like to say something?'

The manager said to me: 'Let's keep calm, shall we? Why don't you just take all that gear back out of your pockets? House'll make it worth your while.'

'No,' I said. 'No, not a chance.'

'Then we might just have to take it off you,' said Earle, starting to get up. 'Rough, like.'

I said to him: 'In your place, I should be very very careful what you say and do.'

Earle turned to his audience and sneered: 'Oh look, the little man's coming on very strong.'

I said: 'And I can afford to, I'm a police officer.' Silence fell suddenly throughout the room; those were two words that were instinctively heard at every table, and every punter, herding his bird by the waist, began drifting urgently towards the doors. I flipped my warrant card out and said: 'I am now going to caution you.' I did that and added: 'The property I have in my possession, together with my report, will be forwarded to the Director of Public Prosecutions and may be used in evidence.'

'On what charge?' said the manager.

I said: 'You'll be told, don't worry. Now get Miss Baddeley, also known as Mrs Anne Kedward, in here, I've a word to say in her ear.'

But she was already there, a big woman in her forties with a drooping lower lip and eyes as inscrutable as a banknote. I said to her: 'I don't know how long you've been listening to this, but probably long enough to realize that you've said goodbye to your licence and probably your freedom for a longish time.'

'We'll see about that,' she said, 'the counsel I can afford.'

I said: 'You're going to need the very best there is, by the time we've finished with you.'

She said to Earle: 'You and Charlie, pick him up and throw him to the wolves on the door. I'll give you a hand.'

I said: 'You're completely out of date, love, you're not helping yourself at all.'

'I'd willingly do ten,' she said, 'for the pleasure of doing you, you cunt. Where do you spawn in the dark anyway? Vice squad?'

'No,' I said, 'Unexplained Deaths. I'm here to investigate the disappearance of a Mrs Marianne Mardy and I will say this – that in addition to the trouble you are already in, which will serve as a holding charge if need be, if ever I trace a connection between the Mardys, you, your brother and your husband, you will all three of you be staring at a concrete wall for a very long time.'

Earle had turned the colour of frozen pastry; the little bat burst into tears. The manager groaned: 'I thought he was just a punter,' and the woman said to him: 'You are just a cunt and you have got us all done brown.'

'The less you say in front of me,' I said, going to the door, 'the better for you. I should save it all for your lawyers, not that it'll make any difference, you'll find. Meantime, the session's closed.'

I added as an afterthought: 'The place also.'

14

When I got back to the hotel there was a man waiting for me. I knew him and said: 'Christ, what are you doing here?'

It was Tom Cryer from the *Recorder*. 'Found you,' he said, 'but it took some doing.'

'What's the flap?' I said. 'What are you wandering around here for?'

'I got a hint it was worth making the trip.'

'I don't need you over this, Tom,' I said, 'I could well do without you. I don't need the press in on this at all.'

'Something's blowing up,' he said, 'something always does where you're involved. However, if you're going to be like that about it, it's not far to go from here back to London.'

'Do it,' I said. 'Just do a quick burn back to town. I tell you, I want to be by myself on this.'

'I hear it's a disappearance case. A woman where people who ought to have cared don't seem to have.'

'I'm saying nothing,' I said, 'except fuck off, Tom.'

He shook his head. 'It's gone too far,' he said, 'it's leaked. If you won't wear me you'll have the rest of Fleet Street on your back.'

'Don't talk downstairs here,' I said, 'come up to my room.' I got the key. When we were in there I said: 'At least the short time you're here, Tom, the taxpayer'll buy you a drink before you go.'

'Isn't hubby old and mad and a struck-off quack?'

'Let it drop, will you?' I said. 'What are you drinking, whisky?'

'Why not?' said Cryer. 'It's no more poisonous than the world we live in.'

I gave him his drink and said: 'How's Angela?'

'She's fine,' he said, 'she's very fond of you, you know. Christ, I don't always know why. I wish you'd come over and have supper with us one night.'

'If only I could,' I said, 'when I've got the time, if I ever get the time.'

'None of us do,' said Cryer. 'So, back to work, tell me how far you've gone on this Mardy woman.'

'I can't and I won't.'

'At least give me some reason why I'm not welcome,' Cryer said.

'All I can say is I'm worried what the papers would do with it,' I said. 'I don't want a tragedy dismissed as a death on page three in the rags.'

'The *Recorder*'s not a rag. There'd be no cheapjack stuff. If it's a tragedy we'll treat it as a tragedy.'

'That's not really the point, Tom,' I said. 'What do newspaper sales managers know or care about tragedy?'

'You could say the same about the police.'

'I know,' I said, 'and I do, and that keeps me down in the ranks where I belong.'

'You're really strange,' said Cryer.

'Why strange?' I said. 'It seems obvious to me, the difference between what's straight and bent. At least it does now, though I had to work for it to understand.' I said to him: 'All right, I'll tell you what I'll do. If you'll be patient for a day or so, long before any other paper gets here I'll give you a story on this case and this town that'll make everyone sit up – but it's going to be done my way because I know it's the only real way; try and understand what neither of us yet knows.'

In the night I went out on an impulse and was walking swiftly towards the edge of town when a man ran at me out of a sidestreet and seized my arm.

'Who are you?' I said. 'Let me go.'

'My name's Brad,' he said, 'I'm Dick Sanders' brother.'

'Come out under this street light where I can see you.'

He edged out from the wall – a sallow individual in his late twenties whose hands dangled without apparent purpose on his wrists. He wore a black plastic jacket and torn jeans that told of much rough work done for not much money.

'You the copper from the smoke? You on the Mardy case? I want to talk about them.'

'All right,' I said, 'but not out here in the street.'

'We'll take a walk, then,' he said, 'not far, down past the sewage farm where there's an unfinished estate, that's where I squat.'

I followed him into the dark through ruined places and puddles left by the tracks of earth-shifting machines. Projects that had been started by bureaucrats in the wrong area had been abandoned for as little reason; we plodded through rutted clay that splashed with the activities of rats and night creatures.

At last we got to a block of concrete that had been left roofless.

'Basement we want,' he muttered, 'I'll get a light, we got a stove and wood. Wait there, give me the torch, I'll not be a minute.' In that time he was back again with his arms full of oak billets sawn small; I watched as he placed them patiently in and then saw the fire spark between his hands and the paper catch. 'Can't get dry newspapers in February,' he muttered, blowing on the flame, 'not really dry.' Men like him had been part of our protection once. They were the descendants of men who had sat still, stroking their horses' necks as they waited for the cannon to open up across ravines very far from Thornhill but whose spirit, still the same, was now unneeded and abandoned. Next he got a camping gaslight going so that I could see the cement room as it was, damp, the windows left blank and unglazed by the builders when the money for the project ran out. Rags had been nailed up across them to cut the draught, and in a corner lay two old torn mattresses with sleeping bags slung on them.

'It's just a squat,' he said, standing up from the fire once he had got it going, 'but the point is we can't be seen. You want a drink?'

I said yes and he said, it's just home-made but none the worse for that, and reached into a cupboard, emerging with a gallon bottle. 'By the neck,' he said, handing it to me, 'we've no glasses.'

'I don't care,' I said, and drank. I added: 'Does Dick live here with you?'

'When he can. But we're in bother.'

'I know.'

'He talked to me after you saw him,' said Brad, 'and that's why I wanted to find you. You know how it is, he's doubtless told you, we've none of us fuck all to lose. If we got sent up for twenty years we'd be no worse off than we are at Lakes Mill.' He put his hands to the blaze and sang:

> 'Over the hills and a long way off,
> This wind will blow our topknot off.
> Over the hills and far away,
> Here's a wind will snatch my head away.'

That was a song the British line regiments sang as they received French artillery in the Peninsula and at Waterloo. We stood against the Tyrant with Polish lancers and German dragoons believing we were saving Europe, and now here the rest of us were in a ruined unfinished building with nothing proved.

I said: 'Did you know about this trip with dry ice up to the Mardys?'

'We're always pushed for money.'

I said: 'Just tell me if you knew about it.'

'Well of course I did,' he said. 'It was heavy gear, it needed several men. Dick rowed me in and gave me a whack of the money, only natural, but we're spent out again now.'

'You know where that dry ice came from?'

'Yes, and so do you.'

'And you knew what it was for? Did you never stop to think about Mrs Mardy? About where your money came from?'

He said: 'You never stop to think about anybody else when you're hungry and broke.'

'Where is Mrs Mardy now, do you think?'

'I can only guess.'

'Do you think she's still up at their house?'

'Maybe. There was this electricity strike, that's when the dry ice deal was done.'

'With Baddeley.'

'With the undertaker, that's right.'

I said: 'She's dead, isn't she?'

'Once I've been paid,' he said, 'I never ask questions.'

'Maybe,' I said, 'but you're going to answer some, I'll see to it.'

He took a drink and put the bottle down on the floor. 'Before I do,' he said, 'we're all of us boracic up there, we haven't a light between us, nothing to eat. Could you give us any money at all? We're frantic up there, it's desperate.'

'Look,' I said, 'here's twenty quid.' I got it out, it was my own money, and he took it. I said: 'Now talk, and make it interesting.'

He said: 'I don't know what trouble I might be getting us into here if I do.'

'Less than if you don't.'

He said: 'What Dick saw arriving one day at the Mardys' was a big fridge—'

But I interrupted: 'I hear a noise outside, we've got an audience.' I went over to a window and tore the rags away. I looked outdoors and said to Brad: 'Get down on the floor quick, take cover, do it now.'

'We're coming in,' said a man's voice out in the dark. In they stormed with knitted hats over their faces. They came in as a triangle with its point towards me, the head man holding a twelve-bore, the two behind spread out with bike chains, the one on the left of me with a knife open.

I said to the man with the gun: 'Have you got a permit for that?'

'Shut your gob,' he said. 'Who are you anyway?'

'Someone who could cause you a great deal of bother,' I said, 'such as a police officer.'

'What a job,' he said, 'that's really tough, darling. Got metal on you?'

'No,' I said, 'you're running no risk, you pathetic little man, I'm not armed, I never go armed, I don't need to be armed for gits like you.'

'We're not after you anyway,' said the gunman, 'for which you can be fucking thankful. It's that cunt behind you under the table there, that Brad, that's the man we want.'

'We all want what we can't have,' I said.

One of the men behind him wrapped his chain round his left arm and came up with his knife. He held it at me, its blade shining in the light from the stove.

I said to the gunman: 'You make me weep. Am I supposed to be afraid of you?'

'Most people are,' he said. 'Now stand aside.'

'I never do that,' I said. 'I exist to make sure that folk like you do fourteen years apiece if you don't drop all that on the floor, do it now.'

'Don't be a fool, John,' said the gunman, 'this is a contract on Dick and Brad – the folk backing me don't like a grass, and what a pity you was here to spoil a neat scene. Now mind your face.'

'I know the undertaker that called the contract,' I said, 'and the fact that I know means it's gone rotten on you, you load of poofs. The man's going up the spout, I should know, I'm in charge, and incidentally my name's not John.'

The man behind on the left, who hadn't spoken or moved yet, except to let his chain swing from his wrist in an idle kind of way, now said to the gunman: 'There's too much chat here, and knocking the law down, that can mean grey days, lots of them.'

'At last someone's talking sense,' I said, 'I didn't think any of you were capable of it. You put me away and there isn't a copper in Britain that wouldn't wring your necks, and some of them have got big hands.'

'Get that cunt behind you off the floor,' the gunman said, 'that's all we want.'

'You waste either or both of us, make up your pitiful minds which. Go on, fire, then – what'll it prove?' I thought if he does

I'll go somewhere, but where is where? Meantime, to know what justice is, you must still have a head, balls and kneecaps – the only way to find justice is to live without shelter, since all the messages are gloomy now.

The man with the knife said: 'This is fucked,' as if it were a failed orgasm, and suddenly closed his knife. The other villain who had stood swinging his chain still stood there swinging it, only now patches of sweat, even on that February night, were breaking out under his armpits.

The man holding the gun said: 'We've no interest in your getting hurt unless you get in the way.'

I said: 'It's my job to get in the way.'

The gunman said: 'That individual on the floor behind you has a contract on him, he's a grass.'

'You berk,' I said, 'I decide all that, I'm the law. Now break that gun and drop it; you'll do life if you don't, and I'll lean on the parole board to make sure you don't do less than ten, if I live.'

We stared at each other. 'You won't have Brad unless you have me first,' I said, 'you can be sure of that. You kill a police officer and you're in real shtuck, you realize that, I repeat it, now decide. Shoot or wank.'

'You're a right runner, you are,' said the gunman. He broke the weapon, kept it in his hand and dropped the shells. He said past me to Brad: 'We'll meet again, sweetheart, don't you worry.'

'If you do,' I said, 'it'll be in court and then look out – ten years, three to a cell in Canterbury, but they say you can hear the cathedral bells if the wind's right.'

The three of them faded, becoming part of the darkness they had emerged from. I watched them leap into a shattered Ford with no plates on it; the back-ups jumped on, bottom gear went in and the tyres yelled on the bad road. 'Bye-bye, cuntie!' they shouted, now that they thought they were away. I thought, you poor pricks. Where I came from, a contract was a serious affair.

I turned to Brad and said: 'You can get up now.' He already had. I said: 'We can be quiet now. What was it you were going to say?

Stop shaking, you're alive, aren't you?'

He started to tell me about a heavy load that he and Dick had delivered three years ago, telling me about it and thanking me for just now.

When he had finished I went back to the hotel and had a bad night, what was left of it. I was thankful when dawn came, but in February the sun rises late, if at all.

15

My most murderous inquiries are into my own life, which is really less my own than of my friends. Most of my few friends, thank God not all, are dead or disabled – Jim Macintosh dead, Ken Hales also, Foden shot through the spine and Frank Ballard paralysed for life. I know my friends, they're like myself – we were all intelligent, sure of our own thought; we knew what we believed and were never afraid. But I feel nearly alone now, though I stand in for my sick and dead, I believe. There are times when I feel alone in the face of our society, its hatred and madness, its despair and violence. To go on drawing my pay, to go on living in Acacia Circus, to go on acting on my own, just to go on at all, I have to be very careful. I feel the edge of the precipice with every step I take and have to be most particular how I tread; the path isn't solid, and under it is the mist and that vile slide towards a bottomless death. I am a minor figure for whom no god waits. The state that pays me laughs at me; my own people at work find me absurd.

I dream across the altar of my past, have many enemies.

I once read about a man who was obliged to take poison for being too honest. He was given time; he was told to take his own life in his own time. His crime, as always with those who value life instead of taking it, was honesty, and his friends helped him to die, giving him the poison disguised in wine as he lay in a hot bath after supper and conversation in which all the questions that had lain between them were discussed. The dying man said calmly that since all men must die we must from the earliest moment examine everything we have known so that good can reign; he said that to find out the best in man through logic, analysis and friendship, discussion and love, was far better than obedience to any state.

There was a man whose help I would have been glad to have in any obscure investigation – he was Greek, I think, and I gather another awkward bastard like me.

My conception of knowledge is grief and despair, because that has been the general matter of my existence. The Hampstead girl that I once loved, and of whom I spoke earlier, fetched a book once in the night that she had been reading and after we had made love stated the position of tragedy:

'There, where the earth's asleep, wedded to night,
Under dead gardens mortgaged to the stars I see my past.
A dream in white slips past, a passing gasp of light
Imagined in pale light;
My folly's all attached to me,
Dark bombs trailing at my sleeve;
I'm lost, but do intend to find the right way soon
As clouds, moving, alter the subtlety of weather.
I dream and suffer in the sweet clasp of lost arms;
Love's cast-off language from my past
Makes my lone waking, sleeping, strange.
I sigh and sigh upon my past, my green past,
My once pasture of knowing.
But now I am checked at last with nothing achieved
But perdition in summer leaf and stand at last
Faced by the screaming young disasters of my past.
There was nothing from father, nothing from the mother;
Her milk was not for me, nor her body for him;
No, nothing but new disasters for the other.
Nothing but a bullet and a flag,
Memories faceless, death in a fucking bag.

A graven angel passed through a second of fire
Then laid the grey pen of her brain aside for ever.

So we caught the train to work,
Laughing together.'

'There are other ways of dying than being killed by a bullet, you know,' she said after reading it, 'just as risky. An idea can be a firing squad, a whole army – the continuing terror of loneliness can be its own trench, the long necessity of thought itself can rot you, leading you to the conclusion that the conditions of existence itself are intolerable: flesh shrinks, blood pales, bone fritters. Fear can kill you,' she said, 'and it makes it all the worse if you can think. I understand that now too late – intelligence is an introduction to fear, it's no defence. Fear can really kill you,' she said, her hand in mine.

And I think fear did kill her.

Sometimes I wish my mind would go away and leave me in peace; I would give all that I understand and feel and know, my very existence, to get out of my situation. I would grovel for the superb gift of stupidity, to be able to smile at my own death without knowing what it was, like the sheep did that I saw killed with my father when I was small – I don't know what I would pay not to see through what I see, feel through what I feel, sense through what I sense, know through what I know, finding only the rottenness of others. All our agony is a short wonder to be forgotten like a day's rain, as when the lights go down after a play and it begins to snow outside the theatre. But in my role how can I ever say what I intend – for language, like life itself, has become irretrievable, hobbling after what's left of nature.

Few people have time to age in the face of beauty and terror, and I have been trying to do both for too long.

Do you see now why I detest the Charlie Bowmans, the bullies of this earth?

A child, a little girl, came up to me one night at Waterloo Station and begged me for a pound. She was so small, dirty and cold; the last dark daring was in her eyes that faced me like a gambler's one card. She had single roses in her hand wrapped in plastic and I said, thinking of my own daughter: 'How old are you, my darling?' and she said: 'I'm ten.' Then I looked at her and saw at once that she had been sent out into existence far too soon and would go to the dark; poverty would push and pull her to the slaughterhouse without her ever having known the air of love, as you manage cattle. But she was brave and human. In the rush-hour crowd around us I gave her ten pounds, all I happened to have, and she dashed away skipping, while I turned away to my train, holding her rose. When I was alone in the compartment I read the message printed round the frozen flower: *the pleasure of giving*.

I took both rose and paper back to Earlsfield with me and have them still among my few souvenirs, both of them wrinkled and dead now. Yet I keep them carefully in a vase on my mantelpiece; there's a flower that will never die for me.

I was in difficulty for a while as a child myself for some time after the war and went through trouble in my head; I caught it from my father's nightmares.

Pity, terror and grief.

16

The blanks on Baddeley, everything I needed to know, arrived by police courier at twenty to four in the morning. The phone rang, and I struggled out of a bad sleep. The clerk said: 'There's gear come for you,' but I was already getting my trousers on.

The courier handed me a fat envelope, said sign the book, Sergeant, looked at his watch and was gone.

The night clerk had a bad cold. 'You people never stop,' he moaned, bubbling through his left nostril. He wiped it on the sleeve of his woolly. 'It's a strain I can tell you, my job is.'

'It's a doddle compared to the strain of what I do,' I said, but he had picked up his porn again.

'This is really hard stuff, this is,' he murmured from behind it, 'like lurid, yes, very fruity.'

I kicked his desk so hard that he dropped the book. 'I hate you,' I said.

'It's the time of day,' he said philosophically, picking up his book again and whispering his fingers through the pages, 'when emotion gets on top of you.'

'I don't hate you so much after that,' I said, 'it's true. Have you logged any calls?'

'I'm an unmarried man,' he said, 'and likely to remain one on my wages, that's why I like reading *Dare*. It's a sort of vicarious relationship I have with women through the snaps and the print, you know.'

'About calls?'

He said: 'Yes, now I think about it, someone did come round looking for you.'

'What was his name?'

'He didn't leave one.'

'Did you ask him?'

'I didn't bother.'

'Did he tell you his name?'

'He may have, I wasn't listening. He left a card, but I'm afraid the cleaners threw it away, they're quite ignorant.'

'I'll bet they're brighter than you are,' I said. 'Now pull your finger out of your fundament with a loud pop and try to describe him.'

'Couldn't,' he said, 'I didn't look at him, I was busy reading. Anyway, fewer questions you ask, fewer you have to answer.'

'It's just the reverse in my job,' I said.

'That must be tough,' he said, turning a page, 'hey, look at this one.'

'You're great fun to be with,' I said. I ripped the book out of his hand, tore it in two and threw the pieces on the floor. 'But try and be useful, will you?'

'Oh, God, now look what you've gone and done,' he groaned, 'it belongs to a mate of mine and I'd only got a bit of the way through it, there was masses more. That'll cost you a tenner.'

'It'll cost you a tenner,' I said. 'You're the taxpayer.'

'I don't believe in taxes,' he said, 'I'm a sociologist and I think taxes are robbery.'

'In my job,' I said, 'I reckon robbers are robbery and if it weren't for taxes I couldn't do my job.'

'Good,' he said, 'I can't knock that, I cannot stand the police myself.'

'Say that again when you've had your throat cut,' I said.

I went upstairs, opened the packet and started reading. On top was a note from Harrison which read: 'This was what I got by checking on Marianne Mardy with the Aliens Registration Office. Maiden name Vayssiere. Born Lyon, France, April 4th 1941. Married William Mardy October 14th 1963 at Russell Square Registry Office, London WC. Enclosed is a photograph of that date from the *Evening Standard*. Her father, now deceased, was Jean-Luc Vayssiere, area director of the Credit Lyonnais. Had money, property in France. Daughter Marianne sole issue of marriage, sole heir. Mrs Mardy also, before marriage, worked for Credit Lyonnais and was posted to their London, City branch and met Mardy socially. Hope some of this will be helpful, Barry.'

I spent some time looking at this other photograph of Marianne Mardy. With her was a man, holding her hand. It was William Mardy, but I barely recognized him. Spruce, elegant and alert, he was gazing down at his wife. She was smiling up at him; it certainly looked as if they had been in love.

I got out everything else in the envelope and spread it out on the bed. There were twenty-two sheets of photocopied cheques, all Walter Baddeley's and Wildways' major transactions over the past year. Kedward's were there too. Kedward received a cheque from Wildways on the tenth of each month, not that I had doubted it. The sum, two hundred and fifty pounds, never varied.

I also very soon singled out the cheques drawn on a company called Clearpath in favour of Wildways and signed William Mardy. They were all dated the first of the month to start with, but latterly the dates had become irregular. The first ten were each for a thousand pounds, the last five for five thousand apiece.

I got the area telephone book and looked up Clearpath. I didn't seriously expect to find a listing for it – nor did I. Nor did I care much, because I could get such information as I needed about the cheques just by leaning on Mardy's bank manager. It was a Thornhill bank, and if I was lucky I might get hold of a manager that had never been properly leaned on before.

Once I had got what picture I could from the cheques I cleared them away and went to bed, trying to make sleep come for a few hours. It was hard. Facts, theories, chased themselves in my mind; my brain wouldn't give up the hunt.

I had to get into a position where I could give Baddeley and the Kedwards a hammering and, what with one thing and another, I was getting on. But Baddeley himself remained. I could get people down to go over his books with a comb so fine that it would clean a louse out from between two hairs. But that was just for formal proof; I had to break him first. Mardy would have to be questioned over his payments to Baddeley too. But Baddeley, I had to get him down on his knees.

I fell into a feverish state that passed for sleep at times. In it I dreamed that I had lost my suitcase on a train. A shrouded woman was sitting opposite me in the same compartment and the train, unlit, halted at a big country junction. The woman, though we hadn't exchanged a word, was important to me. Next, both woman and suitcase disappeared. I knew I had to find both immediately and searched the train, which was packed, without success. Finally I got off it to look on the platform; it was blinding down with rain. Thousands of people were hurrying about round me, jostling each other. When I found no sign either of the woman or my case I turned to get back on the train again, only to find that it had left; now I was alone under the glaring lamps, the wet rails.

I woke unrested and soaked with sweat.

Death is its own best friend, and our dreams know it.

17

Cryer rang at half past eight in the morning. I said: 'Were you round here last night?'

'Yes.'

'Why didn't you leave your name?'

'The man on the desk couldn't be bothered to take it; I nearly stuffed my card down his throat. And where were you?'

'Out looking for villains.'

'Find any?'

'A few.'

'You always find a few. Any story yet?'

'It's shaping.'

'Anything I can print now?'

'No. Maybe tomorrow. I told you. And perhaps there'll be parts that I'll never let you print.'

'Ah, Christ,' he said, 'those'll be the parts I want to print, I don't mind betting.'

'We'll see,' I said. 'Anyway, what have you been doing?'

'I've been to the pub. A pub run by an army-type gent called Goodinge, where I found a man called Baddeley.'

'You shouldn't have done that,' I said, 'I told you not to go rummaging about.'

'It was almost an accident.'

'I know your kind of accidents,' I said. 'They're the kind where you just happen to drop on the man you want to see. All right, tell me about it.'

'I found him very interesting.'

'I'm not surprised,' I said, looking at the time. 'Come and have breakfast with me; the kitchen's not shut yet.'

When we met downstairs the clerk said: 'If it was breakfast you was wanting you're too late, the kitchen's shut.'

'Oh, come on,' I said, 'don't be absurd, it's only twenty-five to nine. You could make an exception.'

'I could,' said the clerk, 'but I'm not going to. If I started with you folk I'd have people wanting breakfast at any old time – why, we'd be serving breakfast all day.'

'All part of the profit principle, I should have thought,' said Cryer.

'I'm not paid to think,' said the clerk. 'That comes extra and nobody seems to want it, so I just carry out hotel policy without doing any thinking, see?'

'Give it up, Tom,' I said, 'it's hopeless. There's a transport café just down the road anyway.'

'Yes, that's where I send 'em,' nodded the clerk. 'We get any amount of complaints about breakfast.'

'Well, fancy that,' I said.

The windows of the transport café, the OK Joe, were steamed up from the frost outside; inside it was filled with the roar of men, the crash of plates, the smell of tobacco and food. We ordered double egg, sausage, tomatoes and chips with tea, bread and marge. We had to shout to make ourselves heard above the truck-drivers. ('How are you, Jack my old son? You off to Wales again?' 'Yeah, I never seem to get anything but Swansea.')

I said to Cryer: 'Well, what about Baddeley, then?'

'The news editor wasn't best pleased when I rang him and told him where I was – said I was wasting my time.'

'He didn't think there was a story in it?'

'You know what they're like,' he said as our meal arrived. 'He'd got me lined up to cover a jewel robbery at some old titled bat's in Knightsbridge.'

'You might be a news editor yourself some day,' I said, 'and I can just imagine a son of yours saying to a mate, Christ, Dad doesn't half dig up the rubbish. And so?'

'I told him I was going to stay down here a while longer,' said Cryer. 'Whatever the editor thinks, I believe there's a story in this. I know the sort of things you uncover. I know you.'

'I'll say this,' I said. 'Some people around here are going to get the loud pedal on this music, some people are going to get the soft pedal. You can be the loud pedal if you want.'

'Baddeley?'

'Most certainly,' I said, 'because I can make it stick.'

'What'll the charge be?'

'Heavy,' I said. 'Blackmail. Accessory to a murder, manslaughter at any rate, that'll depend on the DPP. Eat up.' I had a sudden thought and said: 'Have you been round to see Baddeley at his home by any chance?'

'Yes,' said Cryer, 'I have as a matter of fact.'

'You've got a fucking nerve,' I said, 'you really have. Christ, you move faster than I do.'

'Don't worry,' he said, 'I haven't let you down.' He added: 'Walter certainly makes a lot of money, you should see the place.'

'I know he makes money,' I said. 'Did he give you any idea how?'

'I'll tell you how I played it,' said Cryer. 'I played it direct. I went up to the house bold as a whore, rang the bell and said Press.'

'Sounds promising – what's the point my doing my nut with you now you've gone and done it? And how did that approach go down?'

'Not bad to start with. Press – he's a vain old bastard.'

'Let's have the background. Rolls in the garage? I've heard he's got one.'

'No, it was out on the drive being washed – custom-built, the kind the Americans buy. House worth two hundred long ones and horrible with it.'

'Shrivelled little old wife to pour the drinks into the cut glass?' I said. 'Disadvantaged foreign slavey for the pots and pans?'

'I don't know how you guess these things.'

'They smell,' I said, 'and from a long way off.'

'Yes, the wife's a poor little woman – dead red hair, no bust, the kind of woman no one ever wants to sin with and who dreams of murder.'

'I get the feeling he's queer myself,' I said, 'if he's anything.'

'Funny you should say that. I had a word with the Portuguese girl in the kitchen and it seems he's got a boyfriend called Prince, but he was out.'

'You haven't been wasting your time, have you?' I said.

'He came back while I was there. Big, blond, about thirty, nice blow job for a hair-do, pretty clothes, you know, sharp, tattooed I Love You Irene left forearm, heart and arrow, London accent, East End, Hackney or Bethnal Green, I've a feeling I've seen him before somewhere.'

'Probably in some court.'

'His name's Johnny. Anyway, Baddeley wanted me all to himself – so much so that I thought I was going to have to hang on to my chair and think of Angie, and he sent the wife and the blond help out of the room fast.'

'You've been doing very well,' I said, 'I've got to hand it to you, as long as you didn't mention me.'

'Not a chance.'

'The whole thing stinks all over,' I said, 'I do love a villain when he appears to settle down like that, settle down to make money I mean. So go on.'

'He snowed me a bit first, he was cagey, but I told him he hadn't a thing to worry about – I was doing a piece for the paper, the property page, called Big Shots in Little Towns. He liked that. I asked him if he was interested in property dealing still and he said well of course, I'm the biggest estate agent in Thornhill, I'm always ready to buy at the right price. Thornhill, he said, is now a very popular part of the world, connections to London, the Midlands, where you like; it's picturesque, which of course means select. Talking of people buying into the region I'm careful, no rubbish wanted, I'm not in the business of driving the market downhill. I had a nice Indian gentleman the other day after Longstreet Manor, I'll pay cash he said and I'll up your commission on it don't worry, but I said regretfully, sir, and quite frankly, the only colour we have here in Thornhill is white, we don't want splashes on it do we, ha ha. Got some big properties on your books right now? I said. Plenty, he said, mind, they don't hang around long with me, I get them out at a keen price to the right buyer. Have you got a building firm to do them all up, together with the rest of what you do, local undertaker and all the rest of it? I most certainly have, he said, I can price work better if I'm employing. Of course I don't pay high wages, but there's still some youngsters around who'd rather do an honest day's toil than draw sup. ben. Besides, I'm running for mayor shortly as you may or may not know, and that naturally means I take pity on the numerous Thornhill unemployed and try to slot them into a job when I can. I said, I find you disarmingly open, Mr Baddeley, and it must be money for old rope, but he curled a bit on that one and said I think that's putting it rather stark, Mr who was it you said again? I gave him plenty of soothing flannel to get him round and then said well, what with property and funerals, I suppose they almost go hand in hand, Mr Baddeley, you certainly seem to have backed the favourites in life's great race. I wouldn't put it like that at all, he snapped, and if you print that in your paper you'll have my lawyers after you in no time flat.'

'Messrs Carrow & Carrow,' I said.

'All right, I said, now there's another thing that comes to my mind – could you shed any light on a matter that seems to be mystifying people in this area, the disappearance of a Mrs Mardy who lived up the road from you here? I could see he didn't like that brought up, but naturally he couldn't say so. Seems funny a property journalist raising that question, he said, or is that what you're really down here about? No, I said, but things get about in Fleet Street, that's why it's full of newspapers, you know, and what's livened the dish up is the rumour that the local police here haven't been doing their job over it, and it seems that there's even a police officer been sent down from London to like stick a pin in them, as I say it's just a rumour of course. It's the kind of rumour that had best remain a rumour, he said coldly, otherwise some people might find themselves running into a writ server. All right, I said, however, as a leading figure in Thornhill you must have some view on the matter. He turned his eyes up at that in his best funeral way and said, I'm afraid I can't tell you anything, if only I could, poor Mrs Mardy, a wonderful woman, her disappearance is, and I fear will remain, a complete mystery and it is of course very very sad. Do you know her husband, Dr Mardy, at all, I said, and he wrung his hands and said no, hardly at all, poor desolate old man. I see, I said, well thank you very much indeed for your time, Mr Baddeley – here's my phone number, home and office, and thank you again for your valuable help, I'll show myself out, I said, and that was that.'

'Isn't it weird?' I said, when I had thought about what he had said for a while, 'your job's exactly like mine in many ways. And don't you get fed up with being lied to all the time? Talking of time,' I added, 'what is the time?'

'They're open, if that's what you mean,' said Cryer. 'I've found a nice little pub called the Eddystone Light and I'll buy you a drink if you like, the last round was yours on the McGruder business.'

So we went over, he set the drinks up on a table and I said: 'You know, I could have made some sort of a detective out of you.'

'I wouldn't have liked the money or the hours, cheers.'

'No,' I said, 'they're certainly both rotten, it's no job for a married man and tell me some more about lovely Angela.'

'Well,' he said, 'I've protected her from her worst errors so far.' He took a drink of his beer and sighed: 'Errors such as going out on her own at night while I'm at work and chatting up villains in pubs in Paddington and along the Baize. She's trying to write a thriller of all things and says she prowls around to get what she calls local colour.'

'It's a colour that could turn bright red one of these days,' I said. 'You must be mad, you ought to stop her.'

'Try stopping an express train with your foot.'

'Maybe if she had a kid she'd stay at home more, I know that's what I used to think with Edie.'

He shook his head: 'You're completely out of date, it doesn't work like that at all. Not any more.' He added: 'You got over all that business well.'

'Half over,' I said, 'it never really finishes.'

'What are you telling me to do about Baddeley?'

'Get after him in your own way,' I said, 'but not till I tell you, and leave the Mardy end of the whole thing to me.'

'Couldn't you give me some angle on the blackmail part of it now? Like how Baddeley got his hands on the Mardys? Anything?'

'I'm sorry,' I said, 'I couldn't. Not yet.'

He said impatiently: 'I can't stretch this job out for ever.'

'You won't have to,' I said. I finished my drink and stood up. 'Keep in touch with me – but always remember, there mightn't be a story after all.'

'I have a feeling there will be,' Cryer said.

18

The light was failing and it was snowing on a north wind as I drove back up to Mardy's; a last shred of sun, a blood-spot in a lazy eye, clouded in grey, fled to sink behind the land that reached back to clumps of naked oak. I wound down the window, but freezing air whipped at me through the gap and I shut it again quickly. The gates by the side of the road were wide open and I edged in past the rotten pillars.

Now I saw by the final light what I had only sensed in the dark the time before. Now appeared the murderous abandon of the park – shrubs that had once been planted in orderly groups shrank like wet beggars; they flailed and thrashed, unpruned, under diseased elms staggering in the gale. I stopped the car, got out and looked up at the ruin of the house, high, wet and hideous.

As I stood there I suddenly felt afraid – not of what confronted me but in a general way. I thought and felt that the secret of existence was perhaps to get old with beauty, ironically, coming closer and closer to you as you aged; innocence, everything that you had rejected or ignored as a young man, entering you like music all the time until in the end there was no more time. Then much of what had seemed so hard would be over, after too much work in cities, after patrolling too many streets for too long, after studying too many faces with the sly, fixed look of the dead.

Intelligence is at the service of us all and I believe that curiosity and investigation, like a chicken's beak, are intended to kill the viper that threatens an egg. Powerful curiosity is the source of all detection and is surely its own end, a field cleared and well ploughed – but it is too simple for us only to have justice and logic; what use are either without mercy? The eternal cycle, the beginning, middle and end of a human being, the incomprehensible dance in the magic of our own theatre will continue for ever. But ignorance of our birth and death makes us largely mad; the majority of us clap at our disasters as though they were a play; but it is a work that we cannot possibly understand. Throughout our obscure race in life our entire frame is intended, is inclined to return to the earth on which our parents lay flat to conceive us; from a great distance our planet is an extraordinary sight, more so than most of us can yet understand, and I think that in the meantime we ought to be very careful about how we treat the flesh that we are. As I looked up at the house I found myself thinking, I don't know why, of men in fields leaning on the wind, their arms crossed on the working end of their rakes, their clothes blowing round their motionless bodies. Whether in heat or cold they stared off beyond their farms to judge the clouds and the sun; in each season they were wise over the earth. They planted at the right time and lived mostly alone in fields that were never theirs, trapping a bird for food with a wire or stones, stripping mushrooms from dead bark with the vast patience that a people has.

Now they have been carried off to the night. Their grand-children work in banks and tax offices, often commit murder and rape at weekends; because of war, because of our past, a catastrophe has occurred which no single man, though he may endure it, can ever solve – chatty, puffy ministers, over the past century, have committed the greatest crime of all; it was made up of expediency, self-interest and indifference. But all I can do about it is to go on catching criminals until I get too old.

Now I could see the gravel of the drive cluttered with the masonry that had crashed outwards from above. A mass of the corner wall had broken away, leaving an angle like the ruin of a tooth to rise in unsteady pinnacles to the sky. I turned my collar up, my face peeled by the cold, and walked along under the facade of the house, gazing up at the tons of rubble bowing overhead. Then I went to the great double panes of the front door and passed through them.

Much that I hadn't been able to see on my last visit was now apparent. The hall was at least fifty feet high and rose to a glass ceiling. Three galleries ran round the hall, serving the storeys; soaring above them was the organ, the round windows of its loft like the portholes of a liner. Ranks of pipes spreadeagled upwards, leaning into or away from each other at absurd angles. Half-effaced saints painted on them in red, blue and gold indicated the Gothic script that described their sayings or lives; draughts cracked and snarled across the hall, booming into the pipes which responded with groans or howls. I turned slowly on the marble floor, half an inch deep in rain, listening to the branches thrashing in the wind against the walls, listening for anything.

'Dr Mardy?' I called out.

There was no reply. I walked over to a wall on which a great canvas hung, its lower part half lost in the shadows. By my torch I saw that it was titled *The Inspiration of Alphaeus* – a young man with wings for hands and feet, demons yawning blackly after him, ascended to the ceiling. I walked off down the hall, opened a door at random and was met with all the desolation that I had seen before; I was in the remains of a dining-room. Chairs were pushed back from some ancient dinner party and ten glasses filled with rotten liquid stood on the table, cutlery lying where it had been flung down. The smell in that tight-shut, soaking place was terrible, like the smell of death itself. The poles at the windows had broken and collapsed, hurling the velvet curtains across the floor. The shutters had come unhinged and were shored up with planks; a rat nodded at me and scuttled into a corner. Beyond the cracked or absent panes, against the freezing dark sky, I watched the wild branches as they continued to sway and batter each other in the wind, and still Mardy did not come.

At that moment I became aware of the voices again.

I hadn't been altogether sure about them the time before, but now I definitely was. Besides, they were louder. I couldn't yet make out what they said because they were too far off but I could tell that a man and a woman were having some urgent conversation –

was it a quarrel, or that violent pleading which comes almost to the same thing?

'Mardy!' I called out again. 'Dr Mardy!' But my voice only rang emptily back at me.

I also wished immediately that I hadn't spoken; my words seemed to have provoked a new sound, for there came the crash as of a fist on a table from upstairs and a man shouted, quite clearly now: 'Don't you see I can't go on?' There was a woman's answer but it got fainter again, as though the people had moved into rooms further off.

Now I was sweating, yet I felt icy cold. I was convinced that the woman's voice I was listening to was dead, that it was Marianne Mardy's; but that didn't alter the fact that I was sure I was hearing it. She sobbed on as I stood in the dark downstairs and I felt as cold as we all do in the presence of madness and death.

I thought: 'I've got to find the stairs.' I did find them and climbed until I found myself at the banisters of the second gallery. The moon shone for a moment, glaring through the glass roof; far down shone the marble of the hall floor, glittering in water. Around me, draughts groaned through the doors, many of them open, of what had been bedrooms; cold, bitter air blew in, mixed with the soft scent of decay. I shone my light into one of them as I stole past. Wet bedding lay tumbled on the floor; clothes from another age sprawled half out of a wardrobe. I went on, and the two voices got louder all the time until there was no further to go at the end of the gallery and I was faced by a shut door. As far as I could tell I was at the wrecked end of the house, and by putting my ear to the panels of the door I could for the first time listen clearly to what they were saying in there.

'Do you trust me, Marianne?'

'You know I do.'

'Even if it comes to the worst?'

'Of course.'

'I'm torn, Marianne.'

'I'm not.'

'I couldn't bear to lose you to the ground and yet I—'

'I wonder at times if I really want your solution, William. I wouldn't know the world I was coming back to any more, and how do I know if you'd be in it with me? I sometimes wonder if I know what it would involve, coming back – I couldn't go through hell twice and please don't let's quarrel now, darling, I feel so ill.'

'We're not quarrelling. It's just the state of your face, Marianne, and what must be done about it.'

'We're talking about life and death, William; we both know it. I'm very sick, just help me to die.'

'I can't do that; I want us both to go on for ever.'

'I don't see how that can be.'

'Not now, but in fifty years. They'll have the answer to everything in fifty years. Do you truly believe in me as a surgeon, Marianne?'

'You know I do.'

'Still, you realize there are people better able to help you, better qualified than I?'

'But not better qualified to love me.'

'Struck off as I am, I'm not qualified at all. And I haven't the equipment, I haven't the help I need for major surgery.'

There was a silence and then she said, moaning: 'It's this terrible, unrelenting pain, William, and my face in the mirror, my mouth.'

'There are no more mirrors, Marianne. I have destroyed every mirror in the house.'

'Thank God.'

There seemed to be a break at this point, because when they began again she was speaking in a different tone, as though it were some other day.

'So we're going to take the risk?'

'There is no risk, Marianne. I've been studying cryogenics for forty years.'

'But there is a risk. Where will you be in two thousand and thirty?'

153

'With you, of course, and by the same means.'

'Oh,' she sobbed, 'how can you turn base metal into gold?'

'I need your decision, Marianne. Am I to carry out this last operation?'

'Yes, of course, darling. You know I believe in everything you do. That's why I live with you, that's why I exist, and nobody is ever going to touch my body except you.' She sighed and said: 'I just wanted to talk about it, it's for my confidence.'

I heard tears grind out of his face and felt dirty listening to such things secretly behind a door, and believed that I knew everything that was most repellent then about police work. After what seemed a long time she sighed and said: 'May I have my shot now? It must be time.'

'Yes. Marianne, you realize you should be in hospital, don't you?'

'We've been over that hundreds of times, William. I believe in everything you do. If I die, I die. Oh, please, my shot.'

'Yes, of course.' There was the sound of instruments, syringes being moved and she said: 'All this must be costing a fortune.'

'As if I cared.'

Yes, I felt sick with disgust at my being in sone way present there as though I had, by the fact of listening like that in a hidden way, torn away the poor wall that stood between myself, the world, and the dignity of people's lives.

'Ah,' she said after a little while, fading.

When I could tell she was asleep I heard him say: 'The truth is atrocious. A woman of such brilliance, my only love, her concerts, all her sweet outgoing, how can it be decreed that she should walk in public with her diseased face, watch her rotting features in a mirror?'

Then I listened to him fall, shouting Marianne, Marianne! Our bodies mixed! Transpierced! Transpierced! – then I knew what agony between two people really was.

After a time he began to mumble how her death had been a day of sunny nightmare. 'August the fourteenth: I disentangled the diseased parts from her small head, smelling our love, our smell,

both our flesh and her life while existence ignored her sickness –
oh, it was such a fine day. I felt I was going to lose her from the
start, and began working with a sense of chill and doom. I gave her
her pre-med and she yawned comfortably in her lipless mouth as
though death were just a fine evening, the end of a busy day. She
turned her face to the wall but I saw all kinds of things about her
as I bent over to give her the anaesthetic – her breast and
shoulders, her hands, part of her head, it was like plucking the bird
of our memories while I straightened and prepared her but I
thought, I mustn't be nervous now, mustn't flinch, must think just
about the work that's to be done. Dear Christ how I fought to buy
us time when I felt her begin to fail and yet later, at the end, when
she died uttering a little sound and was gone I found I now had
all the time on earth to remember her, a timeless time, and I took
her and held her to me as though that would prevent what had just
happened, watching her eyes turning in ancient interest to
questions that were now beyond both of us. I could not
immediately understand that she had gone – that took me many
hours and days – I only wept that I might have had that second
more with her that I would never have any more, just one more
chance, just that little time it would have taken me to explain my
pettiness, my stupidity in many ways, perhaps my identity.'

On that fatal word the voice stopped, yet I continued to crouch
like a dog outside that door, disgusted with myself at having
listened to such private, final matters; I can't say how long I stayed.
Yet in the end I did get up and remember turning the door-
handle, filled with comprehension and dread. The shrunken boards
of the door swung freely away from me into the room, giving on
to close darkness. There was no one in the room. I shone my torch
in; its light picked out sodden sheets that trailed around a bed. It
hovered on a dressing-table and the smashed glass of its mirror; I
knew at once that it was her room; I picked out feminine clothes
and several medicines in my weak light. Frightening and absurd
words crowded and crossed through my head as I looked:

'First we march in, then we stamp round
With a scream and a stagger and a shout,
We bang and we batter,
We drum and we chatter
As we dance all our nightmares out.'

I called to Mardy through the frozen gloom of the house and said that I was coming down.

19

Mardy said: 'I must tell you this; I had a revolting dream just two years before Marianne died. I dreamed I was walking on a common, it was a very fine sunny day. It must have been a Sunday or a bank holiday; anyhow, there were hundreds of people about.

'All at once I noticed what I thought was a large grey dog rolling about on the turf, as though basking in the hot weather. But coming up to peer at it, as everyone was doing at its antics, I suddenly saw that it wasn't a dog at all but something else, and that it was writhing in a transport of agony, not delight, surrounded by a heap of its faeces and foaming in some kind of fit. Yet nobody but me seemed to find it repellent; innocently they went up to the creature, petting it and stroking its matted fur. Others, in loose, intelligent groups, strolled around, discussing the phenomenon.

'However, I was filled with loathing and disgust as I watched this sick thing – the fat grey woolly back that it kept snapping at in its dementia with its broken teeth; even though I was standing behind crowds of people I felt alone, filled with doubt and doom, and was glad I had a stick with me.

'What I wanted to do was to kill it before its sickness could spill over to us, and I couldn't understand why nobody else seemed to feel the same. No, instead, children, quite unafraid, were going up to it and fondling it. Convulsed in its fever, it was oblivious of us at first, and I could see no reason why, out of everyone, it should have singled me out. But once it had become aware of me it fixed its yellow gaze on no one else and seemed to take its health from me, rolling upright to trot towards me, threading its way intently through all the people.

'Even though to begin with it seemed to nose its way up to me in a random way there was an inevitable quality in what it did and as it got closer to me the greater my hatred of it became, because now I could smell it and see how its pelt was teeming, putrid with lice. Yet still everyone stood politely aside, smiling, and encouraging it to come to me. Some even stooped to pat it as it passed, while I wanted to yell at them not to; I tried to shout at them not to touch it, only to find my voice had jammed in my throat. I implored them with my eyes to turn it away from me but they only smiled and waved – happy, peaceful faces.

'I walked swiftly away from it, affecting nonchalance, but it followed me through bushes towards a series of distant hills, shambling after me under the cloud of flies that pursued it, saliva swinging from its muzzle in bright chains.

'At last I found a bush tall enough to wait behind, took a firm hold of my stick and then when I judged that the beast was close enough I aimed a terrific blow at its head, only my stick was nothing but a stem of grass that broke off above my fist. As soon as it realized that I had failed to kill it this presence stood perfectly still and watched me for a measureless period of time; it knew its own turn had come now. I looked around for help, but everyone had got much further off; it was dark, and I watched a few scattered people making for home against a night horizon.

'Then I began to run as I never have before.'

Later he said: 'One evening, not long after Marianne died, my dog ate one of my own teeth which had broken off, embedded in a piece of meat I had been eating. The dog ate it because I was sickened by the sense of my own mortality and so threw him the whole lot, tooth and all, whereupon he snapped that small part of my body up and looked at me expectantly, wagging his tail for more. Oh, I tell you, what I thought of myself as a lover, student, intellectual as I examined this new gap in myself!

'Yet I soon learned to smile in a new way, sideways; we are all quite alone.

'So time drops on us all like a shadow.'

We stood in the icy hall, talking. 'We married in a fragile spring,' he said. 'I always felt afraid for our love as though the weather on our wedding day – cloud, blossom, rain and some sun, all these constantly changing, too much going on in the sky at once – threatened our love. But you think that I'm perhaps being sentimental?'

'No,' I said, 'just go on talking.'

'Now I've started,' he said, 'it's a relief to talk. I had to make you listen to that tape just now. I felt there was no other way I could get you to understand.'

'I know,' I said, 'it's all right.' While I listened to him I found I was also thinking about a report I had found on my desk the other day at the Factory. It droned: 'Murderer, convicted, of three old women, no recommendation for release, this individual is unfit for any prison work and now rarely leaves his cell at Wakefield prison. He had one friend, another killer, a transvestite, but they quarrelled over a cassette-player and the friend killed himself.' Nobody at the Factory would have cared one way or the other, of course, if he hadn't been wanted as a witness in another case. But if it had been me – unfit for prison work – I'd have thrown a spade at the bastard and thrown it hard and told him to get on with murdering a few sacks of cement for the rest of his days: I don't see why the taxpayer has to work for these people and keep them. Eight hours solid in all weathers, like the rest of us, or else no snout soon makes you forget your wanking habits and gets you to be of use to someone. At least better to build a wall or paint a traffic sign than strangle, rape and rob some blind old biddy for twenty quid. These charmers often blind the victims so they can't be identified.

'You can't grasp the music of the dead,' Mardy was saying. 'I remember Marianne's, but can't seem to catch it, not really. Every tragedy is in the past; I hold that those who live after the dead suffer with them. Mine carries on; hers is over.'

'All right, Dr Mardy,' I said. I knew the moment had come. 'Where is your wife?'

'Downstairs.'

'Shall we go and see her together?'

'Yes, of course.'

We went silently through the house, and I thought the long flight of steps into the basement would never end. Mardy said only, as he held his gas-lamp up for us to see by: 'I've felt like a hunted beast up to now.' He looked even more frail in that fluttering light, crouched in his anorak; wet walls shone around us. At last we got down to a cellar with a concrete wall built across half of it; there was a steel white-painted door set into this wall. Mardy took keys out of his pocket which opened two locks in the door; at that point he turned to me and said: 'You heard our tape.'

'Yes.'

'Before we go in,' he said, 'it's very important that you should remember what you heard.'

'I remember it all.'

'I'm appealing to you as a human being,' he said, 'whatever happens to me, whatever you do to me, you have heard Marianne and me argue our situation out.'

'Yes.'

'I wonder if I'll get justice for my wife and me?'

'We seldom do, but still.'

'Wait till I switch the light on,' he said, unlocking the door and going through it into the dark. 'Of course, I know this place by heart.' Yet it seemed to me to be a long moment, as the uneasy beam of his lamp ran along the wall, before he found it. Then a small square place was filled with ruthless light which focused on a deep-freeze in the middle of the floor. The device was chained and locked, its motor whirring. A green light glowed from its control board and a bouquet of wild flowers lay fading on the lid. 'I pick them for her every day,' he said.

'Would you open it, please?'

'Yes, but it won't be a long look,' he said, pulling out another key, 'will it? Not very long. The bulk to be kept chilled is considerable and the temperature must never rise above minus sixty-five centigrade, it kills the tissue.'

Now I understood everything about the delivery of dry ice. 'Was there an electricity strike at some point?' I said.

'Yes, yes,' he said. 'Life is so complex, we can none of us know each other's problems.'

'Some of us profit from them, though,' I said, 'don't they, Dr Mardy?'

'Must I talk about that now?'

'No,' I said. 'Tell me rather, how long has she been in this?'

'Since she died last August,' he whispered. He bent mechanically to check the temperature at the outer case. I read it over his shoulder; it recorded minus seventy.

'Who built this machine?' I said.

'I had it built for the two of us,' he said, 'by a firm in London to my own specifications. I told them what I wanted, they built it and I paid for it, that was all.'

I knew I would get the name of the builders and just store it in case; there weren't four firms in the country that built fridges like this – the size for two bodies and the temperature for a corpse. 'Open it now,' I said.

He nodded and swung the lid up. A cloud of frozen vapour rose from the inside, where lay a shocking bundle of green plastic in the rough shape of a human being. It lay on its back, masked, bound and tied.

'I'm going to be frank with you,' Mardy said.

'You'd do best to be.'

'It's her face you'll want to look at, of course.'

'Yes, to identify her.'

'There isn't much left,' said Mardy, 'I'll explain,' reaching in as he spoke. The head and face were also swathed in green plastic. He added: 'I uncover her face sometimes, a minute or two never hurts.' The freezer's motor hummed under her. 'I spend a lot of time down here with her, at night mostly. Yet I need to be careful. It's her brain that needs most protection against any warmth. The vital organs too, of course, heart, liver – and her face.'

'What did you do to her?'

'Loved her.'

'Did you kill her?'

'I don't know,' he said, starting to cry. It's terrible to see an old man cry. 'It depends what you mean.'

'Try and go on.'

'Marianne was very beautiful.'

'Yes, I've seen photographs.'

'She'll be beautiful again, of course.'

'Please tell me what you mean.'

'I mean when she rises again,' said Mardy, 'when she comes back. She's only resting here. In fifty years' time science will be so far advanced that everything about Marianne will be cured. My task is to preserve her during that time; you heard that tape.' He was leaning in over his wife's body as he spoke, busily loosening the straps that bound her bust and head. 'Every limb must be separately encased,' he muttered, 'an arm frozen to the ribs, or one leg to the other, that can cause frightful damage under ice.'

'You packed her yourself?'

'I did everything myself, now do you understand what hell is? Losing your entire world? I mean to cheat her death, what else could a doctor be for?'

'I'm afraid I must see the face,' I said.

'Yes, I've unpacked it,' he said, 'she's all ready for you.' He coughed. 'She's not as she was, not yet.'

'My nerves are all right,' I said.

'It's like the face of someone waiting for a train just at the moment,' he said. He leaned over her and took the plastic away from her face: 'Now don't be alarmed.'

It was frightful; it wouldn't have been so bad if it had been an animal, but this was a human being like us who had once been happy and given concerts. She had no lower lip at all; the dubious teeth of a middle-aged woman grinned in a jaw locked solid in ice and her eyes, no longer startled, shook only the onlooker. They were milky in colour and hard as glass.

'I see you're looking at her eyes,' said Mardy in a professional way, 'it's only natural you should, but that's not as serious as it looks. At minus sixty-five she lives in a different world, but her sight will come back with the rest in fifty years.'

I said: 'Why is she bald?'

'That's nothing,' said Mardy, 'I'll explain it to you. Her hair will grow out again, as beautiful as it ever was. But I had to shave her head so that I could operate.'

I said: 'I think the best thing we could do is for you to close Mrs Mardy up again for now, and for you and I to go upstairs and talk.'

'Yes.'

He relocked the freezer when he had finished repacking the body. He made sure the temperature was correctly set. He picked up the flowers that had fallen when he opened the lid and replaced them. He got out the keys to the cellar door to lock that after us, but I held my hand out and said: 'I'll take the keys.'

'Of course.'

I pocketed them and said: 'Look, I know nothing about surgery or the year 2030, but I'm a policeman, and as far as the police are concerned your wife is judicially and clinically dead.'

'Metaphysically—'

'It's no use talking to a judge about metaphysics,' I said, yet as I spoke I wondered if there wasn't something wrong about that. As for the police, I thought it's a good thing he's got me and not Charlie Bowman to deal with.

'I didn't murder her,' he said. 'She was my love. I was trying to save her, not kill her.'

'But from our point of view she died under your knife.'

'If a surgeon were to be told that each time he lost a patient, there'd be no more operations carried out at all.'

'But you weren't qualified to carry it out.'

'That's why I wanted you to hear the tape.'

'I understand all right,' I said, 'but prosecuting counsel won't. You have to realize that. Now tell me formally why you didn't report her death.'

'Because they'd have buried her. She'd have rotted in the ground.'

'That's going to happen anyway, I'm afraid,' I said. 'There's no way either you or I can prevent it. The autopsy, the coroner's verdict and then—'

'I'm sixty-three,' he said, 'it doesn't matter for me. I wouldn't mind dying – I've had enough of horror and loss. It's for her.'

I studied him and realized that madness is the last defence of the mind when it can't hope to reconcile itself with events; I, too, was standing between routine and the unknowable. I could not say what I ought to have said: we all have to die. Why prosecute a mind at the end of its tether when far more villainous people get off scot-free? The morbid desire that bores have for a headline?

I locked the door to Marianne's cellar myself and we stood outside it, talking in low voices.

As we started to go back upstairs by the light of our uneasy torches he said, without turning to me: 'When I think how I started. I was one of the most brilliant students of my year.' He added: 'What is brilliance, I wonder? The refusal to accept an end?'

20

We were upstairs in Mardy's room. Four walls can suddenly become a heart too full for words, a space of indescribable pain, unspoken yet felt. Love's unseen but broken wings batter on window panes as words most urgently meant, and your own anxiety is sharply fastened on the invisible. I sense death in houses that I go into, even ancient murder – the short stab, the red glare of a pistol, the ungovernable tension of a moment, the trigger word that nobody can revoke.

Mardy had crossed to a corner. He looked at me and said: 'I'll be lucky to get out of this.'

'Out of what?'

'It's been a long time to the crisis is what I mean.'

'I'm sorry I have to be here,' I said. I felt myself to be what I was, a public agent sent to weigh up and destroy values.

'I'm sorry too.' He said: 'I want you to listen to this. Do you know how a person, like my wife, can get a better understanding of existence in a foreign country sometimes than they can in their own?'

'I believe I can imagine it,' I said, 'but it's no use trying to persuade me out of being a policeman.'

'That's not what I'm trying to do,' he said, 'I'm trying to get you to see something I feel.'

'All right,' I said, 'well?'

He said: 'My wife wrote this – she wrote and sang our language better than I do. "I looked out when the cuckoo sang, Winter had gone, now summer ran down from the sun. No dreams or rest, no final sleep be mine, Your love and breast be mine. The fruit turns red now, swelling in the dark. And can we ever touch with love, the dark? Passion's all colours, beauty only one. I'm glad to go into

165

the dark with you, our comprehension singing, for blindness is nothing black if we come out singing like a season after the long dark and after madness, after sighing, after the hatred and the losses, our fighting and our dying." "Poor prince, cold prince, your hands are cold." "I'm dying Sweet queen, your passion in my absence flying away, hold us to all our tears, our nearness dying. No dreams or rest, no final sleep be mine, your love, sweet breast, be mine."'

He had forgotten me, as he was justified in doing, and I saw him as he was, quite absent from us in his wasted shape, his hair and poor clothes, bent in that grief which is the terrible element of amusement for the uninvolved, the temptation to laugh as a primitive form of hiding from sadness being the most terrible kind of ignorance.

'It was just a pimple to start off with,' he was saying, 'on the left corner of her lower lip. Yes, at first we both laughed it off as a cold sore, but then it didn't go away.

'The horror of loss,' he said, 'the immutable ruthlessness of existence that you can only be young to ignore.

'The horror,' he said. 'I walk the narrowest of ropes. Do you think that I sleep? The walls round my bed, if I go there, are spattered with the mad figures of dwarves in the plaster, sneering deities, insane judges with Habsburg lips and half their head missing, a peasant coming at his wife with an axe, she laughing in a corner, and God is a middle-aged man with a moustache like an army officer's whose stare varies from wicked to kind according to the sun's position behind the curtains, which I always keep drawn. Cryogenics?' he added. 'The Americans go far too low. They freeze theirs at minus 196 degrees, but sixty-five's ample in my opinion.'

I said: 'Explain why Walter Baddeley was blackmailing you.'

He said: 'Because there was an electricity strike and the temperature started to rise. The only solution was to go to the undertaker's to get dry ice.'

'That was a delivery that cost you thirty thousand pounds,' I said. 'I've got the cheques.'

'I had to keep her temperature down,' he said. 'I don't care about the thirty thousand pounds.'

'Whether you do or you don't,' I said, 'I do. I care very much indeed; I loathe blackmailers; it's a form of bullying and cowardice I can't stomach.'

'You shouldn't have interfered,' he said.

'I had to; it's my job.'

He groaned in despair.

'I'm a police officer,' I said. 'I can't help it, but it's against the law to conceal a death, you know that.'

He hid his face in his hands. 'Why can't you just go away,' he said, 'and leave us both alone?'

'You know that's not possible.'

'I know,' he said, tears rolling down his face, 'but she was my wife.'

'I'm not here to argue that,' I said, 'your counsel will have to.'

'I don't care about any punishment I might get,' he said, 'not at my age. That's not the point. What matters is that if they take her away we'll be lost to each other for ever.'

'I want to help you,' I said, 'but there's a point where I can't. I know it's absurd, but I've my own people to deal with. Who brought you the dry ice?'

'Do you know anyway?'

'Nearly all of it.'

'It was a man called Prince and a man I used to have as a gardener called Sanders.'

'Employed by the undertaker.'

'Yes,' he said. 'He bled us white. He started by offering us an annuity when Marianne first looked ill. I refused, but when death happened and then the electricity strike as well, I had to go to him to keep her temperature down.'

'And you never had any trouble from the local police?'

'No, that was in our contract.'

'Between you and Baddeley?'

'It wasn't put like that. It was between two companies.'

'Baddeley set them up?'

'Yes.'

'I know what they were called,' I said, 'Wildways and Clearpath.'

'That's right.'

'And with all the gossip about your wife going round Thornhill,' I said, 'why didn't the police down here intervene?'

'The inspector's wife and Baddeley are brother and sister; they're also in business together.'

'Yes, gambling,' I said. 'I know. Kedward's tame, a tame copper, but I wanted to hear you say it.'

'Well, now you know.'

'But they weren't going to leave it at that, were they?' I said. 'I can guess. Baddeley and Kedward were just going to wait till you ran out of money, then force that annuity on you in exchange for this place, and for their continued silence.'

'Yes,' said Mardy, 'and I'd never have done it. This place is for Marianne when she comes back, and for no one else.'

'But they'd left you no way out.'

'It may look like checkmate on the board,' Mardy said, 'but I'd have found some way.'

We paused for a while and then I said: 'This will probably go to trial, I have to warn you. I'm not cautioning you now, but just make sure you're well represented. You'll get good counsel for nothing; no fair-minded man likes a blackmailer.'

Blackmail an old man who has lost the wife he hopes to save? What land is this whose laws I operate?

'I couldn't stand a trial,' he said. 'I'm in enough pain.'

I said: 'It'll depend on the coroner's decision, and of course the DPP.' I thought, I'll have to tell him this, too. 'There'll be a lot of publicity about it as well, I'm afraid – we might as well go on being frank with each other.'

'No,' he said, 'no, I couldn't.' He said to me: 'Won't they ever stop?'

I thought, no. The lower levels of the Sunday press will have fun with this for ever.

Mardy bit into the side of his cheek and said: 'If you had been there! If you could have seen her! I told you, it looked like nothing but a cold sore getting worse on the outer edge of her lower lip. We laughed about it to begin with, though I never liked the look of it from the start. But she was so proud of her looks – and rightly so – that what could I say? However, I remember one evening in May last year, we were having supper, she said to me, William, I don't like this spot I've got on my lip here, don't you see that it gets bigger all the time? I know you've had it some time now, I said, describe to me exactly how it feels. Well, it's hurting me, she said. I said, is it like a throbbing pain? She said, it is, rather. A month later it looked quite wrong for a cold sore. It was the wrong colour. It had become angry, a purple colour, with a hard cracked scab on it. For several weeks she had taken to gnawing on it and I said, don't do that, dear. She said I can't help it, it's driving me mad. You're the doctor, do you think it might be malignant? My blood ran cold in the face of my opinions; I had absolutely put it off that she could be right. You know how we're all weak? My weakness was that I laughed at her and told her not to be so silly, though of course I knew much better. But a fortnight later, one evening, we were out in the garden, she suddenly said to me, William, I don't think I can stand this place on my lip any more. Are you in pain? Yes, I'm in pain, and I don't see how you can go on kissing me on this place any more.

'Then I knew what death meant.

'Of course it could be removed, I said, that place, only a sample of it would have to be taken first and sent for analysis. She turned to me among the roses and said simply: I want you to do it, William. Marianne, I said, I'm not qualified to do it, I'm struck off, you know that. But if you want, I can send you to some of the top surgeons in London, men I know, we were students together. But she would keep going on: no, no one but you is going to touch my body, I love you and I have faith in you. This is how it happened, Sergeant. Why, William, she said, you can do it, I know you can do it and it must be done; you're not getting soft, are you? She said, you had the most brilliant future ahead of you as a surgeon.'

'But something happened to it,' I said.

'Yes,' he said, 'I'll tell you about that in a minute. Meantime I yielded to her. You know what women are? Or any people? I ended by going up to London and equipping myself with everything I should need. Where she is downstairs, that cellar, I turned that into a theatre for her. She came down with me and said, half curiously, I've never performed in a theatre like this before. It was such hot weather. We decided the date over dinner the night before, and I said, have a good dinner now, and then nothing till after the op. We ate everything we liked most; I remember it was oysters to start with, then roast beef, potatoes and a green salad, also two very good bottles of wine. You'll be on a drip after this, I said, and she said yes, I know. All our tragedy was in our happiness over that meal. It's for tomorrow evening, then, she said, and I said yes, if you're sure you agree. I insist, she said.'

He turned to me and said: 'Oh, what a fool I was ever to agree, but you see it was our love.'

I said: 'You took the sample?'

'Yes.'

'And had it analysed.'

'Yes,' he said, 'and it was malignant, a sarcoma. Of course, I had had to cut her lip a little for the sample and she already looked different because of it. We had another dinner but she couldn't keep it down. Later we toasted each other with champagne and she said, William, it is malignant, isn't it? And I said yes, because we've never had any secrets from each other. She said, I knew it was, deep down.'

'Then what happened?'

'I told her that the whole growth would have to be removed but I said, Marianne, listen, you'll have to go into hospital for it. No, never, she said. I've got no anaesthetist, nor possibility of any help, I said, you've got to understand, and that growth on your lip has got to be removed. But she said, no, I believe in you, and only in you, William. I said, and supposing I won't remove it? She said, well then, I shall die, shan't I?'

'And the deep-freeze?' I said.

'We had that already,' he said and added: 'It was for me, I was twenty years older than Marianne. It was I that was going to come back in fifty years' time, not Marianne.'

We were silent for a time.

'All right,' I said, 'what happened next?'

'I said, it's wrong of you to insist that I do this, Marianne.'

I said: 'But you did it.'

'Yes, as soon as I was equipped and ready. I did it at night. It was a terribly hot night, not a breath of wind. I removed the whole growth and cleaned the wound.'

'I know nothing about surgery,' I said, 'but you'll be questioned by people who do. Are you satisfied in yourself that you carried out the operation as you should have done?'

'Perfectly satisfied.'

'And do you believe that another, impartial surgeon would say the same?'

'I do.' He wiped sweat away from his forehead and added: 'You realize, of course, that I couldn't be as dispassionate as an uninvolved surgeon would have been.'

'I understand. And then she got worse?'

'Very soon afterwards. She had discomfort with her mouth at first; then she was in pain and finally in agony, complaining of pain not just where the growth had been, but higher up inside her cheek, in her throat and in her ear.'

'How did you treat the pain?'

'I could only alleviate it.'

'And how did you do that?'

'With morphine.'

'And where did you get it?'

'You can get anything,' he said flatly, 'if you're prepared to pay for it.'

'Go on.'

'I examined her. There were secondaries in her left cheek, in the throat, and the beginnings of a growth in the left mastoid. I said,

Marianne, you'll have to do now what I should have made you do all along, and that's go straight into hospital. She said, and if I die there I shall be buried in the usual way, and we'll never meet again in fifty years. But I can't treat you here, I said, I haven't what I need and I've got no help. She said, I'm not going into hospital and that's final. I said, Marianne, you're very seriously ill – how can I just stand here and let you get worse and worse? It was like a nightmare, Sergeant.'

'Yes,' I said, 'I can see it was.'

'I said, Marianne, don't you want to get better and see your friends again and sing? I'll never sing again, she said slowly, I know that, and I don't believe I'll ever get better now. You mustn't talk like that, I said. You must go where you'll be properly cared for, and that means hospital. I've got all that on tape as well. I listen to it over and over.'

Now I knew really what the voices I had half heard were saying – the dread, desperate arguments.

He continued: 'It's my face too, she said. I've looked at it. William, I want you to smash every mirror in the house, and I did. She said, if ever I do go out I shall wear a veil.'

I said: 'Did you continue to operate on her?'

'Yes. Part of it was in her vocal cords.'

'And you operated there?'

'Yes.'

'Do you consider that you carried that operation out in a proper way?'

'Yes.'

'Under those circumstances?'

'The test of any surgeon is his courage.'

'Were you successful?'

'I removed everything that I had to, but still I couldn't halt it.'

'Did you operate on her any further after that?'

'Yes. I removed the new growth in her cheek. I had to go through the cheek, of course, but that was nothing; it would have left the smallest of scars. But you may know how it is with cancer.

You remove one secondary and then almost immediately another one—' He stopped.

I said: 'And the mastoid?'

'I had to do it,' he said. 'Don't you see that otherwise she would have died in worse agony than she did?'

'So that was why she was bald.'

'Of course. I had to shave her.'

'I'm asking the kind of questions that you're going to have to answer at your trial.'

'I know,' he said, 'but you must remember that I had to do everything alone. Normally I would have had a team. But this was like being back in the war, trying to work on a battlefield.'

'Where did she die,' I said, 'and when?'

'It was on August 14th at teatime, in her bedroom. It was three days after the last operation.'

'Was she in pain?'

'No more so than usual. It had got to the point where at the first signs of distress I would give her morphine with a whisky base, and she would lie there dreaming and smiling.'

Half bald, I thought, and no lower lip. Dressings on her cheek, her throat and on the left side of her head. 'Could she speak after the throat operation?' I said.

'No, just a croak,' he said, 'but she was most often on morphine anyway.'

'What finally killed her?'

'Shock, I'm afraid,' he said. 'She was so weak after what she had already undergone that in her last hours I could watch her just slipping away.'

'Do you think that any treatment could have made her well?'

'No, no,' he said, 'and a woman – think of her face. In fifty years, of course—'

'How was she when she died?'

'Happy – I saw she was going and I put my arms round her, and she died looking out of the window at the sun, whispering old songs and stroking my face. I've come a long way from my own

173

country, William, she said, but I'm going back there now. The morphine had really removed her from me already, but I could tell what she wanted to sing; we used to sing it together: *Les filles sont volages, fréquentez-les donc pas; un jour elles vous aiment, un jour elles vous aiment pas.* I sang it for her, and when I had finished she turned to me in my arms and thanked me very gravely, went grey and was gone.'

'Did you take her downstairs yourself?'

'I had to.'

21

'When did Baddeley first start to bite?'

'That was in November, about three months after Marianne had been downstairs, and the electricity strike happened. I was taking her flowers to her when the alarm from the freezer suddenly started. I looked at the thermometer; the temperature was only minus forty, so I rang Baddeley about the dry ice.'

'Was Sanders working for you at that time?'

'No, he had left; he was doing odd jobs for Baddeley.'

'There was no trouble about Baddeley giving you this dry ice?'

'Not at first.'

'He didn't ask you any questions? Didn't ask you why you wanted anything so unusual?'

'No, he made no trouble about it at all.'

'You didn't think that was strange?'

'I was only thinking about Marianne.'

'So you packed the dry ice in with her and then the strike ended. Then what happened?'

'About a fortnight after that Baddeley came up to see me.'

'Alone?'

'No, there was a man called Prince with him whom he described as his assistant.'

'What kind of person was he? Prince, I mean.'

'Unpleasant.'

'Tough?'

'Big, from London, six foot two, hair crew-cut, sharp clothes. I saw them in this room. Baddeley sat in that corner there with his arms folded and said, I'll let Mr Prince do the talking.'

'And what did Prince say?'

'It's not the sort of language I use, but as near as I can recall he

Derek Raymond

said: listen, you old cunt, what did you want that dry ice for a fortnight back? We think it was for your wife. Now you'd better play this straight up with us, otherwise the law'll be round in less than five minutes and you'll be right in the shit. And what about you? I said. Never mind about me, Prince said, you just worry about yourself.'

'That makes sense,' I said. 'Yes, I can hear that music.'

'So then he said, we want to see the body, darling, to make sure, and that sharply. I said, and if I won't? If you won't, he said, I'll turn this stinking old barracks over from cellar to attic and find out what we want to know anyway, and in a very short time. There'll be some damage done in the process too, he added – in fact, by the time I've finished you won't know your arse from your elbow in this place, and you could even get hurt yourself.'

'And Baddeley?'

'Baddeley just sat nodding and smiling and saying, I think you'd do best to cooperate with Mr Prince and myself, William.'

'Had you ever talked about cryogenics in Thornhill?'

'Yes of course,' he said, 'as a theory.'

I said: 'Go on. Did either of these individuals in fact offer you violence?'

'Yes. I was only thinking of Marianne. I was terrified the police would come and take her away. I didn't care about myself so I prevaricated, until in the end Prince said, I'm getting fed up with this – if you don't show us what we want to see, you miserable old bastard, I'll do no more but knock the shit out of you, and what do you think about that?'

'Did you in fact show them your wife's body?'

'Yes. I'm sixty-three, and I'm afraid my courage ran out in the end.'

'I understand,' I said. 'So what happened when you told these two priceless crown jewels what they wanted to know?'

'They put their contract to me.'

'Did that include the reversion of this house to them on your death?'

'It did.'

'And what did you get in exchange for this reversion, and for the thirty thousand pounds you paid them?'

'The promise of their silence, Marianne and I left alone, and no trouble from the police.'

'It's really very very interesting,' I said. 'Yes. Now there's a case that will most definitely go to trial when I've finished, and you will be a valuable prosecution witness in it. I cannot stand blackmailers.'

'I was a fool to think I could keep her death secret,' said Mardy, 'but I was desperate.'

'All right,' I said. 'So then Baddeley set up these two companies, Wildways and Clearpath?'

'Wildways existed already,' Mardy said. 'Clearpath was just for me to make the payments.'

'Anyone else on the board except yourself?'

'My wife. She can be a sleeping director, Baddeley said.'

'I find that really very sick,' I said.

'Yes, they both burst out laughing when Baddeley said that, and then Baddeley said to me, it's all right, she doesn't have to sign the cheques, and her director's fees can come straight to us, OK?'

'The money you paid them,' I said. 'It was too much for you, wasn't it, financially.'

'It broke me.'

'I will tell you something,' I said, 'if it's any relief to you. You will have to go to trial, of course, but I'm the arresting officer, and I will tell you for nothing that there will be mitigating circumstances. Secondly, certain people in Thornhill, some more prominent than others, I have already marked down for arrest, and they will go down with a crash you could hear in Australia.'

'But Marianne,' he said. 'What about Marianne?'

It was the question I couldn't answer.

I thought as I walked back to the car that Mardy had been further abroad in the realm of terror and risk than most people would ever go.

Derek Raymond

As for me, I set my webs in the dark, and wait for my prey to come to me.

My prey is never innocent; it causes me wicked and frightening dreams, I am alone against it. All I want is for our democracy to be rid of violent bores.

I don't mind how it's done if we protect the innocent.

22

Hardly had I ceased thinking about bores when by Christ I was confronted by one. I was just going through the doors of the hotel when somebody darted out of a plastic armchair in the foyer, grabbed me by the wrist and said: 'All right, what the hell's going on with this Mardy business?'

'Hell varies,' I said, breaking my arm free, 'and talking of that place, who the fuck are you?'

I didn't know him.

'I'm Fox,' he shouted. 'Detective-Inspector Fox. Fox by name and Fox by nature, that's me.'

'There's no need to boast about what you can't help,' I said. 'Now get off me.'

'You cheeky bastard,' he said, 'you want to watch your step.'

'And you mind you don't break an arm,' I said. 'Now hop back into your panda, go back where you came from, fuck off out of here, go on, do it.'

'I'm going to put in a report about your behaviour!' he shouted.

'It'll just be ink wasted,' I said. 'Now go away, I've got a lot on my mind.'

'You don't understand!' he screamed, waving his warrant card at me, 'I'm working out of Serious Crimes.'

'Work your way back to them then,' I said, 'nobody ordered you.'

'If you've got to quarrel, gents,' said the night porter, suddenly arriving, 'would you mind doing it somewhere else? The other guests are trying to sleep.'

Fox said: 'We're police.'

'I don't give a fuck who you are,' said the night porter. 'I've not committed any crime so far and what I say in this hotel goes until

179

six in the morning when I go to bed, and I advise you to do the same before I get fed up. If you're both in love or something there are the rooms upstairs, but keep it quiet, will you?'

He drifted off. I said to Fox: 'You one of Charlie Bowman's mob? Yes? I thought so. Well, I know Charlie a great deal better than you do, and let me give you the strength of this, Inspector, and tell you what my thinking is. You've just been promoted, Charlie's been lumbered with you, you're brand new and silly and he's sent you down here just to get you off his back and on to mine – anything to get rid of you for a while, he thinks that by pestering me you might get your motor run in a bit. Now don't be tempted. I'm going to tell you what you're going to do next. You're going to turn quietly round, pretend you've never seen me if you know what's good for you, and steer off back up the motorway to the smoke. Tell Charlie from me that this is my case, I'm warning you nicely, but if I get another sniff of you, you funny little artist, I might well be clumsier next time, are you with me?'

He could hardly help being, and had turned white. 'You're in for a lot of trouble over this,' he said, 'you do realize. I've been sent down here officially to help you clear this business up, whether you want me to or not.'

'It's my case,' I said. 'I'll handle it the way I do all my work, entirely in my own way, and I absolutely will not cooperate with you, I don't need you, now leave.'

'You're only a sergeant,' he sneered, 'you could get fired if you go on like this.'

'They've never got round to it yet,' I said. 'Why? Do you fancy yourself at A14? I'll be blunt, I don't think you're the right material.'

'I think I could change all that,' he said softly, 'about your being fired.'

'Do it, princess,' I said, 'and clear up all the shit if you can, but my view is that you're just piss and wind, wooden-top, so get clear of me.'

'You think you're finished with me, do you?'

'I don't have to think hard about what I know.'

He went red as a poisoned berry. 'All right, Sergeant. If that's the way you want it.'

'I do,' I said, 'now piss off, get back to traffic control, I'm busy. Never ever interfere with a case of mine again, and you might live to draw your pension.'

'For the last time, Sergeant, I'm reminding you of my rank.'

'The fact that you have to remind me of mine,' I said, 'means that you don't deserve yours. Christ only knows how you ever passed for inspector – my God, you must have been on form that day.'

23

The voice rang me at seven thirty in the morning, my last on the Mardy business as things turned out. It said: 'I'm having the most frightful time up here. I've got Detective-Inspector Fox screaming at me that he's going to break your neck.'

'He had his chance to and didn't take it,' I said.

'What the hell did you think you were doing, sending him back like that?'

'I didn't need him at all,' I said. 'I never ordered him, it isn't his case.'

'You cheeky sod,' said the voice. 'He went down by agreement with me and Chief Inspector Bowman to help you along with it.'

'Well, I just helped him back into his car,' I said. 'You should have asked me first.'

'Are you inferring that Fox can't do his job?'

'I don't need a rat to do a tango at a funeral,' I said, 'I'll put it that way — all I wanted to do was get rid of him, and please don't send me people down on these things with new buttons on, he can hardly do without a bib at mealtimes yet.'

'You know this is all going to go further,' said the voice, 'and this time I don't think I'll be able to cover you.'

'I'll survive,' I said.

'Maybe,' said the voice, 'but not in the police, I don't think.'

'Well that'll be just too bad,' I said. 'Now until I'm finished here just keep people like Bowman and Fox right out of my way.'

'We're wondering whether to take you off this case.'

'Keep wondering,' I said, 'but don't do it now, it's solved.'

'What about this woman then? Where is she?'

'In a deep-freeze,' I said, 'and in anybody's view except her husband's she is dead, and has been since last August.'

'Will you stop talking in riddles?' the voice snapped. 'Exactly where does the husband come into it? Tell me what you mean.'

I told him, and at the end of the recital the voice said, Christ.

'So you see,' I said, 'the inside of this town looks like spaghetti junction, everything and everyone's entwined with everything else; Mardy himself is only one factor.'

'Yes, you've made yourself clear,' said the voice, 'you usually do, I'll say that much. I don't know what's going on down in the country these days.'

'I think they've been watching too much bad television,' I said, 'but within twenty-four hours I'll at least be able to make plenty of arrests.' I added: 'Like six.'

'Including this Inspector Kedward?'

'Of course. I've got proof that he accepted bribes. So there'll be him to stay, his wife for running a dishonest gambling club, Mardy, Dick Sanders for accepting money to deliver the dry ice knowing that he was helping to conceal a death, Walter Baddeley and his assistant Johnny Prince for extortion and blackmail. I might need help making the arrests,' I added. 'I can hardly lodge them in Thornhill police station, not under the circumstances.'

'You sent the help back.'

'No, that was a hindrance,' I said. 'I will not be told how to work a job by a man like Fox.'

'You might have to face up to the fact that Bowman'll come down,' said the voice. 'I don't know yet.'

'I do, though,' I said. 'If he does come down it'll be because he can smell a headline in it. I'll have cleared up all the shit; all he'll have to do is make the arrests and cart them off, these people, then take the credit.'

'I will not have you talking about your superiors in that way,' said the voice. 'I've warned you countless times.'

'It's the truth, though,' I said, 'you'll see how it turns out.'

'I've just made peace between you two,' said the voice

mournfully. 'When I think of the trouble I went to.'

'You shouldn't have bothered,' I said. 'Peace can never last long between Charlie and me. In any case,' I added, 'I want Mardy left to me.'

'Why?' shouted the voice. 'He kills his wife as the result of a series of illegal operations, conceals her death—'

'He believes he had a reason to behave as he did, and I can follow it. I will not have him handed over to Bowman. Anyway I've made a deal with him.'

'You had absolutely no right! The law—'

'It was the truth I was after,' I said. 'Wasn't that what we wanted?'

'You'll be telling me you're sorry for Mardy next.'

'I am.'

'We're not in the pitying business,' said the voice.

'No,' I said, 'and may God have mercy on us.'

'There's such a thing as police procedure, Sergeant.'

'I know,' I said. 'Part of it's called resigning.'

'You'll bloody well see this job through,' the voice said.

'Only on my terms, though. No one but me is to interfere with Mardy, understand?'

'You're the only low-ranking detective I've ever heard of who dared talk to a deputy commander like that.'

'We might as well be clear,' I said, 'is it yes or no?'

'I'll have to think about it.'

'Well, make up your mind,' I said, 'there isn't much time left on this one.'

'Oh Christ,' said the voice, 'well, all right then. I really don't know how I'm going to square it though. You know what Serious Crimes are like once they take an interest in A14 – they're better budgeted, better equipped, better manned, and they've got their own folk upstairs to put the pressure on.'

'You just find a way of holding that mob off Mardy for twenty-four hours,' I said, 'I don't care what happens to anyone else. Don't worry, I know what I'm doing.'

'Yes, but the trouble with you,' said the voice, 'is that no one else does.'

'I have to solve these things my own way.'

'Somebody told me you've got the press on it.'

'One man,' I said. 'You know what it is, I feed them and they feed me.'

'I suppose it's that bloody man Cryer from the *Recorder* again, is it?'

'He's all right,' I said.

'You might as well go ahead and marry him, have done with it.'

'You're right in a way,' I said. 'I always protect my own, there aren't many of them. So look after your end of it, but keep clear of Mardy.'

'Why don't you and I change jobs?' said the voice.

'I don't know,' I said, and rang off.

I went over to the tough-looking little armchair that stood in a corner of the room. It held its plastic elbows out to me like a wrestler, and the only way I could think of to get a submission was to sit down on it hard and have a drink. But I had barely had a chance to mix it when Cryer rang.

'We were just talking about you,' I said, 'where are you ringing from?'

'London, I had to go and see Angela.'

'You think of Angela when you think of Mardy, OK?'

'I had a talk with Mardy before I left, I ought to tell you.'

'I should fucking well think so,' I said, 'I told you expressly not to do that. Well, anyway, how was he?'

'Not good. All absent in his mind.'

'You be careful how you play this,' I said, 'you meddling bastard, don't you come on hard-boiled with me. What did you find out about Mrs Mardy?'

'Nothing,' said Cryer. 'Where is she?'

'I'm not going to tell you. Not now.'

'This story's beginning to make a noise where I work. The

sort of noise we're paid to make.'

'I don't care,' I said, 'nor do you. As long as I'm in charge of this case you're the only reporter on it, and that's for past favours and favours to come. But play it my way.'

'She's dead, this woman, isn't she?' he said.

'Yes,' I said, 'she's dead.'

'And the husband killed her.'

'Yes, but it was no ordinary murder.'

'I've got to know more than that.'

'And you will, but not before tonight. Look, don't worry,' I said. 'I keep telling you, no one's going to get in ahead of you. But when you do get the facts, Tom, now you help me, damn you. Let's have a little pity from the fourth estate – it won't do your story any harm. I'll tell you this much; yes, I'm going to do Mardy, I have to, but I'm equally going to make certain that he doesn't do the full bitter trudge in a court of law.'

'What are you asking me to do?'

'Be kind, basically.'

'I've got an editor who isn't kind.'

'Fix him,' I said. 'You can if you've a mind to. What you and he both want is to get in with it first and you will, but you'll do it on my terms. Are you coming back down to Thornhill now?'

'Of course.'

'Good,' I said, 'because I might be going to need you.'

'All right,' he said, 'but what about these other people? I've heard a rumour there's even a local police officer involved down there.'

'Where the hell do you people get these rumours from?' I said.

'All sorts of people talk,' he said. 'They've got tongues in their heads, haven't they? Our job is just to listen.'

'I told you earlier to fuck off, Tom,' I said, 'you didn't listen. I told you to leave Mardy alone – and you've interviewed him.'

'You trying to protect Mardy or what?'

'That's what I'm doing,' I said. 'The rest of the mob, you can go mad on that lot, but I will not have Mardy destroyed, either by us or by you, do you understand? Now will you play this by my rules or won't you, it's as simple as that.'

'OK.'

'Then get down here fast,' I said, 'and stand by, I'm on my own here. Tonight, if you and that editor of yours can hold yourselves in that long, it'll all be finished, and you can start printing.'

'OK, OK,' he said. 'Done.'

I thought, ringing off, that Cryer had hardened up a lot since the McGruder days. But don't we all get harder?

24

(Mardy had said to me: 'Perhaps Marianne and I would have looked tawdry with the dawn now, the candles pale, exhausted; we would have gone out, looking old, to shiver on the terrace, waiting for next summer with the dead beside us. We would only have comforted ourselves with our music and memories, waiting for sunrise.

'Slowly I am feeling my way towards the other line.'

'What line is that?' I said, and he answered: 'It's death, for the other night when I was cold and alone I pulled my blanket over me and half dreamed that I was in the small back bar of the pub behind the hospital where I trained. We were the same nine at our table; we used to drink beer and gossip. Somebody, Ian Richards, I think, cracked a joke and I said that's really very funny but as I spoke I fell from my place, faint, knowing I had gone, falling against the stomach of a big man who was standing nearby, and I heard them say, he's ill, but I was on the floor. It was too late; sound, voices, light had faded to nothing.

'Then the man who always sat on the pavement to draw by the entrance to the pub was there again; he often appears in those dreams. He had no limbs but drew with coloured chalks between his teeth, the Houses of Parliament and London scenes.

'I go down to be with Marianne in the night. She is always near me, I sense her arms tight round me in the evenings and feel her saying hush, quiet your tears, I'm alive in a different place now and would be in heaven if only you could join me. I tell her I'm just coming and by a breath not to shake a spider's web she whispers, I'm always here for you, always, because you kept your word. She tells me there are streams, lands and cities better than on earth and says, I sing all the time now, remade and longing for you. We have to work the fields of heaven, she says, to produce a new seed; there's much to do and we need you.'

He gazed at me and said: 'It sounds banal, the dialogue of bereavement, doesn't it, but it isn't. The power of imagination as well as of science is so great, that thanks to the engines of the brain and heart we create that life beyond death which we are sure must be possible for us.

'Reality is to be questioned, not accepted. Matter dangles on a rail, drawn and dark like a curtain or an overdraft. Our state is an unending crisis and the invisible, crammed with errors, crashes through us. Defeated, broken, my ideas ridiculed, my beliefs punishable by law, I am in an impossible decline, going to the point where life and death squarely cross. Reason steers me to my end; nightly both hurry in against me between damp sheets. But I resist, knowing that life is a short fever.

'And so power is crowned and uncrowned at a stroke, the change between trust and murder.

'I have cost none of you anything. I want to be helped out of myself now, having been here long enough; I want to fly upwards as the white bird of death.

'They will laugh at me in court; everything I have ever done or thought will look absurd. Yet I have been through hell.

'I remember when I was young I went out one September morning into Kent between Maidstone and Rochester and walked through the woods; the leaves were just turning. It was nineteen forty-one; I was on leave. Under slowly gathering weather, vast clouds, I walked for miles, considering what beauty and eternity were, and if I could ever carry off their prize. At last I lay down by a stream near Holborough quarries with my sandwiches and beer – you know what it is, such happiness as is possible for us must be had at once. I still see that day; the world felt bright as a new penny, like 1500; I still smell the smoke from the fields where they were burning off the stubble. I stayed there dreaming until my watch told me that I had to go back to the war. So I got to a pub called The Duke Without A Head, where I was staying on my own, had an early supper, changed into uniform and took a taxi for the train. In that train I leaned out into the dusk as the carriage drew away round the curve from the station; I was filled with passion for all I had seen on my long walk; everything in the land I had seen seemed to me worth dying for, even as an army doctor. I had a case and gas-mask with me, I recall, also a thin book about love. I went on staring out at fields and towns increasingly obscured by night.

'Ever since I have spent my time trying to struggle forward to where I can get into a position to think.')

('During my treatment of Marianne I realized that existence is much more serious than many of us suppose. Just before I carried out the operation on her for the tumour she suddenly took my head into her deep breast and sang to me for a while in the dark. I reassured her about her illness, but she only shook her head at me, that I had already shaved, and smiled and said to me, you've done all you could. I'll always comfort you, she said, now never be afraid of love, and I said, the only fear I have of love is losing it and she whispered, that will never happen.'

He was silent and then added: 'It seems to me all the same that there's nothing in my contract with existence that obliges me to live out every inch of it. I don't know, perhaps I ought to rewrite my entire life, but I've no time now; forgive me.')

25

They rang me from reception to say that a Mr Bowman and a Mr Fox wanted to see me in the lounge.

I went down and walked across the spaces between empty sofas till I reached them where they were waiting at the back of the room. I said: 'What the hell are you doing?' I said to Fox: 'You particularly. I already told you to get lost.'

'Now don't get cheeky,' said Bowman, 'watch your bloody tone.'

'Get your little cocks out of my fundament,' I said, 'and everything'll be OK.'

'It's orders I've got to try and be patient with you, Sergeant,' said Bowman, and Fox sniggered.

I turned to him and said: 'You find me amusing, do you?'

'That's right,' Fox smirked.

I said: 'You think that because you're standing next to a chief inspector you're running no risk, is that it?'

'I suppose that's right,' said Fox.

'You jaunty little man,' I said, 'wipe that smile off your face or I'll smear it over a wall, now shut your boat.' I said to Bowman: 'Have you or your demon apprentice here touched this case at all?'

'We've been up looking around,' said Bowman, 'yes.'

'You've seen my man?'

'It's all quite in order,' said Fox, laughing, 'after all, we are police officers, and so what about it?'

'I'll tell you what about it, darling,' I said. 'If either of you have as much as sneezed on that man I will have your guts for a garter, now is that plain language or isn't it?'

Bowman said to Fox: 'He's always like this, Darenth.'

'Oh Darenth,' I said. 'What a sweet pretty name.'

'Just let him row himself deeper into the shit,' Bowman said to Fox. 'No need to get riled, I've had years of practice with this one.'

I said: 'Tell me what you have both been doing.'

'Up your jumper,' said Bowman, 'we don't have to tell you anything, you cheeky berk.'

I said: 'Have you found out where Mrs Mardy is?'

Fox said: 'We have.'

I said: 'How did you find out?'

Bowman said: 'We came down with a W, we did your work for you. I decided it was a serious crime. We went up, turned the place over, and found her OK.'

'You dolts,' I said, 'and they call that detective work, just bomb straight in, never mind who gets hurt – what have you done to her?'

'Never you fucking mind,' said Fox, 'this is for Serious Crimes from now on, we'll take it from here.'

'What did the husband do when you looked into that fridge?' I said.

'He came on a bit,' said Fox, 'and so fucking what?'

'I'll tell you fucking what,' I said. I went over to him and hit him in the mouth so hard that I cut my knuckles open on his teeth. His problem was that he didn't believe I was going to do it until it was too late; he went down like leaves in a hailstorm. I turned to Bowman and said: 'OK, who's next, do you feel like having a go? I'll wreck that jacket for you if you like.'

He didn't fancy it. He went and examined Fox, squatting down to do it. He said to me: 'You cunt, you have really hurt him.'

'That'll teach him to keep his mouth shut,' I said. 'I've told you before, Charlie – never, never interfere in my business. Your friend can lie wired up in hospital for a month or two and think about that.'

'What a lot of fuss about a killer,' said Bowman. 'Just because we had the current cut off,' he added. 'You know you're going to be disciplined over this, don't you?'

'It won't be the first time.'

'No,' said Bowman with satisfaction, 'but it'll be the last. I've finally got you. You wait and see the report I'm going to put in about this. You're just a cunt, I've always told you that, and you deserve what's coming to you the way a pork chop deserves apple sauce.'

I said: 'Never mind that. What state's Mardy in now? This is one more time you won't make superintendent, Charlie. I'm going to heat this up for you, and so is counsel when it comes to court.'

'You swear against me in court,' said Bowman, 'and that's your career completely fucked, I guarantee it.'

'By the time this comes to court,' I said, 'I'll doubtless no longer be a copper, so get stuffed.'

'You certainly hit him all right,' said Bowman, peering at Fox. 'I'll say that for you. Poor sod.'

'My arsehole,' I said.

'You people in Unexplained Deaths are funny,' said Bowman, 'very funny. Anyone'd think you were on this murderer's side.'

'I am,' I said. 'But it's too complicated for you, Charlie.'

'You're a fool,' said Bowman. 'Anyway, you're a goner.'

The night porter hobbled on to the scene and said: 'Gents, I'm sorry, but you're making too much noise, folks is trying to sleep. Haven't you no bleeding beds to go to?'

I went back upstairs and heard my phone ringing. 'It's me,' said Cryer, 'I'm in a call-box just outside Thornhill, what do you want me to do?'

'Play this my way, Tom,' I said, 'please. I've got myself in bother, but never mind that. Go straight back up to Mardy's place and stick to the man till I can get to you.'

'What's going on up at Mardy's?'

'I'll tell you now what you'd have found out anyway – his

wife's in a deep-freeze in the basement and has been for months. This thing's all breaking, I just want it to break my way and no other. Now this is your chance for the interview, but I want you to calm the man, not turn him on. I know it's not your role, but help me and I'll help you. You just look after the man till I can get up to you there, don't bully him for the story now.'

'What's the rush?'

'The rush is that I'm afraid you'll find him in a terrible state – an interfering jumped-up detective-inspector has had his current at the house disconnected so they can get the body out and take it to the morgue for an autopsy, and if what's inside the fridge there rises far above minus sixty-five centigrade it'll start to go bad, and that's what the rush is, Tom.'

'But what did this man get the current cut for?'

'It was just sadism.'

'Did you get uptight with him? I know you.'

'Yes, I altered his face, and that's the trouble I'm in.'

'It sounds like trouble for you all right.'

'It does, and it is.'

'I heard Charlie Bowman was down around there somewhere, nosing about.'

'He is,' I said, 'I've just left him. But until I'm officially suspended I'm still on this case.'

'What are you going to do now?'

'Wipe Baddeley up while I've the time, plus one or two others. Can you contact me?'

'I've got a phone in the car.'

'Give me the number.'

When I had it I said: 'You'll need strong nerves in that house, Tom, I'll tell you.'

'Worse than McGruder?'

'Just as bad,' I said, 'but differently.'

'No real story's ever easy.'

'No,' I said, 'it isn't. Now for the love of Christ get going.'

I got through to the emergency service of the electricity board and explained who I was and what I wanted.

'I'll have to check.' The man I was talking to was gone a long time, and when he finally came back on the line he said: 'I'm afraid what you're asking for's not possible.'

'Oh?'

'The Mardy electricity supply's not to be touched; it's to be left disconnected, and that's police orders.'

'I am a police officer, and I'm asking you to reconnect it.'

He took my name and rank and said: 'This has come down from higher up than you.'

'Can't you bend the rules just for once? It's this man I'm worried for.'

'It'd be my job if I did. Anyway, there's a lot of money owing on that account.'

'There could be a life owing if something isn't done right away.'

'I'm sorry.'

'What's the use of that?' I said bitterly.

'Why don't you talk to the area manager in the morning?'

'Why don't I talk to almighty God?' I said.

(Mardy had said to me: 'I take dignity and respect among people to mean everything, honour and mutual trust – nothing else seems to matter. In that belief I find it possible to reach across any barrier and, if only in my dreams, retrieve every thing I have lost. I'm sixty-three now and ruined, but others will take up the great path.

'My life and heart scatter on the wind of broken images. It's hard for me not knowing why, for I'm sure I don't understand what's happened to me. Existence, to me, is so closely associated with experiment and risk that it's painful for me to be destroyed by a society that understands neither. I can only say that in my heart I belong to a time when all men were free, and that now I grieve how we went down in our innocence.

'However, my dead remarry in the air I breathe, invisible yet solid, reliving their situations in this wet house – a calm, upright spirit is the one response to evil, and that is our fight.

'At least I know now that what I have lost here I can never lose again.

'Oh God, if I had been born stupid I would have gone to my death like an ox and been eaten for my meat by my tormentors without ever knowing or caring why.')

26

When I got into Baddeley's living-room he was not alone. There was this chunky young sod with him in a white denim jacket and jeans, the latter with some dinner over them. The aggressive stare in his eyes was spoiled by their redness; he was a pisspot to me. You could see he was used to the fighting game by the way he held himself, but I doubted if he had ever seen many rings but stone ones – i.e. a street. When I came in Baddeley said: 'What do you want?'

'Both of you,' I said. I said to the young fellow: 'Who are you? Is your name Prince?'

'That's right, copper,' he said, 'Johnny Prince I call myself, and what is your fucking name?'

'It's here on my warrant card,' I said, showing it to him, 'but that's not what you really need to bother about. It's what I'm going to do to you that you need to concern your brains with.'

'Ho, ho, ho,' he jeered, 'and what might you be going to do?'

'Nick you, turn you round and send you off to an HM Prison workshop for rather a long time.'

There was a short pause that seemed long and then Prince said: 'Oh dear oh dear oh dear, we are in a temper today, aren't we? And what might the charge be?'

'There'll be more than one,' I said. 'Conspiring to conceal a death, then there's blackmail and, who knows, it might even go further than that.'

'You'll be lucky.'

'That's what they all say,' I said, 'right up to the bit where the judge says ten years, no recommendation. So now listen, bunny rabbit, are you the brains in here or just the minder? Why not let the boss get a word in?'

'Watch your fucking mouth,' said Prince, 'or I'll smash it through your teeth, copper.'

'Even if you were able to,' I said, 'that would do you no good at all, the jam you're both in. Now since you are just the minder all you need to do is fuck off, as you are beginning to give me a very big pain in my arse. I can see you're on the slow side, but have you got it?'

Baddeley was on the sofa watching all this. For some reason he giggled. I said: 'I shouldn't giggle, Walter.' I said in a voice as grey as death: 'The real jokes haven't started yet.' I added to Prince: 'Now don't stand there, darling, when I've told you not to. I want a word with Walter here on his own. I've marked your card, now get out of here, you miserable wanker, and do it fast – I don't bother with bunny rabbits.'

Prince turned white. 'Go very easy on that talk,' he said.

'With you,' I said, 'I don't need to go easy on any talk. I can go the distance with you – I can be as deliberate as I like.'

Prince said: 'And you are being. If you weren't a copper I'd have killed you by now.'

Baddeley said to me: 'Look, why don't you just calm down?'

'Walter,' I said, 'this is a free and easy age, I know – but you just don't talk to police officers like that.'

'Why not?' he sneered. 'I talk to everybody else in Thornhill like that.'

'That's an agreeable stage in your life which is about to come to an end, Walter,' I said. 'I'm in a very bad temper with you, in case neither of you had noticed, and I'm no Inspector Kedward – which is lucky for me, because he's about to be nicked too.'

'What's the charge?' said Baddeley.

'That's none of your business,' I said. 'However, I'll tell you: accepting a bribe, you know all about that, you little villain, but that's only a start. Now get rid of this poof, will you, before I lose all patience.' Whereupon Prince said: 'All right, that's it,' and came at me and I said: 'Indeed it is,' and stamped on both his insteps very hard.

'You can't insult and attack people in my house!' Baddeley

screamed. 'Prince is my personal assistant!'

'So is the devil,' I said. I went over to Prince, who was sitting on the carpet moaning and stroking his feet. I said: 'Never ever do that to me again, like have a go, do you understand, because it'll be your fucking head next time, not your feet.' I turned back to Baddeley and said to him: 'What else does this cunt do for you, besides delivering dry ice to unfortunate old men and polishing the grate?'

'He's a bearer in my undertaking business.'

'How nice to take your last journey on his shoulder. Look at him on the floor there, Walter, good old British stock, turn his hand to anything, from burials to blackmail, a bit of an all-rounder, isn't he?'

'We've all got to live,' said Baddeley anxiously.

'Yes,' I said. 'And die too.'

Prince, his head coming and going backwards and forwards over his feet, moaned: 'Why don't we bury him, Walter? The bastard's on his tod, there's none to see.'

'I'm one of those folk that never stay buried long,' I said, 'and I could see you out any day.'

'Look,' said Baddeley, 'I can see you're uptight over this business with the Mardys, but it was just a commercial deal.'

'It certainly was,' I said, 'and it's one of those deals that's earned you a second-class single to a load of porridge. Now get up off that sofa.'

'Why?'

'Just do it, darling.'

'You're not going to have a go at me, are you? What? Are you? Are you mad?'

I said: 'Get up and take your glasses off, I don't want to blind you.'

Baddeley said: 'Help me, Johnny, you can see this fucking copper's going to start.' Now all his pretensions had dropped and he talked like any villain.

'I can't, Walter,' Prince said. 'Can't you see I'm hurt? I'm hurt bad, look at my feet.'

I said to Baddeley: 'Get up on yours, undertaker.'

'No, I'd rather make a statement,' he said. He added: 'With my lawyer, of course.'

I repeated: 'Get up.'

'But I've got a weak heart,' he mumbled, gazing at me like a sick animal, 'anyone in Thornhill'll tell you that.'

'I'm fed up with what I hear in Thornhill,' I said. Prince had realized how tight the moment was for the two of them and was trying to pick himself up off the floor. I said to him: 'If you want a really good kick in the earhole you can have it. But if I were you I'd just go on trying to mend your feet. Keep quiet.'

'Police officers can't behave the way you're going on,' said Baddeley.

'I'm other things besides a police officer,' I said, 'like a man, for instance – I don't like you playing tricks with weak people.'

'What are you going to do?' said Baddeley.

I said: 'Come outside.'

Prince said from the floor: 'Negotiate, Walter. Negotiate.'

I said to Baddeley again: 'I tell you, come outside.'

I pushed him outside to the drive where his Rolls-Royce stood. I said: 'That car, is it locked?'

'Yes.'

'Unlock it. All the doors. Wide open.'

He sensibly did as I told him, then he said: 'Now what are you going to do?'

'I'll show you,' I said, getting my cock out. I pointed it into the car and pissed all over it; I'd been looking for a place for some time.

'You're pissing on twenty-six thousand quid's worth!' he screamed.

'Yes, but the money's not yours,' I said. 'Somehow I just don't care.'

'There must be a way to stop this,' he entreated, wringing his hands.

'That's what Mardy thought when you began bleeding him,' I said. 'But there wasn't, and there isn't going to be with you either.'

I pissed on all over the seats, all custom-upholstered in lambswool.

Baddeley began to cry. 'The stink'll stay in the upholstery for ever!'

'Good,' I said, finishing my piss and zipping myself up. 'But where you're going you're not going to need a car anyway, you can't drive this thing round in a cell.' Prince hobbled outdoors as I turned round. He said to Baddeley: 'For Christ's sake let's top him.' He looked dreadful. He was holding a shooter, but it didn't look very steady. In his other hand he held a cut-glass tumbler full of whisky.

I said to him: 'I very strongly recommend you to put that gun down,' and Baddeley said: 'Yes, I've got to talk to this man, you – fool, and I can't do that if he's dead.'

Prince began to cry. He said: 'Now this cunt's brought me down you don't want to know about me any more, do you? That's the fucking strength of it, Walter, isn't it?'

Baddeley said: 'Now don't be idiotic, Johnny.' At the same time he tried to get away into the dark. Prince fired at him. He missed; the bullet crashed through the windscreen of the car. Prince threw the gun down on the gravel and stood there with tears running down his face. 'I feel so small,' he said with his head down on his chest, 'so bloody small.'

'All right,' I said. 'That's enough.' I went forward, picked up the gun and looked at it; it was a Colt .38 revolver. I dropped it in my pocket. Baddeley said to Prince in a hard voice: 'Johnny, get indoors. Somewhere where I can't see you. Get out of the way, Johnny.'

'So you don't need me,' he said, limping towards the front door. 'You don't need me.'

'That's right,' Baddeley said to his back, 'nobody does.' Prince disappeared into the house. Baddeley turned to me now and said: 'Forget about Johnny. What I want to know is, what can we do about this business, Sergeant?'

'Nothing,' I said.

'Oh come on,' he said. 'Let's be friends. I could give you a cheque for twenty thousand right away. Or cash if you don't mind waiting till morning when the banks open.'

'The banks can open and shut as they please,' I said, 'I'm not interested.'

He turned white. 'You can't mean that.'

'I do,' I said. 'Blackmail, accessory to murder, you're going to go down for fifteen years minimum, you'll see.'

'What about Johnny?'

'He can forget the sunshine for ten years.'

'This is just laughter and jokes,' said Baddeley.

I said: 'Yes, and didn't the Mardys love it.'

'Look, thirty thousand, then. All cash. A nice little nest-egg, Sergeant. I've got ten thousand in notes in my safe, and you can have it to be going on with, the rest tomorrow. So we forget about all this, what do you say?'

I said: 'I've got photocopies of all the payments between Clearpath and Wildways. I've got the proof I need to break you, and I'm going to.'

'You people have no sense of fairness,' he sobbed.

'That sounds really funny,' I said, 'coming from you.'

Prince reappeared on the doorstep. He still held the tumbler in his hand, but now it was empty. He leaned against the stucco masonry of the porch. 'I hate you,' he said to Baddeley. 'I really do, Walter. What's the use of working for a man who makes love to you and then lets you go down?'

'He's going down himself,' I said.

'I want to do myself some good,' said Prince. 'At least let's forget about the shooter.'

'Why should I?'

'The load of dry ice for the Mardys was me and Sanders. That was our lark.'

'I know,' I said, 'and you're going to sing like one.'

Baddeley shouted at him: 'Will you just fuck off, Johnny!' Prince staggered off, and Baddeley said to me: 'Look, for the last time.'

I said: 'The last time was the last time.'

'Give me one chance,' he said, 'just one.'

'You had it and used it long ago,' I said.

'How the fuck did you make Mardy talk?'

'With pity,' I said. I started to walk away. Baddeley tried to hold me back by the arm but I shook him off; I got into my car and drove out of there back to Thornhill in a state of great depression.

27

I walked into Thornhill police station; Turner was sitting there.

I said: 'Is Inspector Kedward in?'

'He's not available, sorry.'

I said: 'Make him available.'

'For someone who's on real bother you like giving orders, don't you?' Turner said.

'Oh,' I said, 'you mean that man's jaw I broke.'

'Yes,' he said, 'and not just anyone's jaw, it was a police inspector's jaw.'

I said: 'It was a cunt's jaw, but I suppose these things get about.'

'You're the living proof that they do,' said Turner.

I said: 'Get Kedward out here, otherwise I'll go in, I'll do it myself. I'm just trying to be polite but I'm not trying that hard, see.'

'You never make much of an effort over that,' said Turner, 'no.' He started to get up, but Kedward came shooting out before he could. He said in a white voice: 'Did you want to see me?'

'You bet your life I do,' I said. 'I suppose this is going to be private, I don't know why, so are you showing me the way or am I going to take it?'

He understood. I looked at myself in the reflection of a window as I went after him. I looked frightful. I looked as if I had slept in my clothes, and I had; since I'd been down in Thornhill I hardly seemed to have had a chance to get them off.

'Well, sit down,' said Kedward when we were in his office.

'No,' I said, 'this is something I prefer to stand up for.'

'Do as you please.'

'I always do,' I said.

He said: 'Well? What is it? I'm in a hurry.'

'You are,' I said. 'You're in a hurry to do bird, because you are a

204

bent police officer.'

There was a silence and then he said: 'Would you care to repeat that?'

'Most certainly,' I said. 'In court.'

'What are you implying?'

'I'm not implying anything,' I said. 'I'm in the business of stating things and I am stating that you are bent.'

'I don't know what you're talking about.'

'Well if you don't I do,' I said, 'because I've been looking through your cheques over the last year, and when I look at the difference between your income and the money you've had, then I want to know a lot more, and so will a judge.'

He swallowed, staring at me.

'How much did you take to sit on the Mardy thing and keep it quiet?'

'Nothing.'

'That's an idiotic answer,' I said, 'because I can see from the cheques that it was nearly three thousand pounds from Wildways. You'd have taken cash if you'd had any sense but you hadn't; thieves never have at that price.'

He said: 'I'm just going to give you a piece of advice.'

'You can shove that up your jumper, the position you're in,' I said. 'What did you do with the money?'

'I say I never had any.'

'The cheques you banked don't agree with you,' I said. 'You used that money to finance a mortgage on that club of your wife's, the Lucky Jack, didn't you? It's no use your saying you didn't, I've got the proof in my pocket.' I remembered what a dreadful woman she was — stank like a jack-rabbit and talked far too much, mostly about money. She wasn't Walter Baddeley's sister for nothing.

'I don't deny my wife runs the Lucky Jack,' he said. 'But it's her own venture, I've got nothing to do with it.'

'Yes you have,' I said, 'and your bank and the building society will tell the court all about it. You're just ad-libbing, and I'll soon split that down.'

'She started the club because she got bored sitting at home all day.'

I said: 'Well now she's got a new home coming to her where she'll be even more frustrated.'

'What about a drink?' said Kedward. 'I've got some nice malt here in the drawer.'

'Not me,' I said. 'Never when I'm on duty.'

'Oh don't be so fucking holy,' said Kedward, getting the bottle out, 'we're two coppers alone in here.'

'I told you no.'

'All right, then,' he said. 'What about that inspector's jaw you broke? You'll be disciplined for that, and serve you right.'

'I think it's very possible I will be,' I said, 'but that won't save you.'

One of his eyelids started to twitch and I said: 'Now, would you like to make a statement about this?'

'Not a chance,' he said.

'You might as well,' I said, 'you're nicked, you know. I've got you, and I never let up.'

'What devotion to duty,' he sneered. 'I daresay that's why you're only a sergeant.'

'Maybe,' I said, 'you interesting little man – but the terrible thing about me is, I don't care.'

'I'm amazed you're still wearing a skin with no holes in it,' he said. 'Quite amazed.'

'There are holes in it all right,' I said, 'and now yours is going to be punctured as well; I'm going to use your phone.' I reached over and picked it up, dialling the voice at its home number. When he came on the line I said: 'It's me. Right away I need a warrant for the following – Ernest and Anne Kedward, William Mardy, Walter Baddeley, John Prince and Richard Sanders.'

'It's all wound up, is it?'

I said: 'Yes, but the experience was much more difficult than the facts.'

'I don't know what you're talking about,' said the voice, 'and I urgently need to have another talk with you about that man's jaw you broke, Inspector Fox.'

'When I get back to London will do,' I said. 'Don't let's fuck this lot up now. Send the arresting officers down from London, you see why we can't use Thornhill, will you do it?' I rang off the moment the voice said yes, before it could start arguing.

Kedward had bent over in his chair. 'I don't feel well,' he said.

'I don't wonder.'

'You've no mercy,' he said.

'Oh I have,' I said, 'only not for you.'

'I'd give anything to get off the hook.'

'No,' I said, 'you're going to go the distance.'

I walked away from the place and the desk sergeant, Turner, eternally scratching in his hair, looked vaguely up at me as I went by.

I drove back to the hotel. 'Society?' an anxious, bearded wizard was inquiring of a TV panel as I passed through the lounge. 'I wonder what we mean precisely by that term?' I could have told him, the silly old cunt. I got up to my room, and as I reached it the phone was ringing; it was Cryer. 'Christ,' he said, 'I've been trying to get hold of you for hours.'

'I can't be everywhere at once,' I said, 'now calm down, Tom, what is it?' He sounded in a dreadful state and I could tell that whatever it was, it was nothing good.

'Get up here to Mardy's at once,' he said.

'I'll be there in the time it takes me to get there.'

'Ah, but there is no time,' he said.

(Mardy had said to me: 'I am the new evangelist. I have challenged life and death now, I have seen heaven and hell. I have lost and won, I suffer for all men that have suffered, I feel for the whole world. I cry all night with my head on my crossed arms; I can see no exit for me, no end to my sighs and tears. Yes, I lie with my brain cradled on my arms and face the great hidden cause. I am a fraction of what was once a great country, and its failure reflects my own downfall.

'But I will see the mockers off. All, all I will carry away in front of me on the black water and regain my love and strength, my wife and youth. Our troubled river runs underground for a while only to come up again and glitter as a fountain and be of great service to the thirst of men. My pride will be reborn, reborn and reborn; we will always be born again.

'The challenge is to be oneself. What you see now is a creature in adversity, dying through the loss of my wife in a hideous and obscure battle. But soon I shall be at ease and know the great words peace and rest.

'But now I am just an insect. It is too slight to decorate with a medal, nor can you bury it with any honours piled on a coffin. No, it dies under a random boot in the middle of pursuing its path.

'I drown in the sorrow and bitterness of Marianne's death; we are all of us forced out of our shape by necessity and by events beyond our control.

'To pray for your dead is in a certain way to be dead oneself.'

And he added: 'Do what you like with me.')

28

Mardy had said: 'I have this terrible recurring dream of monsters gnawing at my arms.'

Between our questions and answers he had crooned part of an old song, thinking of Marianne:

> 'Darling, never never change,
> Keep your breathless charm,
> Won't you please arrange it 'cause I love you,
> Just the way you look tonight.'

'I operated on her for the last time with that song going round in my head,' he told me: 'Impossible agonies, indescribable pain. The weather that day was so glorious – my thinking hideous, my future, none. Oh God, rescue me from this nightmare which I have had too long – my judges will have made no worse errors than I, what have we done to deserve it?

'Oh Marianne, Marianne – appalling loneliness, a void. Only the invisible bears me up; we speak together in the shocking darkness, each carrying the other somehow, unseen.'

It was dark and raining when I went up to Mardy's for the last time. I drove up to the house, edging past the smashed masonry on the gravel, and parked between Mardy's rusted, broken van and Cryer's car. I took my torch and pushed my way in through the open front door. Cryer was standing in the hall under the organ and came towards me saying: 'Thank God you've come.'

'What's the matter?' I said. 'Now come on, take it easy.'

'I can't,' he said. He led me to the steps that went down to the cellars and pointed down them, saying: 'He's down there with her;

I heard him but I couldn't get in.'

'He must have had another set of keys,' I said. 'What did you hear, Tom?'

'I heard him raving, praying and singing.'

'We'll go in,' I said, 'I've got the keys he gave me.'

'Be slow,' he said, 'or by Christ I think I shall go mad.'

'It's all right,' I said. 'Why don't you just stay out here?'

'Oh no,' he said, 'I've got to come with you; if you can do it I can do it.'

'You heard him moving about?'

'Yes, seems like just a few minutes ago, I'm not sure. Shuffling about, and sounds like the opening and closing of a lid.'

'Yes,' I said, 'I know what it's the lid to. Look, I tell you, you just stay out here, this is police work.'

But he shook his head.

'Whatever we find in there,' I said, 'it's going to be frightful.'

'I know.'

So I used the keys I had to open the door. It budged an inch or two, but there was an obstruction behind it of some sort; all I could see with the torch was that it was dark in there of course, the current being cut off. It was also warm and very smelly, like rotten beef. 'Give me a hand and push,' I said to Cryer, 'so we can squeeze in.' So we did that, shoving the door back against this obstacle until we could get past. Immediately we did Cryer, who was just in front of me, slipped and fell on his face on the floor. I shone the torch and managed to get him up, then saw he was bright red all down his front. When Cryer saw what there was to be seen in there he shouted, oh my God.

'Turn away,' I said, 'don't look.' Marianne Mardy sprawled half in, half out of the deep-freeze, her bald head swung over the edge, the melted ice dripping off her face, and Mardy was huddled in the corner where he had fallen in killing himself; my light picked out the glitter of the surgeon's knife he had done it with and which lay beside him. I knelt down in his blood to examine him and by degrees understood that he had begun by opening his left wrist and that when that hadn't worked fast enough he had cut his throat.

It takes love to bugger up a life and smash it to pieces, yes, it takes love in its strange forms to do it, good and evil being so hopelessly mixed up in us. At least I didn't need to look at the figure of the woman lolling out of the icebox, not any more thank God, that was the pathologist's work now, not mine.

Behind me Cryer was whispering: 'Look, there's something written here on the wall.'

I went over to it. Written in Mardy's blood that straggled downwards across the plaster I read: MARIANNE O DARLING MARI

So, suddenly, it was all over, and I understood yet again how everything is far more complex and serious than we suppose as though I had ever doubted it.

'All right,' I said to Cryer when we had got back up to the hall, 'I'll phone and get the mob over.'

'Poor man,' said Cryer, 'poor people.'

I said: 'Remember those words. Now will you be all right for ten minutes? Then I'll come straight back and wait with you till everybody comes, because I think we need each other's company for a time.'

'I must call Angela,' he said. His face was perfectly white. 'The paper too.'

'Of course you must,' I said. 'You go and do it as soon as I get back.'

'Use the phone in my car,' he said, 'and thank you for your understanding.'

'There should be more of it,' I said, 'and it's for me to do the thanking, I'm glad you were here. I may well be finished in the police over this, I'll have to face a board over Fox, but now you see the difference between what some people call channels and what I call justice.'

'I truly do,' he said, 'and I don't believe you'll be finished.'

'No,' I said, going to the door. 'Give me a straight run at the truth and I don't believe I'll ever be finished.'

'I think Mardy was all right,' said Cryer.

'Yes, so do I,' I said, 'it was those braided dolts that killed him.'

As I drove back to London to be suspended the following day I thought in the traffic about everything Mardy had said. He said to me at one point: 'Marianne was the most brilliant and wonderful person I have ever known.

'I suffer and hurt all over. Life means nothing to me now; my heroine will never change, thinking, as she always did, of others. I tell you, just taste the heart and you will find you are thinking about the dead, about people who went off in front and drank death first.

'Speaking for myself, I wonder if in your work you can really imagine what prison's like; over Dorothy's death, I endured the shame of it every day as I endured the heat and the cold there, the rotten food, the bullying of the warders, the disguised contempt of visitors. For a surgeon, a doctor, for a brilliant man, the pain's terrible, terrible. Marianne soothed the pain away for me, and I'm afraid I can't go on talking just now.

'Yet the bitterness of old age and death makes me wonder rather late what we've all been doing in our lives except go down in our own blood and other people's.

'Yes, it's true, love, passion, brilliance and disaster is all I've ever really known.

'Above all, truth is not politics or money, nor indeed anything except itself but love.

'You know, I was so quiet in my mind, happy even, until existence touched me, until I was needed at the moment where others reached for me and begged me for my help.

'Yes, if I were to live now, from now on I would always live for others; everything I would do would be for others, what I would do for myself I would do for them.'

I remember how I went to look outdoors a little while after he had said that; the sky was troubled and overcast, and yet sweet.

'You know,' he said, 'I'm quite certain that envy and greed, blackmail and murder will never defeat us. No, no,' he said, shaking his head, 'not us. Not us.' He turned to me and said: 'You understand how passion changes us back again into what we once were, must have been.'

I told him I understood, even though I wondered if I did.

Perhaps the only true crime is to know too much without really knowing what understanding means, so that as you live for the other, you also die for him.

'Oh yes,' he said, 'watch our reflections as they fade and change, because it may be for the last time.'

THE AMAZING ADVENTURES OF SUPERMAN!

Escape from Future World!

by YALE STEWART

Superman created by Jerry Siegel and Joe Shuster
by special arrangement with the Jerry Siegel family

PICTURE WINDOW BOOKS
a capstone imprint

The Amazing Adventures of Superman
is published by Stone Arch Books
a Capstone Imprint
1710 Roe Crest Drive
North Mankato, Minnesota 56003
www.capstonepub.com

STAR32426

Cataloging-in-Publication Data is available at the Library of Congress website.
ISBN: 978-1-4795-5732-5 (library binding)
ISBN: 978-1-4795-5736-3 (paperback)

Summary: When Brainiac sends SUPERMAN and CYBORG into the distant future, the
super heroes must somehow survive and . . . Escape from Future World!

Editor: Donald Lemke
Designer: Bob Lentz

Printed in the United States of America in Stevens Point, Wisconsin.
032014   008092WZF14

TABLE OF CONTENTS

Time Machine..........................7

Future World.........................14

Saving Tomorrow!..................18

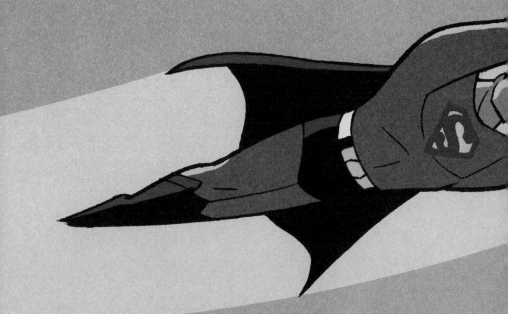

Superman's Secret Message!........28

Born among the stars.
Raised on planet Earth.
With incredible powers,
he became the
World's Greatest Super Hero.
These are...

Chapter 1

TIME MACHINE

One morning, Superman

arrives at S.T.A.R. Labs.

Scientists at the Metropolis

research center have almost

finished a new invention . . .

A time machine!

The head scientist points at the invention. "Once it's finished, this machine will lead to the future!" he says.

"Sign me up for a test drive," jokes Superman.

Soon, Cyborg arrives at

the lab. The super hero is

half man and half machine.

Cyborg greets his pal

Superman. Then he tells the

scientist, "I'm here for my

checkup, doc."

"Let's hook you up to the computer," the scientist says. He places dozens of cables on Cyborg's robot arms and legs.

Suddenly, ZAPPP!!

"Ah!" Cyborg yells.

A face appears on the

nearby computer screens.

"BRAINIAC!" shouts

Superman with surprise.

"I've taken over S.T.A.R

Labs," says the evil alien,

"and all their machines."

"Not this one!" adds

Cyborg. He pulls the cables

off his arms and legs.

"Let's get him!" Cyborg

tells Superman.

"Not TODAY!"

Brainiac lets out an

evil laugh. BWEEOOM!

A beam of light blasts
from the time machine. It
strikes the two heroes. Color
drains from their faces and
their uniforms.

Then they are gone!

Chapter 2
FUTURE WORLD

Seconds later, the heroes wake up in a strange city.

"Where are we?" Cyborg asks his hero friend.

Superman looks around. He is puzzled.

Cars fly above. People walk the streets in shiny metal outfits. "We're still in Metropolis," says Superman. "In the future!"

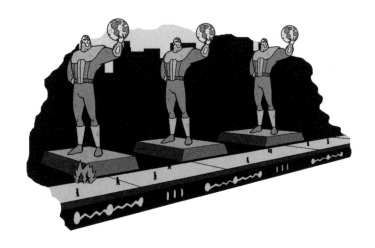

Cyborg points at a nearby statue. It's Brainiac! Statues of him line the sidewalk.

"When did he get so popular?" Cyborg wonders.

"While we're here in the future," says Superman, "Brainiac is ruling the past."

"How do we stop him?"

asks Cyborg.

"Follow me!" replies the

Man of Steel.

Chapter 3

SAVING TOMORROW!

Moments later, Superman and Cyborg arrive at S.T.A.R. Labs. The building hasn't been used in years. Inside, the time machine is covered in dust and rust.

"Do you think it still works?" Cyborg asks his pal. There is no time to answer. A dozen robots enter the room and attack. They all look like Brainiac!

"Brainiac was prepared!"

Superman shouts.

The Man of Steel blasts

the robots with his heat

vision. More keep coming!

"Quick!" Superman says.

"Start the time machine."

Cyborg connects himself

to the dusty machine.

Then . . . **BOOOM!!**

In an instant, Superman

and Cyborg escape from the

future world. They are back

in their own time.

"Nice work, Cyborg,"

Superman says.

"It's not possible!" cries

Brainiac from the nearby

computer screens.

 Superman

blasts the screens with his

freeze breath.

"Wait!" says Cyborg. "I'll shut down Brainiac, once and for all." The hero enters the computer through its wires and cables.

"You won't stop me today," shouts Brainiac.

"Here today," Cyborg begins, "gone tomorrow." The mechanical hero quickly erases Brainiac from the computer. BLIP!

"Your systems seem to be working just fine, Cyborg," jokes the head scientist.

The heroes laugh.

"Another amazing adventure!" says Superman.

"One day Brainiac will return," replies Cyborg.

"Yes," adds Superman, "but for now, the world of the future is safe!"

SUPERMAN'S
SECRET MESSAGE!

Hey, kids! When super heroes need help what's their best secret weapon?

Use the code below to solve the secret message!

checkup (CHEK-uhp)—a medical examination to make sure there is nothing wrong with you

invention (in-VEN-shuhn)—something new that's created or made

mechanical (muh-KAN-uh-kuhl)—made or operated by machine

outfit (OUT-fit)—a set of clothes

popular (POP-yuh-lur)—liked or enjoyed by many people

puzzled (PUHZ-uhld)—confused or unsure about something

uniform (YOO-nuh-form)—a special set of clothes worn by a super hero

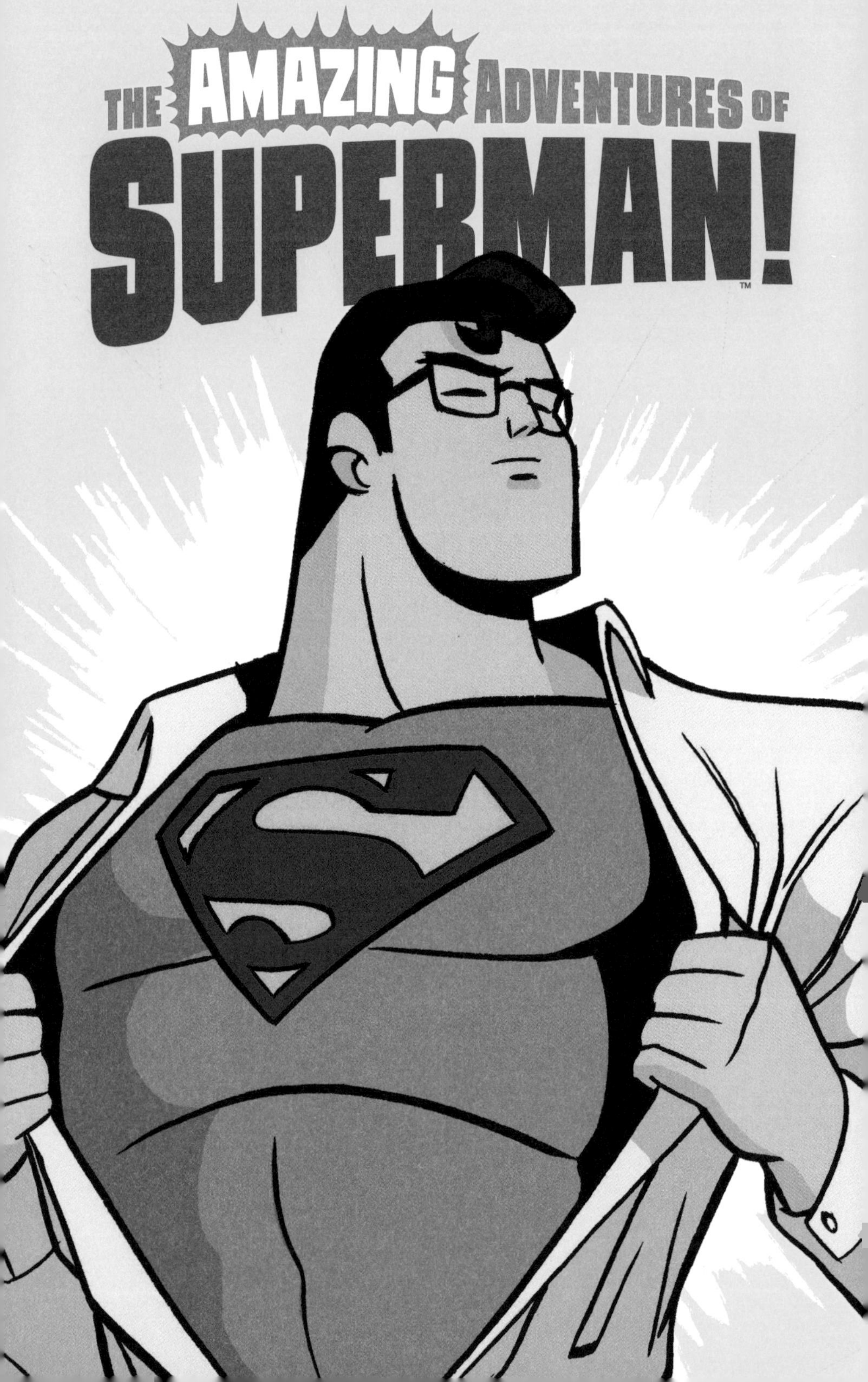
THE AMAZING ADVENTURES OF
SUPERMAN!™

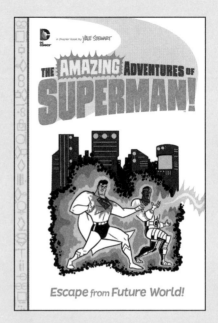

YALE STEWART

Yale Stewart is an independent comic book artist, working primarily on his creator-owned project, "Gifted." His day job is working in the vintage clothing industry. He attended Savannah College of Art and Design and graduated with a BFA in Animation. Originally from St. Louis, MO, he currently resides in Savannah, GA. He is also an avid movie-watcher and music-listener, and eagerly awaits every baseball season.